LAST NIGHT WHILE YOU WERE SLEEPING

A COLLECTION OF WRITINGS BY
MICHELLE KILMER

Copyright © 2014 Michelle Kilmer
Cover art by Michelle Kilmer
Book design and formatting by Michelle Kilmer

ISBN: 0988252287
ISBN-13: 978-0-9882522-8-8

DEDICATED TO MY TUB,
WHERE ALL MY BEST IDEAS COME FROM.

TABLE OF CONTENTS

MESSAGE FROM MICHELLE

Welcome to my head.

Many of these stories were born from ideas that popped into this cranial space while bathing (the cover), showering, or trying to fall asleep.

The individuals whose art pieces are included in this book have my undying love and adoration. Their art sets the tone and helps to bring my words to life. Check the back of the book for bios and websites where you can find more of their work.

I must also thank my family and friends who have lent their eyes, ears, minds, hearts, and sometimes even names to my work. A few of you know this book wouldn't exist without you. I'll never forget all you've done for me.

To my revenge character, who was never supposed to find my writing, but did while I was working on completing this collection... you turned my hate to gratitude, my hurt to happiness, and you continue to teach me how complicated life, love, and loss can be. I have to be appreciative, otherwise I'd go insane.

And to you, reader, thank you so much for opening this book! I suggest you get comfortable and do whatever you would do to prepare yourself for, say, a roller coaster.

Enjoy the ride.

LAST NIGHT WHILE
YOU WERE SLEEPING

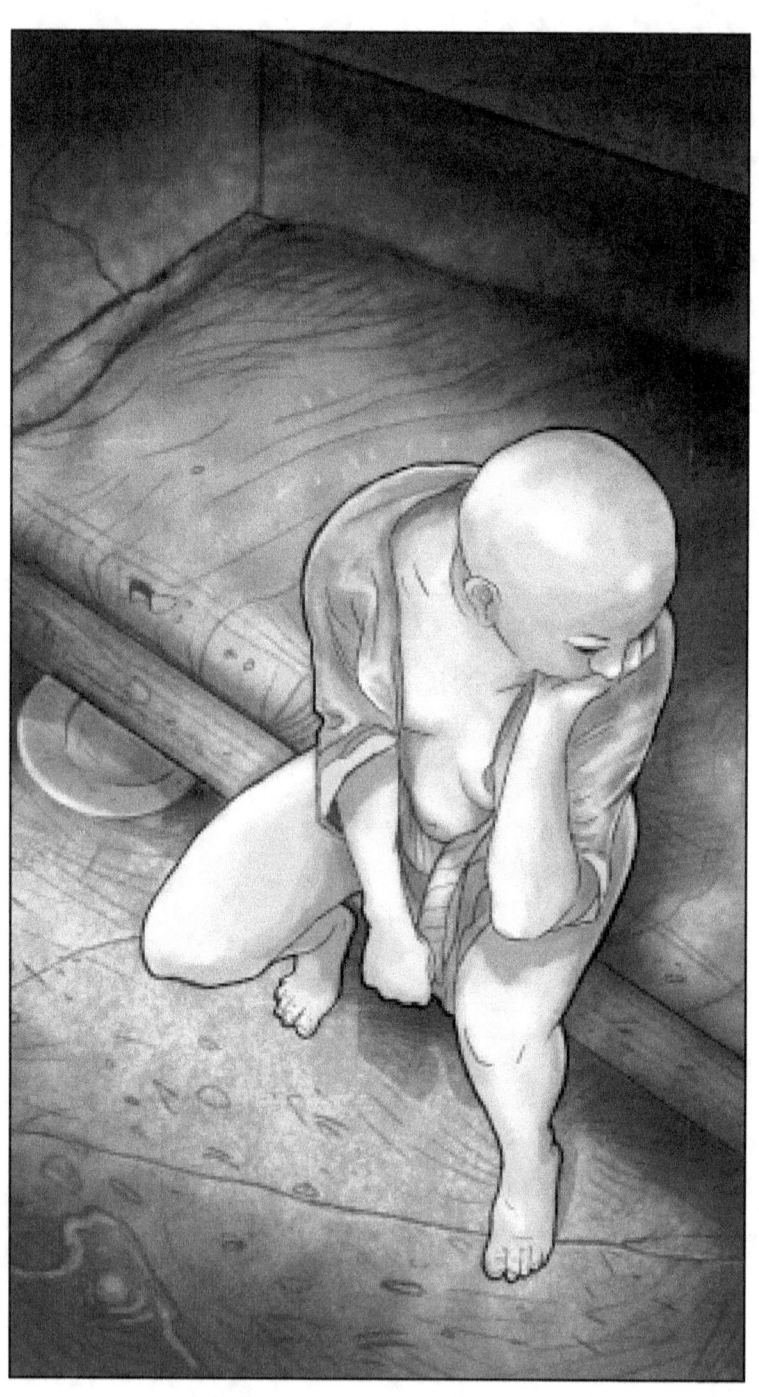

ART BY DARRELL TOLAND

MIRIELLE

THREE AND A HALF YEARS AGO

The room was ready. The beds were made. The gas lines ran perfectly.

FIVE MONTHS AGO
MINA

It was uncanny, the resemblance she had to the others. Her skin was slightly darker from the extra exposure to the sun and her hair had some wave to it, but otherwise she was exact in her perfection. They had met previously when he was in Italy on a business trip. She worked in a café as a waitress and, when he laid eyes on her, Steven was too stunned to order. She laughed at his speechlessness and brought him a small coffee. He visited her every day of that trip. She gave him the feeling of having never left home.

On his return to the country he found that she was still shuffling back and forth in the small café. Her simple life hadn't changed at all. He almost felt bad for what he was going to do to her.

"Mina?" he called out as she hurried past his table. Many of the regulars called her by name, so he knew she wouldn't think it odd.

"I'll be back to take your order in a minute," she said without looking at him. She cleaned a table, collected money from another customer, and then returned to his table with pen and pad in hand.

His heart began to race. He hadn't even looked at the menu. It wasn't sustenance he wanted. He readied himself for introduction, checked his clothes and smoothed out the wrinkles in his lightweight dress shirt. He cleared his throat, extended his hand and put on his most charming smile. "I'm Steven. We met years ago."

Everything was riding on whether or not she would recognize him.

"Oh, yes, I remember you!" She smiled and placed the pen and pad in her apron. "How are you?"

His heartbeat slowed. It would be a piece of cake. He obliged her want to small talk during her break and dutifully played the part of interested listener, but what he really wanted was to get her home with him. When her break was ending, he took a chance.

"I'm world traveling and looking for a companion. Have you ever been to the United States?"

Mina was taken aback. Never had anyone been so direct with her. She loved her life, but part of her wanted to see the world. And there was something about this man, something she couldn't ignore. She'd heard of women being whisked away to other countries by rich, foreign men. Now it was her turn for such an experience. She decided to make the decision when his trip was coming to an end.

A month after his proposition, she was planning a trip to the States. To be safe, she flew separately and booked her own hotel room.

But Mina's precautions weren't enough. Steven was determined to collect and keep her, like a bug in a jar. Like the others.

She flew in and checked into her hotel. They went to dinner. She drank too much wine. He drove her around the city until she fell asleep.

She was the final woman and now that he had her, his project could really begin. But it was bittersweet. He would miss the thrill of the chase, the pleasure of finding another match.

He still remembered finding the first woman, Ren.

THREE YEARS EARLIER
REN

"Found you," Steven said aloud. She was tall for a Japanese but it didn't surprise him for she was a near perfect match. The cheekbones, the build, the delicate and graceful hands. She ended up being the most difficult of the women to find due to the fact that Asia was a rather large continent, even with all the information he had. And she was the first; he'd never hunted anyone down before. But here she was offering him champagne and conversation. He never thought she'd be a hostess at a hostess club in Tokyo.

Another woman had approached him when he entered the club, but he pushed her away. "I want her," he said, pointing to Ren, who had just finished with another customer.

"*Konnichiwa, Gaijin!*" she said cheerfully as she grabbed his hand and led him to a booth.

"Do you speak English?" he asked as she sat down across from him.

"Yes," she answered. "Do you speak Japanese?"

"No, I'm afraid I don't," he said through a chuckle. "You'll have to do things my way."

"Yes, master," Ren said softly. It was a canned response that all of the hostesses were trained to say, yet it still thrilled Steven to hear it. Submissiveness would be an important quality for Ren to have.

He spent a lot of money with her that night knowing that it would be worth it. They were already bonding.

After her shift ended, Ren walked down the winding alley toward the subway station. Steven followed her and skirted around one side of a building. He ran the next block, took a breath, and then stumbled out in front of her.

"You are just like the salarymen! Too drunk to walk home." Ren put one of his arms across her shoulders and did her best to help him to the subway train. Steven continued to act helplessly drunk as the train moved underneath the city.

"I like you a lot, Ren," he said. It was an obvious advance, but he was eager to gain her trust and that, coupled with the alcohol he had consumed, made him bold and forgivable.

She smiled. "Most drunk men like me a lot." It was true. She was never want for company. Steven seemed different to her though. His eyes had a bit of sorrow in them and that made her want to love him. Besides, she knew exactly how much he had spent on her. This American man wasn't hurting in the wallet.

They made small talk until the train arrived at her stop. Ren stood up and said goodbye.

Steven stood up as well.

"This one is mine too," he lied. He had no idea where they were but every moment he could spend with her was important.

They walked together for a while.

"This is my street. Where is your hotel?" she asked, surprised, since they had already passed by all of the hotels in the area.

"I'm lost," he lied again. "I don't think that was my stop." He put on his best "I'm confused" face and made sure to make it look friendly as well.

"Ugh," she grunted and once more took him by the arm. She led him to her small apartment. "You can stay, but in the living room."

While Ren slept he looked through her things. She had been to the U.S. before. From the looks of the photos he found, it was a school trip. Before going to bed he watched her sleep, wishing he could kidnap her that night, but a sedated body would never pass as a carry on. The alternative plan was to make Ren come to him.

The next morning he was gone, but he left a note and an envelope for her. Inside of the envelope was a plane ticket to the U.S. and his phone number there. *Let me know when you arrive,* the note said.

Ren thought it very odd that he left without saying goodbye and doubly so that he left her a ticket to another country. She ignored it for a few weeks, but as the date drew near she couldn't put it out of her mind. Visiting the U.S. in high school was one of her fondest memories. Going back was a dream of hers. There wasn't much for her in Japan; the hostess club most certainly wouldn't miss her. And then there was Steven and his money.

She packed her bags and hoped for an uneventful flight.

Twelve hours later she stood at a payphone in the Salt Lake

City International Airport, the handset pressed to an ear.

"Hello, Steven?" Ren asked. She could barely hear his response over the poor connection.

"Ren! I'll be right there! I have a room for you to stay in if you'd like!" And then the line disconnected.

*

They were both happy to see one another, but for entirely different reasons. He loaded her suitcases into his sedan, offered her the front passenger seat and a bottle of water.

The rohypnol, which he had crushed and dissolved in the water, worked within twenty minutes of leaving the airport. She was now under his control.

Back at his home he smeared her body with hair removal cream and rinsed away all of the tiny hairs, including her eyebrows. The only hair left was her eyelashes. She was a blank canvas, more beautiful than she had started.

He watched Ren wake up in the room. It looked quite different on the monitors with someone in it. She stumbled around, hitting the walls and screaming things in Japanese.

He worked diligently to find the next woman and to bring her in before Ren went completely insane.

ONE YEAR LATER

ANA

Ana awoke on the cold floor of the room, Ren's bald head and eerily similar face hung above hers. Goosebumps raised on her arms. "Who are you?"

"I was going to ask you the same question," Ren said cautiously with a thick Japanese accent.

"Where is he?" Ana asked, referring to the man she had only briefly seen.

Ren pointed to the camera mounted in the corner of the room.

"Did you have something to do with bringing me here?" Ana asked with a hint of accusation.

"No. It was only Steven. I've been trapped in here for a long time."

"Trapped?" Ana queried, alarm rising in her voice.

"There's no way out. He's very careful." Ren looked up to the camera, knowing he was watching the interaction.

Ana took in her surroundings. The walls were windowless and painted the starkest white. No art or photos hung upon them. The furniture, two sets of bunk beds with basic linens and a cheap-looking table, made it look like a dorm room before the start of a school year. She jumped to her feet and ran to face the lens of the camera. She tapped it with a fingernail. "You mother fucker! You kidnapped me!"

"So you didn't come willingly?" Ren asked.

Ana turned to face Ren. "Are you kidding me? He dragged me into a van. I didn't know his name until just now!"

"Oh," Ren said quietly, embarrassed that Steven had fooled her. "Where are you from?"

"Mexico, but I was on vacation in California." Ana looked closer at Ren. She was very thin and very bald. "Where is your hair?"

"Hah!" Ren laughed, surprised that Ana hadn't yet noticed her own lack of hair. "Wherever he put yours!"

Ana brought a trembling hand up to her head. Where there should be beautiful golden brown hair, there was only cold, smooth skin. She looked down the front of her pants. "What the fuck?"

"It will all come back."

"If you've been here for a while, why hasn't yours?"

Ren self-consciously ran a hand over her own head. "I had some before you came. Now it's gone again. He removed it in time for your arrival, I imagine."

As Ren rubbed her own bald head, Ana noticed ragged scars across both of her wrists. "What happened?" she asked, pointing to the damaged flesh.

"I tried another way out, but he wouldn't allow it. He stitched me up."

Steven was relieved that the first two women were getting along. Ren had been a very social person back in Tokyo. He hoped Ana's presence would fill that need and put an end to Ren's suicide attempts.

He prepared the first of many meals the women would be eating together and slid it through a small metal flap at the base of the one door that led out of the room.

Ana tried to count days, but without sunlight it was impossible. She counted her menstrual cycles, but those were far apart and more sporadic than normal. Ren taught her to count the light cycles instead. Steven turned out the lights for sleeping and then back on to wake them up. Whether it was four or seven hour nights, they didn't know, but it was better than not counting at all.

TEN MONTHS LATER

A hissing sound filled the room. It startled both Ren and Ana, but only Ren knew what it was.

"What's happening?" Ana asked.

Ren opened her mouth to explain, but lost consciousness before a word could cross her lips.

*

Steven lifted the dead weight of the third woman's sleeping form onto a cart and brought her into the room. Her dark skin stood out against the white walls and drab linens, but that would change soon enough.

BAHATI

"Wow, this place is nice," Bahati said as she wiped the crusted tears from her face. "Bunk beds and everything."

Ana and Ren awoke from their gas-induced sleep.

"Another one," Ana said.

"Yes, I was about to say that when we passed out. Also, all that extra food he gave us meant that he was traveling again, to find someone else," Ren explained.

"Why didn't you tell me then?" Ana was slightly hurt that her prison mate had kept valuable information from her. "We could have tried to escape while he was gone!"

Ren shrugged.

Annoyed at the poor welcome, Bahati broke into their conversation before they could continue. "Hi!" she said happily to the room. "I'm Bahati."

Ana had heard that level of excitement before, from the mouths of teens coming to camp for the first time. It didn't fit the situation. "You don't find it strange that there are two bald women, who also happen to look a lot like you, in the same windowless room as you?" Ana questioned.

Bahati stood up and stretched from left to right. "Steven said there would be others and that they would look like me."

Ren and Ana stared at one another. Neither could believe what Bahati had said.

"You have been kidnapped," Ren said bluntly. "Like we have been kidnapped. He just wrapped it in a different package."

"No, I came willingly," Bahati replied calmly. "And I've been in worse situations than this. From what I can see we have beds and drinking water. Is there a toilet?"

Ana and Ren nodded. Ren pointed to a door to the right of a mirror and sink. Bahati clapped with excitement.

"You're crazy," Ren said, "and you haven't even been here for years yet." Already the novelty of having a new roommate had worn off.

"You said you came willingly?" Ana asked. "And that Steven told you about us?"

Now across the room and stroking the starched sheet of one of the lower bunks, Bahati nodded. "He knew I wanted out. When he asked me to leave with him of course I said yes!"

"Except he didn't tell you the part where he was going to strip you of your hair and lock you up, right?"

"No, but like I already said, I've been in worse situations."

Bahati picked up a pillow from the bed and pressed it to her face. She breathed in the freshly laundered smell.

"Where did you come from that is worse than this?" Ren asked.

"South Africa."

Bahati truly had been the easiest to bring. They had taken a flight together from Cape Town back to the States. She walked into Steven's home on her own two feet. Of course he'd still had to knock her out to process her, but that had only to do with how intimate those steps were.

5 MONTHS LATER

INTRODUCTIONS

Steven looked over at Mina, still asleep in the passenger seat of his car. She was lovely and hardworking. He could keep just her, get rid of the others. This thought played over and over in his head as he gently unbuckled her seatbelt and carried her to the front door of his house. As they crossed the threshold, he remembered his wedding night. He remembered the effort he'd put into finding the others. He remembered his theory. He remembered *her*, his reason for all of this.

"No, this isn't how it ends," he said.

He brought her to the master bathroom and administered a sedative just as she began to stir. His happiness overwhelmed him and he cried as he rubbed the hair removal cream on her nude form and rinsed her clean. Then, laying her body in the center of the bunkroom, he removed the hair of the other women. They looked like newborns to him. They were his second beginning.

*

"What is going on here? Who are you?" Mina crab walked backward to the closest wall.

The others went through the motions of introducing themselves, blaming Steven, and answering all of the questions that Mina had.

"I'm confused. We were in love," Mina said.

19

"Love," Ren repeated with a mocking laugh. "He does not love. Perhaps like a snake loves a rat."

"He loves me!" Bahati asserted. "That's why he brought me here."

"Don't listen to Bahati, she still thinks Steven is her boyfriend," Ana said with disgust.

Mina searched the room for answers, lifting up mattresses and turning things over until she was satisfied she wouldn't find any. Then she saw the camera. "Are we being filmed? Is this a TV show?"

"No, but we are being watched," Ana said.

Mina pounded on the walls and door. She rubbed at her scalp, willing her hair to return. Frustrated, she eventually sat down on one of several floor pillows.

"So, you've been here years," Mina pointed to Ren and Ana, " and you, months," she looked to Bahati.

The women nodded.

"Why us?" Mina wondered. "I can't wrap my head around it."

"We look similar. Maybe like someone he knows?" Ren suggested. "After all this time and seeing all of you, that is the only reason I can come up with. That or he's just fucking crazy."

*

Later, the women sat together and listened to Ren talk about the time she spent alone in the room and all of the ways she'd tried to take her own life.

Electrocution.

"I dumped water on the floor and was trying to get a hold of one of the wires from the lighting, but Steven cut the power before I could do any damage," she explained.

Drowning.

"But the shower stall is too shallow."

Suffocation.

"I tried it, you know, with a blanket. But it was too thin. I couldn't cut off the air supply."

"He always thinks of everything," Bahati said as she reminisced. "While we were flying here, he got me these little peanuts when he thought I was hungry. It was sweet."

"Anything to keep us alive," Mina sighed.

"Tell them about the screwdriver," Ana urged Ren.

"Ah, the only mistake he ever made!" Ren recalled with a grin. "I cut my wrists with a screwdriver he accidentally left in here. By the time he got to me there was blood everywhere. He tied me to the bed, stitched the wounds closed, and left me like that for days as punishment. I was very sad. When he finally untied me, I was going to try to poison myself with the shampoo, but then he brought Ana and it wasn't so bad anymore."

"Why don't you have any scars?" Mina asked, unconvinced that Ren had attempted anything.

"I did, but they started to fade after Ana got here. Right, Ana?"

Ana nodded. "Here and here," she said as she gestured to her left wrist and then her right one.

Ren showed the women her wrists and after generous amounts of poking and prodding, Mina and Bahati were equally amazed at the lack of remaining evidence.

"It's like it never happened," Mina said.

*

They speculated on how many more women would wake up in the room.

"Maybe three more," Bahati guessed. "He told me there were only a few women in the world as special as I was."

"You are special, Bahati. Very, very special," Ren said with an eye roll.

"There could be other rooms like this one. With other women," Ana suggested.

"No more," Ren said confidently. "There has always been four of everything. Four beds, four pillows on the floor, four toothbrushes, and four hand towels."

Mina agreed with Ren. "So the question is, now that he has all of us what does he plan to do next?"

Steven had dreamt of this moment years ago. These four women in the room together, bonding over a shared captivity experience. Becoming closer by the minute.

CYCLES

Bahati awoke to a sensation she was unfamiliar with, *ease of movement.* She sat up in bed and realized that her breasts felt much lighter than she was used to. She risked a glance down her shirt and was astonished by what she saw. Her breasts were at least three cup sizes smaller than they were the night before.

"Strange," she muttered. There were no stitches, no pain, but somehow they had changed.

"Eh?" Ren yelled from the bunk below. "*Nani?*"

"What does 'nani' mean?" Bahati asked as she climbed down to the floor.

"It means 'what'," Ren translated. "I won't fit in my bra now."

Bahati looked at Ren. She was wearing a fitted tank top and, due to the unexplained enlargement of her chest, the top was nearly splitting at the seams.

"Look at mine!" Bahati said, proudly displaying her more streamlined form.

Ren was even more shocked by Bahati's transformation. Her breasts had been very large and sloping, but now they were much smaller, more athletic and pert.

Mina awoke and followed her morning routine of teeth brushing and face washing before speaking to the other women. Even when she was finished, she went about thumbing through a *Better Homes and Gardens* magazine Steven had put in the room.

Ren sat down in front of her and cleared her throat, "Ahem!"

Mina looked up and couldn't believe her eyes. "Where did those come from? You were flat as a board yesterday!"

"Hey!" Ren cried out as she slapped Mina for the insult. "Are yours different?"

"No, I don't think so." Mina felt one of her breasts. It *did* seem slightly firmer. "Maybe a little bit, but I'm close to my period. Are you?"

"No, and they've never gotten this big. I can't believe they aren't sore," Ren said as she looked once more at her new acquisitions.

"Your cycle could be changing," Mina suggested. "When women spend a lot of time together sometimes they sync up."

Ren shook her head. "This is more than that. Look at Bahati."

As Mina did, she dropped the magazine. "Holy shit! Where'd they go?"

Ana slid out of bed and lifted her own shirt without discretion. She was dismayed by what she saw. Hers too had decreased in size. "No! I love my *chichis*! My husband is going to freak!"

"Wait, you're married?" Mina asked. Steven had taken all of their jewelry and she'd never heard Ana mention a husband before. She'd also assumed that Steven targeted only single women.

"Yes, and he's a boob guy!" Ana shrieked. "How is this possible?"

"Hormones, maybe," Mina said as she re-examined her own for any difference, "he could have put them in our food."

Ana ran to stand directly under the security camera's gaze. She pulled her shirt up once more. "What's going on?" she yelled. "Are you giving us drugs? I know you know something about this!"

The camera adjusted slightly and focused in on Ana's exposed chest.

"Pervert!" she screamed and stormed back to her bed.

"Look by the door," Bahati said, pointing at a small pile of red fabric. "He's left us gifts!"

Ren looked through the pile. "New shirts and bras. All the same size."

"He *did* know," Ana said angrily from her bunk.

*

Steven watched the women changing into the new clothes, hoping to catch another glimpse of the first change. Ren's healing wounds made him hopeful, but this newest development confirmed that the process had begun.

PERSPECTIVE

Ren had a daily routine of doing morning calisthenics, something she learned as a child in Japan. She did a series of standing poses, throwing her arms in the air in large circular motions and bending occasionally from side to side. Mina sat on the floor and watched as though Ren was putting on a performance, a seemingly random mix of yoga, ballet, and basic stretches. On this morning, Mina noticed that Ren was wearing a brown shirt instead of the red one they had been given just days before. She looked at her own and it too was a golden brown.

"Where'd these shirts come from?" she asked Ren, but Ren couldn't be interrupted during her exercises.

"The shirts didn't change," Ana said as she approached Mina. "Mine still has a stain from when I spilled soup on it yesterday. See?"

Mina looked at other items in the room. The colors were less varied, less vibrant. The floor pillows had been green, but now they were tan. "Whatever he drugged us with is making us colorblind!" She went to the mirror. Her irises, also green just yesterday, were now blue. "And my eyes have changed color. If we get out of here, I'm suing him."

Ana joined Mina at the mirror. She leaned in close and opened her eyes widely. "Yeah, mine were blue, but this is a darker color."

Ren finished her calisthenics. "Let me see!" she said as pushed between Ana and Mina at the mirror to look at her own.

"Oh, my god, your eyes are blue too!" Mina said to Ren. The change was dramatic as Ren's eyes had always been a very dark brown.

"I'm going to... kill him," Ren said, still short of breath from exercise.

"Let's wake up Bahati," Ana said. Bahati's eyes had been as dark as Ren's, darker if that was possible, and against her dark skin any other color would be startlingly brilliant. They pulled her out of bed and to the mirror.

Bahati shrugged. "I like it," she said as she stared at her reflection. "Blue looks nice on me."

"You really do find the good in everything," Ana said sadly.

*

Later that day, Mina sat alone on her bunk, her eyes closed. She thought about the garden she was growing back at home in Italy. How weeds must overrun it. She pictured with her mind's eye the beautiful red of the tomatoes and the lush greens of the vines and leaves. She prayed she would see it all again in the right colors, with her own eyes.

ROOTS

On another morning, several days after their eyes and eyesight had changed, Bahati awoke and felt the beginning stubble of her returning hair. Would Steven remove it again or let it grow? Either way, it didn't really matter to her. She'd enjoyed not having to worry about hair care. The other women, however, were elated.

"Finally!" Ana squealed. Her hair was down to her low ribs when Steven kidnapped her. She missed the security blanket that it was. For it to grow back would be one step toward normal.

"Now that it's coming in, it's growing so fast!" Mina said as they ate lunch together. She couldn't wait to have long hair again and to regain some sense of a separate identity.

Ren spent hours in front of the mirror. The hair growing in on her head was light brown. It wasn't right, it wasn't her own. She didn't know what color Mina or Ana's had been before, but they didn't seem alarmed. Bahati looked like she was wearing a wig.

"You don't think it's weird that your hair is coming in the wrong color?" Ren asked her.

"It will darken up after awhile," Bahati said confidently.

Ren sighed. Bahati really was a hopeless case.

Their hair grew to shoulder length in three days time and then stopped growing altogether. Mina tied hers back with a strip of fabric from her pillowcase. Ana wore hers down. Ren did a mix of both, depending on whether she was exercising or not. Bahati couldn't figure out what to do.

"I don't know how to take care of this! It's so flat!" Bahati said as she tried to tweak sections of the hair one morning.

"It's straight, Bahati, not flat," Ana corrected her.

"Straight, flat, same thing," Bahati replied. "All I know is that it won't cooperate!"

"Flat just sounds so negative," Ana explained.

"Let her be negative!" Ren said. "At least she found something to complain about like the rest of us."

*

Steven watched on a monitor in his kitchen. The golden, light brown hair that now adorned each head was just like *hers*.

LAYERS

It had now been months since Mina had seen sunlight and a year or more for Bahati, Ren, and Ana. The harsh glow of the fluorescent bulbs made them all look sick, even though they were nourished and well-rested. It was poor lighting even in the best of circumstances.

Bahati was dealing with skin problems beyond anything caused by lack of sun. Spots of discolored flesh were showing up all over her body. They didn't itch or hurt, but they were spreading.

"A skin disease? Bed sores?" Bahati asked the others.

"No, I don't think so. They aren't open or *sore*," Mina said.

Ana stayed in her bunk. "Just don't touch me, Bahati. I don't want to catch it."

Ren placed fingers on either side of a particularly large patch of lightened skin, pulling and stretching it. "You have that Michael Jackson disease. You are turning white."

Bahati pulled away from Ren and went to the mirror. The sandy hair on her head and her now blue eyes looked less out of place as the pale flesh overtook her chocolate skin. Still, tears welled up from the blue pools and splashed down the patchwork plain of her face. She'd spent her entire life being told by her black community that black was beautiful and, even in apartheid-era South Africa, she had grown up believing it.

"This is where I draw the line, Steven." Bahati approached the camera and waited for a sign that Steven was watching her. The camera moved, scanning her body up and down. "You see what is happening to me? This must stop! I am a proud *black* woman. Do not take that away from me!" The camera ceased movement.

"Do you hear me?" she roared. "I am done with your games!"

Mina and Ren sought shelter with Ana on a lower bunk. Bahati had never raised her voice before and it was terrifying. There wasn't much to destroy in the room, but Bahati did the best she could, tearing open the floor pillows and flipping the low table, screaming as she did. She then returned to the camera and looked straight into the lens.

"You're not my boyfriend anymore!" she declared, her voice hoarse from her rampage. Next she ripped the camera from the wall and threw it on the ground, breaking it into several pieces.

Gas hissed from tiny holes in the walls.

*

Steven had no way of knowing when the gas had knocked them all out. With the camera destroyed, he was entering blind. He lay on the floor outside of the room and unlocked the flap on the bottom of the door. Peeking in, he was startled by a hand lying just on the other side. He poked it and was relieved to find it unresponsive. Standing up once more he unlocked and opened the door.

All four of the women were unconscious and accounted for.

He wanted badly to be with them, but his project, this process, wasn't over. Instead he caressed a cheek here, a slightly freckled hand there. Memories flooded his mind.

He swept up the camera parts and set to work installing a new camera, higher up on the wall. He cleaned up the light dusting of pillow feathers that blanketed the room and righted the table.

"Time to speed things up," he said to the sleeping women before leaving the room again.

PROXIMITY

Mina came to before the others. The camera had been replaced but not the pillows. Bahati was tied to her bed. Then, she took the usual ten steps to the sink and mirror, but arrived at them in six.

"That's odd," she said aloud.

The wall was closer.

She followed its length to a corner. They had all assumed they were in a sealed room, but on closer inspection, the walls didn't actually meet. A thin crack ran from floor to ceiling in each of the four corners. Mina pushed with as much force as she could. Her grunting and cursing woke Ana and Ren. Bahati was still out cold.

"What are you doing?" Ren asked.

"The walls have moved. The room is smaller," Mina explained.

"Is he going to crush us? Like in a horror movie?" Ana asked, terror rising from her gut. She had so far managed her claustrophobia, but if the walls were closing in, panic wouldn't be far behind.

Steven felt no alarm over Mina's discovery. The movable walls were solid and locked in place. No amount of pushing from inside the room would affect them. He laughed when Ana thought he would crush them. *Why would I damage such beautiful things?* he thought.

*

Three more nights passed by and each night Steven moved the walls, stealing space and forcing the women closer together. Urging the changes to continue.

SPEECH

"Wake up," an unfamiliar voice said in Ren's ear. She stirred and wondered if another woman had come after all. Steven seemed like a man who was never happy with what he had, always wanting and taking more. Maybe he'd grown bored with the four women.

"Only four beds-" Ren stopped herself. The voice coming from her throat was different. It was no longer carrying the Japanese accent and it was slightly higher than hers.

"Ren, it's me, Ana," the other voice spoke again. It too was missing an expected accent. "Are you hearing this or is it in my head?"

"I think we sound the same," Ren said.

"Are you surprised?" Mina asked from her bunk. "These changes won't stop until there is nothing left of us. Ren's healing injury wasn't a miracle. It was the beginning of something."

"What kind of torture is this?" Ana screamed, pounding on the door.

"This," Mina too began to scream, "is murder! You are killing us."

"Let us out, Steven!" Bahati joined in the yelling, hoping that a unified front would somehow change his mind and set them free.

"It's no use. He'll never let us go," Ren said from a corner. She rubbed her throat and cleaned her ears with a finger, but nothing would bring her own voice back.

*

Steven turned up the speakers on his computer to listen to the joyous sound. Every scream, every word, regardless of tone or meaning, was like a love letter to him. It felt so good to hear her again.

REFLECTIONS

Four fair-skinned, golden-brown-haired, blue-eyed women of athletic build went about their day in their cage. With their bodies now identical it was impossible to tell who was who unless the women were in their bunks. Someone stood at the door, tugging on the handle as though a bored child might, with a lack of enthusiasm, but not enough want to stop.

"Bahati! There's no way out," Ren called to the woman.

"I'm not Bahati," the woman at the door responded.

"How am I supposed to know?" Ren shot back.

"Well, Bahati is mostly happy here. She'd never try to escape."

"Yes, but she likes to damage things so you can understand why I might be confused. If you aren't her, who are you?"

"I'm not you, whoever *you* are. So that leaves two possibilities," the woman said.

"This isn't a fucking game!" Ren screamed. "I came here for his money and now he and all of his bitches are fucking with me!"

"Whoa," the woman said as she ceased her half-hearted escape attempt. "I am not his bitch, I'm Ana! And excuse me for trying to have a little fun!"

Next to the door, Bahati sat below the camera and began to speak. "Steven," she pleaded, "please take me back. I promise to be good."

Mina viewed the other women's slow decent into madness from a short distance, as far away from them as she could be in the ever shrinking room. She prayed to go crazy herself, to be free of this place and these people, even if only in her mind.

"Why do we have to be the same?" she screamed.

*

He wasn't *all* monster. It did pain him to watch the women struggle to accept the changes. He wanted to hold them and tell them things were fine, but they wouldn't allow that. Besides, it would all be over soon. There was no point in interfering now.

He spent hours in front of the monitors, watching the clone-like women. They were beautiful and it was working.

TOUCH

Days later Ana awoke to find that things had become gruesomely worse. In the dark, she could feel a body lying next to hers on the lower bunk. She tried to move away from the form, but her inside arm was tied to its arm with several strips of fabric.

"Wake up!" she yelled as she began to untie the bindings. She had them all off by the time the lights came on and she could see that it was Mina next to her on the bed.

"Thank fucking God," she said. She was expecting it to be Steven, who was bound to be more interested in the women now that they looked like the same woman, whoever she was.

Her relief was short lived, though, when she saw that their arms were still stuck together.

"Ahhhhhhh!" Ana, and Mina who was now awake and fully aware of the situation, both screamed in horror. Where the flesh of one arm ended the other arm's flesh simply continued. Any pulling to separate caused pain and they quickly found that there were no seams or stitches to explain the connection. The flesh had crept together overnight.

In the bunk next to them, Bahati and Ren were also on the bottom bunk and joined together, but it was each ones inside leg instead of arms.

"Help us!" Bahati yelled to Mina and Ana. "We're stuck together!"

Mina and Ana orchestrated getting out of bed the best they could. They helped the other women swing their legs over the edge of their bed and pulled them up to standing.

Bahati and Ren immediately fell over. On the floor, Bahati tugged her leg roughly, trying everything she could to separate from Ren.

"Stop pulling on it!" Ren yelled as she was dragged to and fro.

The other changes had been bearable and, to some, beneficial. This, however, was unlike anything they had known to be possible in the world. Veins connected under the skin. Tendons and nerves as well. Ana could feel when Mina scratched her own arm.

31

"We have to stop this before it gets worse!" Mina forced Ana to sit with her on the floor in the middle of the room. She tore several sheets of paper from a magazine and, holding them as straight and firm as possible, dragged them across the thin flesh where their arms had joined. She was able to saw back and forth several times before the pain was too much for them to bear.

"Please, no!" Ana cried. She looked down on the large paper cut on the skin they shared. "It hurts."

*

Steven jumped back in his chair. He could see blood starting to seep from the shallow wound. It was time to talk some sense into them before they really hurt themselves.

He gassed them and used a flatbed cart to bring their limp bodies to the kitchen. There he propped the two sets of women on high-back benches that were bolted to the floor on either side of a wooden dining table. His brow covered in sweat, he took a moment to rest before wrapping large chains around their waists and legs.

Mina's eyes opened first and she struggled briefly, but gave up when she saw the chains locked around her. She looked around the room and cringed. Where their white-walled prison was spotless and bright, this room was the exact opposite. It was dimly lit. A heavy curtain covered a small window above a sink. Flies hovered around dirty metal food trays that lay abandoned in a haphazard stack on the counter.

Steven sat at the head of the table with a plate of food in front of him. He ate quietly and calmly.

"Take me back to the room," Mina protested. It was her first time seeing him since they went to dinner on the night he kidnapped her. She couldn't stand to be near him.

Steven ignored her and waited for the other women to rouse.

Moments later, when they did, Ren and Ana both shouted obscenities at Steven while Bahati screamed for help.

"You will sit here quietly and I will tell you everything about *her!*" He stabbed his fork into the wooden table so hard it stuck. "So that *maybe* you'll accept this gift I am giving you!"

The women quieted.

"Gift?" Ana scoffed. "Gifts are things people want."

Ren began to cry. Her tears saturated the wood of the table.

"If you unchain me, I will wash the dishes," Bahati offered. "Like a good girlfriend."

"That might have been true when you first came here, but not anymore," Steven responded. "I know better."

Curiosity grew in Mina. "This woman, who is she?"

"Her name is Mirielle." Steven stood up from the table and walked to the fridge. Many items covered the face of it, including a plane ticket to Tokyo with a date three years in the past and a photo of Bahati standing next to a run down shack. He pulled another photo from under a magnet and brought it back to the table, placing it in the middle where all of the women could see it.

Mina gasped. "She looks just like us."

"No, *you* look like *her,*" Steven corrected.

Ren looked up between sobs. Upon seeing the photo, she cried harder.

"Where is she?" Ana asked.

"She's dead," Steven answered matter-of-factly.

"Are you going to kill us as well?" Bahati slammed a fist down on the table.

Steven leaned toward her and moved to slap her across the cheek, but stopped short of impact. "How dare you suggest I would do anything to harm her!"

"We have only *this* to go on, Steven." Mina gestured to the merging flesh of her and Ana's arms.

"You are right and I apologize for any discomforts you have had. It will be over soon."

"Over? What does that *mean?*" Ana asked, her eyes wide with fear.

"You are Mirielle's doppelgängers. When she died, I remembered Mina, whom I had seen years ago. I wondered if there were more women like her, and like Mirielle. This was all a hunch. I didn't think it would work, but I was right." Steven smiled proudly.

"But this is wrong! *How* is this happening?" Bahati asked.

"We all have doppelgängers throughout the world. Land and seas usually separate us. This is what happens when we get too close. You aren't meant to be together."

"No shit, we aren't!" Ana yelled. "So take us the FUCK apart!" Ana lunged to reach for him with both arms, taking Mina's conjoined arm along for the ride.

"I don't think I could, even if I wanted to," Steven said as he touched the photo of Mirielle lovingly. "And I don't want to."

Bahati began to cry as well.

"Why do we look like *her*?" Mina queried.

"She is missing from the group. If she were here, perhaps you'd all make something much more amazing. Or if any one of you were missing instead, I think the others would become you. It's wondrous. Mysterious."

"It's hideous," Ana said as she noticed that the joined flesh had reached their wrists. Soon their pinky fingers would connect. "Only a fucked up man would come up with such a ridiculous idea."

"I lost my soul mate. That fucks one up," Steven explained.

"You kidnapped me on my honeymoon! My husband probably thinks I ran off on him!" Ana bellowed. "Why do I have to pay the price for *your* lost love?"

Whether Steven had an answer for Ana's question or not, he didn't respond.

"Would Mirielle want you to do this?" Mina asked.

He stood up, took Mirielle's photo from the table, and returned it to its magnet on the fridge. "I'm sure she'll be quite happy to be back."

*

When they awoke next they were in the room again. The bunk beds had been removed and the walls had been pushed in further.

Two mattresses lay on the floor, a bucket sat in one corner.

"If we sleep, things change faster. Maybe if we stay awake we can slow it down." Ren pondered.

"Slow it down until what? Someone rescues us?" Ana huffed. "No one is coming."

"This house is in a desert in a place called Southern Utah," Bahati said from Ren's side. "I know what it looks like, he walked me to the front door."

"Knowing these things doesn't help the fact that we are stuck inside, and staying awake will never work. He can just knock us out." Mina was tired of talking. Her right arm was almost completely merged with Ana's left one. Only the fingers were sorting themselves out.

*

When the lights went out that night, Ren tried to lie as far from Bahati as she could. Closeness seemed to strengthen the attraction their bodies had for one another. They now shared a leg and their arms had begun the same joining. She lie awake on one of the mattresses imagining Bahati's flesh stretching and crawling toward her in the dark, long tendrils snaking and intertwining with her own hide.

*

Their bodies continued to merge. Most of their hours awake were filled with crying and struggle as they were forced to adapt to the changes and manage the pain. Mina and Ana made a better team than Ren and Bahati, who fought constantly.

"My bones ache," Ren sobbed. She and Bahati now shared one set of legs and a very wide torso.

"They are *our* bones," Bahati corrected.

"Don't talk like that," Ren whimpered.

"Yeah, Bahati. Unlike you, we didn't sign up for this!" Ana spat.

Mina shifted her side of the body and grimaced. "There's an

itch that won't go away. It's inside of the legs. I can't scratch it."

"I feel it too," Ana commiserated. She rubbed the joining legs that they shared. "I'm sorry."

*

In two weeks time there were two bodies, each with two heads.

Ren's thoughts once more turned to suicide, but it was difficult to plan one's death with another person's head next to your own.

"Maybe if I choke and die, my head will shrivel up and fall off," Ren said.

"No! Don't do it!" Bahati said with a start. "We share a body. I'll die as well!"

"Do you *really* want to live like this?" Ren asked sadly. Her life hadn't been bad back in Tokyo. This was hell compared to it. She couldn't comprehend how bad Bahati's life had been in South Africa that she would prefer this.

"Steven said it would be over soon," Bahati reasoned. "Or maybe someone will resc-"

"And what will they do then?" Mina's head interjected. "Put us in a museum or on a dissection table? We aren't normal anymore."

Ana said nothing. She could feel their body being drawn to Ren and Bahati's and it terrified her.

*

Steven removed panels and pushed the walls closer and closer, until there was only enough room for one mattress. The conjoined women were forced to lay down shoulder to shoulder. Soon the flesh of the two bodies crept to touch, and once more bones and organs were made to find placement or be absorbed. The floor became a slick mess of excrement as the women lost control. Steven had to disinfect the room often. He wouldn't lose his work to infection.

Whenever he could be near them he examined them. Fingers protruded from the core of the form where the two torsos had begun to merge. The union had three legs, the middle having one large foot with ten toes. Four identical heads sat in a row along a five-foot long collarbone. And only once, back in college, had he seen two pairs of breasts this close together in person.

"My love," he said. He kissed each mouth and then left the room.

*

The women slept for the final forty-eight hours of the union. Steven was unable to get any rest. Though the merging of the heads, from four to one, was gruesome to say the least, the process transfixed him.

PRESENT DAY
THE UNION

It had been four months since the changes began. On this, the final day, one body and one head with no physical abnormalities awoke on the floor of the room. The brain connections were still arranging themselves and so the body had poor coordination. Inside the mind, the women's souls spoke to one another and wept together.

Will our thoughts join as well? Mina asked, but no one knew the answer.

I was wrong before. I don't want to die, Ren said. Her sudden and late interest in living, made the others cry more.

The internal suffering eventually forced tears from the new eyes of the body.

Steven entered the room and held the body, stroking the fine, golden hair of its head in an attempt to comfort.

"I knew you'd come back to me, Mirielle," he said as he kissed her head.

The Union ripped its head away from Steven's mouth.

"She isn't in here!" it screamed with four voices at once, echoing and cascading over one another like a waterfall.

"In time," he said hopefully. "In just a little more time." He wiped a tear from its face and licked it from his finger. "Things are already starting to work properly."

*

The Union was falling in and out of consciousness. Fear grew in the mind that the final change was occurring.

We have to do something, Mina whispered to the others, but as they tried to speak back, their voices began to fade. Mina could feel a shift in power and sensed that she was now in sole control of the body. She stood at the door of the tiny room and tried the handle, but it was still locked.

She fell to the floor in defeat and then closed her eyes for good.

MIRIELLE

Steven watched the monitors impatiently, pacing back and forth and willing it to be done with. He waited for ten minutes and then grew anxious that perhaps the body had died along with the women inside of it. He rushed down the hallway to the reinforced door of the room, fumbled with the keys, and opened it.

Mirielle lay on the floor motionless, but for a tiny rise and fall of her chest. He ran to her and knelt by her side.

Her eyes opened.

"Steven, I've missed you," she said.

"And I, you," he said, kissing her warm forehead. He helped her to stand and he would have collapsed himself, had she not moved forward to hold him in a loving embrace.

It was her. Mirielle was back. She moved and smelled as she should. Steven couldn't believe that he was holding his love once more.

She hugged him tighter until he felt as though she was crushing him.

"Too tight," he squeaked.

"Just right," Mina said as she watched him struggle in her new arms.

SIX HAIKU BY SATAN

Hideo, the most recent Japanese pedophile to arrive in hell, has taught me Haiku. Enjoy. - Satan

BEWARE OF DOG
sic cerberus sic
bite the bad motherfuckers
good dog cerberus

THIS ISN'T DISNEYLAND
Dante had it right
abandon all hope, enter
eternal darkness

SERIOUSLY, SHUT UP
save your sob story
beginning, middle, and end
I have heard them all

I LOVE THIS PLACE
underworld domain
beauty in flame, burning, red
endless suffering

THIS IS MY HOUSE
Richard Ramirez
ugh, thinks he owns the shadows
serial killers

WHACK-A-MOLE
hell is getting full
no more room for the wicked
messy housekeeping

ART BY SARAH ALTENBURG

OBACHAN

Miyu was seeing her grandmother, even though her grandmother was dead. After a long life, one hundred and three years to be exact, the woman died peacefully in her sleep in the room down the hall. That was a week ago.

But now her ghost was in the back garden feeding the *koi*, watering the plants that she had tended in life, and humming old songs just above the sound of the breeze. Miyu slid her shoes on as quickly as she could and ran to the pond, but her grandmother was no longer there. On the rocky edge of the water, on top of a flat stone, sat a porcelain plate with a single *wagashi* at its center. The dessert was heart-shaped and pink in color. Miyu made sure her mother, Jun, wasn't watching from the house, then picked up the treat and ate it. She could see there was a small design painted on the plate, but the plate disappeared before Miyu could discern what it was.

*

The next day, Miyu again saw her grandmother's ghost. This time it was inside the two-story house that she lived in with her mother and her father, Takahiro. Her grandmother was sweeping the dining room. The broom made a soft whooshing noise as it caressed the wood floor. Miyu snuck as quietly as she could up to her grandmother, but when she reached out to touch her, she disappeared. On the center of the dining room table was another porcelain plate and in the middle of the plate were two balls of *mochi* ice cream. Miyu made sure her mother wasn't near, and then ate the cold desserts as quickly as she could. Again she saw that the plate was decorated, but it disappeared before she could see what the drawing was.

*

Later that night, Miyu once more saw her Grandmother's ghost. In the kitchen, bent over a steaming pot on the stove, the old woman watched something as it cooked to perfection.

"*Sobo!*" she called out to the ghost, "Grandma!" But it was gone as soon as the words crossed her lips. The steaming pot was nowhere to be found, but sitting in the middle of the stove were three cups of *kuzuyu*. Miyu had only tasted the sweet and thick drink once before. She greedily consumed the contents of each cup and saw that inside, at the bottom of the ceramic cups, there was a decoration just like the plates. It looked like a dog or maybe a cow, but again the cups disappeared before she could really understand the art.

*

Even though Miyu enjoyed seeing her grandmother and eating the treats that she left for her, all Miyu wanted was to hug her again like she had before she died. The next day Miyu couldn't take it anymore. She went to her bedroom, collapsed on her small bed, and cried into her pillow. A chill came over the room.

"My poor Miyu," her grandmother's ghost said. "What is wrong, my child?"

Miyu sat up and saw that her grandmother was standing in the corner of the room. She sat very still in her bed for a moment and fought not to speak for she didn't want the ghost to disappear again.

"I asked you, what is wrong?"

"*Sobo*," she addressed her older relative, "I just wanted to hug you. I wanted you to talk to me."

"I didn't want to frighten you," the old woman said as she floated across the room. She stopped at the foot of Miyu's bed.

Miyu crawled towards her "But you are my *obachan*! Why would

I be scared of you?"

"Because I am a spirit now. And spirits are scary, wouldn't you say?"

"Maybe the *tengu* or the *yokai*, but you aren't one of those, right? You are just my grandmother."

"That is right. Death could not keep me from you. I missed you too much!" The ghost smiled.

"And you brought me those nice treats!"

"A sweet girl like you deserves the sweetest treats."

"Will you come and see me again?" Miyu asked.

The spirit nodded and then disappeared.

It was easy for Miyu to fall asleep that night. Talking with her grandmother's spirit had calmed her and she was looking forward to seeing her the next day. But hardly two hours could pass before she saw her again.

*

The blankets were pulled from atop her. The cool air of the evening and the chill brought in with the ghost caused Miyu to wake from her dreams. Her eyes still closed, she reached around for the blanket, but instead found what felt like a plate, set on the end of her bed. She opened her eyes and saw that it was another delicate, porcelain plate, this time with four large cookies on it. Standing again at the foot of the bed, her grandmother's ghost smiled down at her.

"Look, Miyu, I made you some more sweets!"

Miyu shook her head and pushed the plate to the side. "*Okaasan* will be very mad."

"I won't tell your mother and I'll even hide the plate!" The spirit didn't touch the plate, but somehow it slid back in front of the little girl.

"Maybe one." Miyu put a cookie in her mouth and when it hit her tongue, she was pleased by the taste. It was sweeter than anything she'd ever eaten before; more delicious than the red bean cakes her mother made for dessert.

"*Oishii!*" she squealed. She picked up another and held it out in offering to her grandmother.

The ghost shook its head. "I can't eat them, so they are all for you." The plate slid closer still, until its dainty edge was touching Miyu's leg.

She ate cookie after cookie and when they were gone she could finally see the design on the plate. It was a pig, painted with thick, black brush strokes.

Miyu traced the lines of the painting with her small fingers. "He's cute!"

"I thought you might like him!" the spirit said. "I picked the dishes just for you!"

"I love him! He looks happy."

Her grandmother's ghost smiled and then disappeared along with the plate.

*

She awoke the following morning, the taste of cookies still in her mouth. At breakfast, Miyu couldn't stop smiling and she even found room in her belly for the bowl of rice and *miso* soup her mother made.

"It's nice to see my little girl so cheerful," her mother said. She hadn't expected much from her daughter so soon after the loss of her beloved grandmother, Jun's mother.

*

Later that day, as Miyu was walking home from school, she saw her grandmother again. She greeted her around the corner from the family home, a dessert-covered plate floating above her hands.

"How was your day at school, my sweet child?" the spirit asked.

Miyu shrugged. "Okay."

"Perhaps you'd like some sweets to brighten your day?" The plate lowered to Miyu's eye level and she could see it held five perfectly made slices of cake, each one a different flavor combination of filling and icing.

"Oh, *sobo*!" Miyu danced a little on the sidewalk and took her time choosing the most delicious looking slice of cake from the plate. "We can't tell *okaasan*."

"Don't worry, Miyu. *Obachans* give their grandchildren whatever they like without having to let anyone else know!"

Miyu chose the chocolate slice and gobbled it up.

The plate hovered toward her and tapped her chin.

"Have another slice," the ghost said.

"But *Okaasan* is making dinner."

"This cake is very light. You'll have plenty of room for all five pieces."

Miyu found a spot of grass and sat down. The plate lowered into her lap. She ate another piece and decided that was enough. But when she tried to stand up, the plate grew heavy like a rock, and kept her sitting on the ground.

"*Sobo*, help me!" she whined. "Make the plate float away!"

"The plate is too heavy. Your poor grandma can't lift it. You'll have to eat all the cake to make it light again!"

Miyu did just that and as soon as she swallowed the last bite of the fifth slice of cake, the plate floated from her lap and disappeared along with her grandmother's ghost.

*

That night, Miyu slept with her head under her quilt. There was no room in her belly after five pieces of cake and dinner. She didn't want to see her grandma that night. But again the bedroom grew cold and her blanket was torn from her.

"Miyu," her grandmother called.

"No, *sobo*. I'm sleeping. Give me my blanket!"

"We have to respect our elders, now don't we, Miyu?"

Miyu nodded.

"Then we shouldn't make demands."

"But it's cold in here." Miyu began to shiver. "Can you at least stop making it cold when you come?"

"I'm sorry. I can't control that." A bowl appeared in front of her grandmother's ghost. "But I do have something that will warm you up."

"I'm not hungry." The thought of food made her small belly ache.

"But you are cold. I have a bowl of *o-shiruko*."

"No!" She loved the thick bean soup and would have gladly eaten it at any other time, but there was no room.

"Grandmother has asked you to eat, so you must do as I ask."

"But I told you, I'm not hungry!" Miyu threw her face into her pillow.

The room became even colder and her pillow disappeared.

"*Okaasan! Okaasan!*" Miyu yelled for her mother.

"Your mother is fast asleep. She won't hear you."

The room was so cold now that Miyu could see her breath. Beautiful curls of steam rose from the surface of the sweet bean soup. The bowl floated toward her and Miyu put her hands above it to warm them.

"It will warm you better from the inside. Eat it!" the ghost demanded. "And I know you like to see the pig. He's waiting for you at the bottom of each bowl."

She put her lips to the bowl's edge and sipped the soup. She ate the large lump of *mochi* that sat in the middle of the bowl. As soon as the bowl was empty, its warmth left her and she began shivering once again. She looked at the pig drawn on the porcelain. He looked even happier in his meadow than he ever had before.

"I have another for you. This one is extra warm!" A second bowl appeared in front of the spirit and floated toward Miyu.

She ate it quickly to feel its warmth, but mostly because she wanted to go back to sleep. "How many more?" she asked, knowing that her grandmother always seemed to have more food than the last time.

"There are four more bowls."

The remaining four bowls appeared. Miyu's stomach churned unhappily, but her teeth were chattering now and she was starting to lose the feeling in her toes and fingers. She ate slower and slower as her body filled with the sweets.

Finally when she was done the empty bowls and her grandmother's ghost disappeared. Her pillow and blanket reappeared and she fell asleep holding her stuffed belly.

*

The next day was a special day at school and that meant that lunches weren't served to the children. Miyu's mother, like all the other student's mothers, had packed her a healthy *bento* box of rice, steamed vegetables, and grilled fish. In the lunchroom, she sat with friends and they opened their lunches together to compare what they had to eat. But when Miyu opened her *bento*, it was jam packed with miniature *taiyaki*, a fish-shaped dessert made from pancake batter and filled with chocolate, cheese or other things. These *taiyaki* were filled with thick, sweet custard.

"Wow!" one of her friends said. "My mom just gave me meat and rice."

"Your mom is the best," another said.

She couldn't tell them that it was her grandmother, and not her mother, that had packed this lunch for her.

She ate three of the *taiyaki* and pushed the lunch aside. The custard was too sweet and she had been looking forward to the fish and vegetables her mother had made. When her friends finished their lunches and left the table, Miyu tried to follow, but found that she was stuck to the bench of the table. It felt as though someone was holding her legs, but when she checked beneath the table, no one was there. When she raised her head again, she saw that her grandmother's ghost was sitting across the lunch table from her.

"Miyu, you can't leave until you finish your lunch."

The *bento* box slid back in front of her. Four custard-filled *taiyaki* remained. Miyu needed to use the bathroom and get back to class, but no matter how much she tugged on her legs, she was unable to break free.

"They're too sweet," she whined.

Her grandmother's ghost waved her arms about as though she

was casting a spell. "Try them now." The bento slid closer to the edge of the table.

Miyu put another in her mouth and bit through the outer crust. The filling was still sweet, but not as much as before. She ate one more and again stopped.

"I have to use the toilet," she said.

"Two more and then you can go."

Miyu sighed and willed herself to finish. When she did, she could see that decorating the bottom of the *bento* box was another painted pig. She swallowed the last bite and then the box and her grandmother disappeared. In front of her on the table, the untouched boxed lunch that her mother had packed for her appeared. Miyu put it in her bag, left the table, and returned to class.

When she got home, she took out the uneaten *bento* box and gave it back to her mother.

"I made this special for you today. Why didn't you eat it?" Jun asked. "You've wasted a good meal, Miyu!"

Miyu had no words to explain, none that her mother would believe anyway. She could still taste the custard and her legs felt tired from struggling to leave the table at lunch.

Dinner that night was *tempura*, one of Miyu's favorite meals, but there was little room left in her small stomach for the shrimp and vegetables her mother had fried.

"First you leave your special lunch untouched and now you refuse your favorite dinner? What is wrong with you, Miyu? Have you been sneaking sweets?"

"I haven't been feeling well," Miyu lied.

*

After dinner, her family took turns soaking in the tub. Her mother would always soak with her to make sure she didn't slip under the water. Sometimes, after a long day of housework, and from the heat of the water, Miyu's mother would fall asleep in the bath. That evening, no sooner than her body felt relaxing water, Jun did fall asleep. Miyu knew to let her rest for a while and to wake her mother when she wanted to get out.

Miyu was blowing on the water's surface, watching the ripples fan out and bump gently into her mother's shoulders.

"Look here!" a voice yelled.

Miyu jumped from surprise and looked to the source of the exclamation.

Her grandmother's ghost was sitting on the small stool on the bathroom floor, a plate of eight steam buns hovered over her lap. "I've brought you some buns!"

Miyu lowered her head to hide from her, but the water was too high. There was nowhere to go. She peeked over the side of the soaking tub at the spirit. "Go away, *sobo*! *Okaasan* will be very angry that you brought food in the bathroom!"

"Are you yelling at me, your *obachan*?" the ghost screamed.

Miyu looked to her mother, but Jun was still sleeping.

The plate floated to sit atop her mother's head. Miyu giggled, for it looked like a hat.

But then her mother began to sink slowly, lower and lower into the tub. The weight of the plate was forcing her below the surface.

"*Okaasan*! Wakeup!" Miyu screamed, but Jun did not wake. She shook her mother, but still she slumbered and sunk lower.

"My grandchild, the buns are too heavy. You must eat them to save your mother!" her grandmother said.

Miyu grabbed a bun in each hand and stuffed them into her mouth. She ate six of them, but two buns still sat on the plate. She took them and threw them into the bath water, hoping to dissolve them, but they reappeared on the plate. Miyu tried to lift the plate from her mother's head, but it was unmovable as though it were attached or a part of her mother's body.

"You mustn't waste them. Eat!"

"My belly is full!" Miyu tried to lift her mother's body above the water line. She was too heavy. The plate, heavier still. "*Okaasan*! Wake up!"

"Your mother's face is beneath the water. She will die."

"Help her, *sobo!*" Miyu screamed.

"My hands are useless here. You must eat all the buns."

Miyu stuffed the last two buns in her mouth and swallowed them whole.

The plate disappeared. Her grandmother disappeared. Her mother rose back to the surface and awoke to Miyu in tears.

"Why are you crying?" Her mother asked.

"*Sobo.*"

"I know. I miss her too." Her mother stroked her head. "Let's get dried off and go to bed."

*

Jun invited Megumi, another mother, over for tea the next afternoon. She needed someone to talk to, as her husband Takahiro was either working or drinking.

"I'm very worried about Miyu," Jun said suddenly as she gripped a small cup of tea. "She hasn't been feeling well and she's been gaining weight much too quickly. If she gains any more, I'll have to buy her new clothes."

"Overeating can be a natural response to loss," Megumi offered. "I gained ten pounds when a cousin passed away."

"That's the thing! I haven't seen her eat more than usual. In fact, she hasn't been finishing most of her meals."

"And she's still gaining all this weight?"

Miyu's mother nodded. "Do you think she could have internal issues? She isn't in pain."

Megumi shook her head. "Does she seemed stressed to you?"

"Not at all. She's back to her regular self, other than the food thing. But she has withdrawn. She hardly ever sings anymore."

"Give her time. She'll come around again. The pain is still raw."

*

It was her father Takahiro's day off from work. Normal children would be excited to see their dads, but normal fathers didn't fill their guts with beer until they passed out in their own vomit.

50

When he was home, Miyu stayed outside as much as possible to avoid hearing the arguments between her parents, or being caught in the middle of one herself. This day she stood by the koi pond, watching the fish swim in circles by her reflection. They were always hungry it seemed; always ready to grow bigger.

Miyu no longer wanted to eat anything at all.

She stayed by the pond until the sun set. When she turned to leave, she found the path back to the house was gone and the plants had grown up tall around her. She could only stand next to the pond and look to the clear path on the other side of it.

Across the pond, on the path that could lead her home, her grandmother's ghost appeared.

"I don't want anything! I just want to go inside!" Miyu yelled before her grandmother could speak.

"But you have to cross the pond to go home. I have something that will help you do that."

Miyu ignored her and chose instead to try to walk along the stones that lined the pond. After only two, she slipped and fell into the shallows. Next, she tried to wade in the shallows around the edge of the pond, but a stand of reeds blocked her way. The only way around it was to swim into the deeper section of the water. Miyu didn't yet know how to swim.

Defeated, she walked back to where she started. "All right. What do I have to eat?"

Her grandmother's ghost smiled. "I've got it all figured out. You'll need nine lily pads to cross."

A plate appeared. On it, a tower of *wasanbon* was stacked. The neatly pressed cakes were more sugar than Miyu had ever seen in her entire life. Her teeth ached. She thought it might be better to sleep outside beside the pond than to consume that amount of sugar.

"Each *wasanbon* has been pressed into the shape of a lily pad. When you eat one, a real lily pad will appear and build you a path across the pond."

"You can't fool me! I can't stand on lily pads!"

The spirit's face grew stern. "We should always graciously accept gifts that others bestow. Without doubt. Without question. Do you want to go inside?"

Miyu nodded.

"Then you know what you have to do."

The plate floated beside Miyu as she ate all nine of the sugar cakes. On the plate, beneath the sugar lily pads, the drawing of the little pig was made with thick brush strokes. He was so fat and his skin stretched so taut, Miyu feared he would burst. As her grandmother said, a real lily pad appeared each time she finished eating a candy one. They held her weight and she made it to the other side without falling into the water. Inside, Miyu went straight to bed. She had no room for dinner or energy to answer to her worrying mother.

*

That night, Miyu pretended to be sleeping. She waited for the room to grow cold and when it did, she opened her eyes just enough to see her grandmother's spirit.

What she saw was *not* her grandmother.

Where her grandmother had had long, grey hair, the spirit was now bald. And where her grandmother had worn a beautiful smile, the spirit now had very crooked, pointy teeth. Her grandmother's hands had been different too, certainly not the sharp claws she now saw. Miyu shut her eyes tight and willed the thing to go away. Under her blankets, She decided that she would tell her mother the next morning all about grandmother's visits and the treats she had been sneaking.

The room warmed and she fell asleep.

*

"Wake up!" Jun shook Miyu. "Breakfast is ready."

Miyu's eyes were open, but she wasn't responding. Every so often she would blink her eyes.

Jun felt her forehead and found that it was a bit cool to the touch. She dressed Miyu in the only dress that still fit her thickened body and carried her downstairs for breakfast.

Miyu sat silently at the table, a glazed expression on her face, and she didn't touch her food. Her mother kept her home from school and tried to take care of her, but there was little she could do.

*

Later that night, Takahiro returned from work reeking of alcohol and went straight to the living room to sit in front of the television.

Jun carried Miyu into the living room and stood in front of her husband.

"What?" Takahiro asked as he tried to see past to the TV.

"Something's wrong with Miyu! She's been like this all day!" Her mother was frantic. "She only goes where I take her! She won't eat or say a word!"

"Calm down," he said. "She's sick."

Jun took one of his hands and placed it on Miyu's forehead. "No, she doesn't feel feverish."

"She's cold. Maybe she's had too much candy?"

"Not that I know of!"

Takahiro shooed Jun away. "Put her in bed. Let her sleep it off."

Jun sighed. "Just once I'd like you to worry about her, to care about us."

But her words went unheard, as Takahiro had just drifted off to sleep.

*

For three days Jun tended to Miyu, attempting to interact with and feed her daughter, but nothing changed. Jun's hair began to fall out from the stress and her back began to ache from carrying her daughter from room to room. Takahiro was spending more time at bars after work and going straight to bed when he finally came home.

53

On the fourth day of Miyu's strange coma-like existence, her mother brought her to the table for dinner and kneeled beside her. "Miyu, you really must eat!" She took a portion of fish with her chopsticks, and held it up to the girl's mouth.

But Miyu wouldn't even look at it.

Jun's face twisted into a horrible shape and she cried. "Say something! Tell me what is wrong!"

"Jun, sit down and eat!" Takahiro barked. "You look like a monster."

She sat down and ate a few bites, but it was difficult to swallow when she was sobbing.

Just as Takahiro was standing to clear his plate, Miyu's chair collapsed beneath her. She fell to the floor, but did not react.

At first, her father laughed, but then Jun screamed.

"Enough! I have had enough! We have to take her to the doctor!"

"He's probably gone home for the evening and I'm not fit to drive."

"Call him and tell him to meet us there! We'll walk!"

*

"She is so heavy!" Takahiro complained as he held one end of his daughter.

"It's as though she's gaining weight with every step we take!" Jun said in agreement as she carried the other end.

They were halfway to the doctor's office and entering the middle of town. The other villagers stopped their after dinner errands and watched as the trio passed by. It was a sight to behold. An ailing mother, hunchbacked, her hair so thin one could see her scalp. A drunken father, still in his business suit, though his shirt was untucked and his tie, loosened.

And the *thing* they carried.

Once inside the doctor's small office, they set their overweight child down on a chair in front of him. The doctor stared for a while at the chair. Miyu's father was too drunk to find the other chair and so sat in a corner of the room that, to him, was spinning. Miyu's mother lowered to her knees on the floor and hung her head in shame.

"Doctor, please help us! Our daughter isn't eating, but somehow she has gained all this weight!"

He looked for a while longer at the chair. "I'm not sure what I can do for you," he said. "You've dressed it up."

"Of course we dressed her up!"

"I'm sorry, Jun. This isn't my specialty."

"What do you mean, you are a pediatrician, aren't you?"

"Yes, oh yes." The doctor stood up and walked around the chair, examining what the parents had set in it. "But this requires the help of a psychiatrist."

"I don't follow. Do you think she has an eating disorder?"

"Not a psychiatrist for her. For you."

"I am not the issue here! She isn't eating!"

"You say 'eating'. How does it eat?"

"Why do you keep calling my daughter 'it'?"

"I don't know how to say this, but, um, this 'daughter' of yours is a rock."

"A rock? What do you mean, a rock?"

"A boulder, a stone. You've brought a rock, in a dress, to my office."

"No, this is our daughter, Miyu. You've met her before."

"I am familiar with your daughter and that is her dress, but this is not Miyu."

Takahiro stood, staggered to where his daughter sat in the chair, and placed a hand on her shoulder. It felt cold, hard and rugged. He felt the drunkenness leave his body, as though it were a cloud lifting, or a veil.

Jun raised her head and looked to the chair, to her daughter. She crawled to the chair and placed a hand on Miyu's leg, but her hand fell through it to the chair beneath.

The doctor called in his secretary, who had also come in for the call. "Can you see them out?"

She nodded and went to help them lift the rock, but Jun swatted her hand away.

"No, don't touch her!" she yelled. "Takahiro, take the other side."

Miyu's parents lugged the rock all the way home, fearing their daughter was trapped inside and might break free. Once home, they laid it down on her bed and sat beside it.

"How long has she been missing?" Takahiro wondered aloud.

Jun looked at the rock. "How long have I been trying to feed and bathe this thing?"

Takahiro hung his head. "Did we ever have a daughter?"

"Don't say such things! Of course. She was full of life. This is something different."

"If we have any hope of finding her, it must be in this room." Takahiro swung his legs over the bed and his feet hit something beneath. He lie down on the floor and looked under the bed. Stacked there were porcelain plates, cups, and bowls, each one hand painted with a chubby, happy pig. On each dish, the pig grew fatter and fatter. He picked one up and showed it to his wife.

"Where did these come from?"

Jun examined the plate. It wasn't like anything she'd ever seen. Definitely nothing she'd ever purchased for their home. She jumped from the bed and tore through the room, looking for any more clues, but the closet only held Miyu's clothes and the toy chest, only her toys.

"Move the rock!" she screamed to Takahiro. So he did.

She pulled the heavy quilt from the top of the bed and found the answer for which she was looking.

There, on the crisp white bed sheet, a large brush-stroked painting made of blood.

It was the happy pig, larger than ever, plump and prime and being led to slaughter.

AN ENTRY FROM
BLOODY MARY'S JOURNAL

Saturday, June 27th. I was called to another birthday party tonight. During my dinner nonetheless. Sweet little Ashley Bennett. I'm really getting burned out on the whole 'screaming girls in pajamas' thing. Did you know that ghosts could go deaf? Yeah, me neither! And she said my name twice and I had to fucking wait around for ten minutes before she completed the calling. Don't they know I put on the blood after the second call? That shit dries and starts to flake off. Totally loses the effect. I need to talk to my blood guy. Anyway, she was a brunette girl of average height who looked to be around thirteen. Maybe she was younger? They all look like sluts these days, so its even harder to tell in the dark of the bathroom.

She had her eyes wide open, almost like she was forcing herself to look no matter what. When she saw me she let out a "heep" kind of noise, a brief squeak, then she covered her eyes and peed her pants. SHE PEED HER PANTS. Sometimes I wish my face could show more expressions than 'terrifying' and that I could do more than scream back. Because I wanted to fucking laugh. I wanted to point and laugh.

Instead I did what I usually do, I scratched her eyes out. Usually I drink the first girls blood, because that isn't as messy and more of them will crowd into the bathroom before they realize she is dead, but like I said, I had been eating dinner already when she called. I wasn't hungry.

So I took this girls eyes and threw her body in the bathtub.

I went back to the mirror and waited. This part never gets old. I like to listen to the whispers coming from the other side of the door. Things like "did she come?" "is Ashley okay?" (or Gina, Meg, Stacy…) "should I go in?"

They always come in eventually; at least one other brave soul. Or, more likely, the girl with the smallest bladder in a one-bathroom house.

Once the portal has been opened, I can do as I please. Well, as long as the cops aren't called. I like to slaughter them all and make it look like one of the girls went crazy. This time it was a girl with my namesake, Mary. Only I left her alive and shivering, covered in her friends' blood and mumbling my name, which is *her* name. See where I'm going with this? Knowing she'll be spending the rest of her life in a mental hospital telling stories no one will believe, well, it made my plate of remaining cold food at home well worth it.

I'm not entirely over the aged swingers party I was called to last week. When I arrived, they were all wrinkly, naked, and sipping the disgusting drink that shares my name. "I told you!" they said. "I knew it was true." I couldn't stop staring at their junk. It was like a bad joke and they were laughing too hard. I slit their throats. I can still smell the tomatoes.

Vine fruits reminds me, I heard through the grapevine that Satan was expanding his writerly efforts with a foray into Haiku. That dick stole the idea of journaling from me. I'm sure Haiku weren't his idea. He is way more impressionable than you might think. Jumping on every bandwagon that drives through the Gates of Hell. The worst part about it is that he's usually pretty skilled at whatever he puts his mind to. I'm only good at scaring the shit out of pre-teens.

Speaking of, I hear my name again. Two parties in one night. Must be the full moon.

Coming, my darlings. Be. right. there.

Last Night While You Were Sleeping

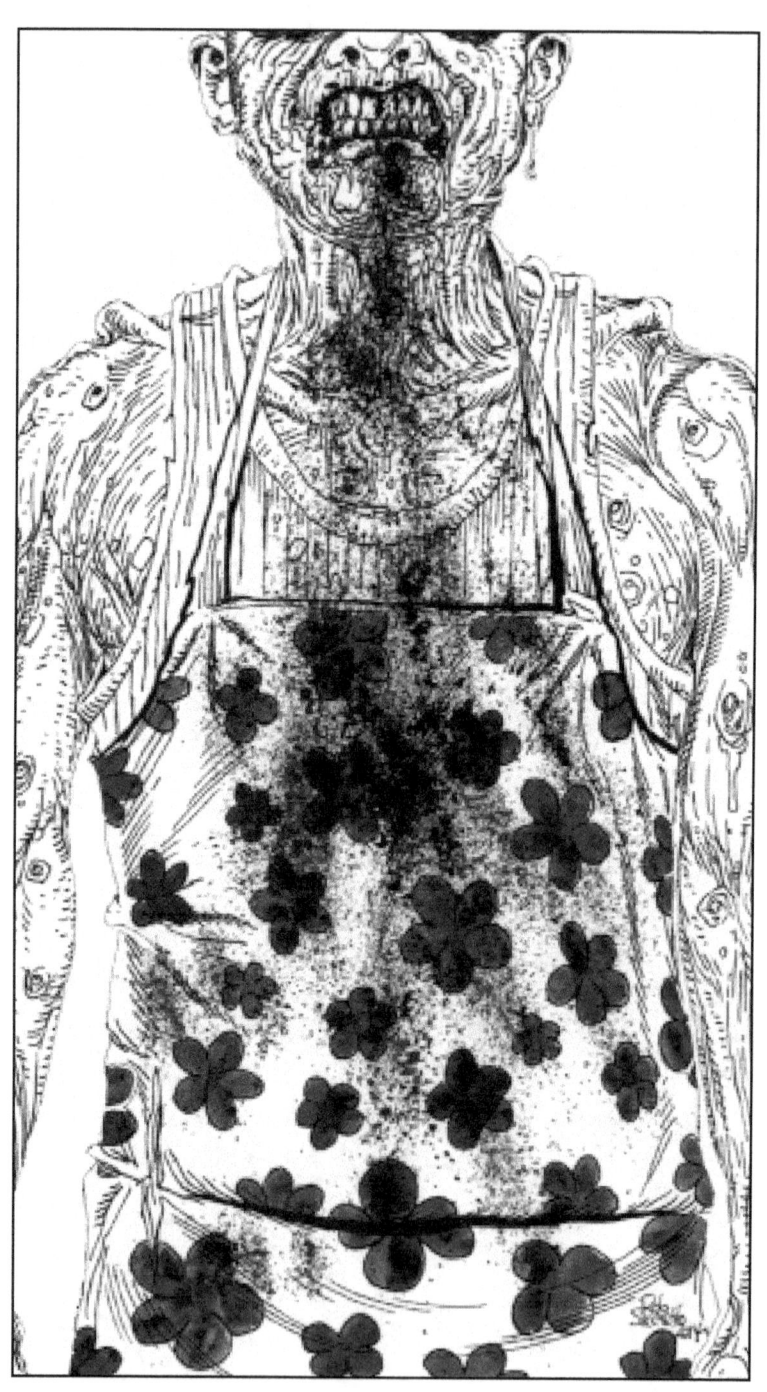

ART BY ROB SACCHETTO

HOUSE HUSBAND

When her husband leaves for the day, Marcy throws dinner into the crockpot, puts her pajamas back on, and grabs her cellphone from her purse. Her favorite show is about to begin. Two houses down, Jenea does nearly the same thing, except she's divorced, still in her pajamas, and she turns off the soap opera playing on the television. She has something better to watch; it just hasn't started yet.

It wasn't that they meant to watch, not in the beginning anyway, but the houses on Pine Street were built so close together, one could trade recipes cards or swap spit through the side windows.

One day, shortly after the new neighbors moved in, Jenea glanced out her dining room window and saw them in their kitchen. There, a man with a fork in one hand and a white knuckled fist in the other, is pressing a woman against the kitchen counter. Jenea could only assume it was his wife. Tears streaked her face and her neck was tight from sobbing. Naturally, Jenea called Marcy and told her about the entire encounter, right down to him pressing the tines of the fork into his wife's neck, laughing and then taking a beer from the fridge before leaving the room.

Thinking a small amount of neighborly love and attention might help the situation-a "we see you there" type thing-Marcy bakes a cake, something she always did for new neighbors, and Jenea puts together a bouquet of flowers. When they drop them off, the woman, now sporting a black eye, answers the door. She graciously takes the gifts, tells them she isn't feeling well, and closes the door. Jenea and Marcy chat briefly back and forth about how rude and sad the situation is, Marcy reads a piece of mail left on the stoop, looking for their last name, and as soon as they return to their homes, Marcy gives Jenea a call.

"Can you tell if *he's* home?" Marcy asks because she can't see the husband on her side of the Orcutt's house.

"Oh yeah. In the kitchen. He's standing in the doorway, watching, but she doesn't realize he's there yet. She put my flowers in a vase and is now cutting into your cake."

"What do you think he's going to do?" Marcy asks, excitement building in her body.

Dallas is getting angry.

"You think you're going to eat this?" He asks Deborah as he takes the cake from her. "I won't let you be Dumpy Deb again."

He likes to remind her of how "big" she used to be. A year ago she weighed fifty pounds more, but she was tall and for her frame, it wasn't large at all. Dallas thought differently and the weight came off quickly when he started denying her a plate at every meal. His leftovers were all she could consume.

Deborah looks at the floor and mutters "It's not like one piece is going to hurt." She wants to eat it badly. The thick frosting is making her mouth water.

"What did you say?" he screams as he picks up her chin to force eye contact. His fingers are pressing hard into her face and sending pains through her gums.

"Nothing, just throw it away," Deborah responds. "I'll tell them it was delicious."

"And waste a good cake?" He pulls a large knife from the block, even though she already has one, runs the blade across Deborah's cheek lightly, and forcefully cuts a large slice of the dessert for himself.

Marcy can hear Jenea breathing heavily into her cellphone. "What's going on?" she asks.

"He called her a name and threatened her with a knife."

"Oh my god! Should we call the cops?" Marcy moves to her

dining room to see if she might be able to catch a glimpse of the domestic scene. She can see Deborah's profile through a crack in the curtains.

"It's not that bad! He's eating the cake now, but he *is* making her sit and watch. He won't let her have any."

Marcy watches a tear drip off the end of Deborah's nose. "What an asshole!"

*

The next morning, Marcy hears screaming from the house next door, but her husband Martin hasn't left for work yet and she knows Jenea won't call if his sedan is still in the driveway. Marcy makes breakfast, starts a load of laundry, and irons her husband's work shirt all while listening with one ear turned toward the noise.

Dallas is pitching a fit.

"You stupid bitch! I told you I needed clean shirts today! You can't do anything right!" He feels the urge to hit Deborah, but he knows she'll start crying if he does, which will cause her to burn the bacon. He sits down at the dining room table and waits, rather impatiently, for his breakfast. "Don't you fucking bring me runny eggs either."

Deborah's hands are shaking as she sprinkles salt and pepper over the eggs in the pan. She is trying her best to not cry and to cook everything according to his specifications.

"Would it kill you to hurry the fuck up?" he yells and slams a fist down on the table.

She plates the food, delivers it to him, and then says "Please don't yell so loud, the neighbors will hear you."

Too late, Marcy thinks. Her own husband is now awake, humming a game show tune, and buzzing around the house to get ready for work.

"Those neighbors going at it again?" Martin asks after kissing Marcy on one of her plump cheeks. "Aren't you glad we don't fight like that?"

Marcy doesn't want to talk to her husband about Dallas and Deborah and she especially doesn't want to wax poetic with Martin about their own marriage. After ten years, they were simply going through the motions. She'd rather talk to Jenea. So she shrugs, hands him a travel mug filled with hot coffee and shoos him out the front door.

As soon as the sound of his car engine fades, Marcy picks up her phone and calls her neighbor two doors down.

"I know," Jenea says as a greeting. "I can hear it. They woke me up."

Marcy sighs. As entertaining as the drama is, she feels bad for Deborah, who can't seem to catch a break from her husband. "Should we invite her out or something?"

"And risk turning his wrath on his? No! She'd say no anyway."

"Fine, but if she ends up dead, I am *not* to blame!"

Sometimes, Deborah still loves Dallas; the way his eyes wrinkle when he smiles at the television, the way he chuckles when he laughs at his own jokes, the way he smells after he's been away all day at his job as a mechanic. It was easiest to love him when he wasn't there and as soon as he left for work, she was loving him as she ate frosting off the cake in the trash. She scoops a big glob of pink frosting with a finger and licks it. The sweet frosting and the calm of his absence gives her an idea.

"Hmmm," she says. *A life without Dallas*, she thinks.

Jenea has started a load of laundry and has some time to kill before her eBay sale ends. Last she checked, the bid was over two-hundred dollars. She'd really make out for the piece of china she found at the thrift store. The glassware, already packed and ready to ship, sat on her coffee table. She sat on her couch, casting side glances out the window into Deborah and Dallas' bedroom. Marcy is on the phone. "She's on the computer in the bedroom and she keeps looking out the front window," Jenea says.

Marcy has Jenea on speakerphone because she needs both her hands to clip coupons. "Oooh! Buy one get one!" She celebrates the savings find. "Do you think she's chatting with someone?"

"No, she wouldn't risk that."

"Do you have binoculars?"

"Ha! Of course I do! I didn't want to freak you out though."

"I'd buy some myself, but my husband would never believe I'd taken up birding."

"I have to put you on speaker." Jenea says as she puts the phone on the floor. She finds the square box in her coat closet and removes the heavy binoculars. They haven't been used since a house fire erupted across the street five years ago. She almost auctioned them off when her bank account was getting low last year. Now, thankful she didn't, she kneels on the floor next to the side window in the living room and rests her elbows on the sill.

"Can you read the screen?" Marcy has put down the newspaper and scissors, no longer able to divide her attention between savings and spying.

Jenea steadies the binoculars and squints her eyes. She can see only the right side of the screen. "There are only a few words I can make out."

"Well?" Marcy, so eager to know, is shifting back and forth from foot to foot as though she has to urinate desperately. She does have to pee a little, but not nearly enough to miss the play-by-play. Her manic pacing is creating a wind, sending coupons to the floor.

"Absorption, metal, brain, systemic...shit!"

Marcy can hear Jenea shifting around and then a loud thump as though she has dropped the binoculars. "Hello?" she calls out through the phone.

"Sorry. Deborah stood up and came to the window. I had to hide!" Jenea laughs. "Man, that was a close call."

"What could those words mean? Is she sick? Or pregnant?"

"She looks well enough and she isn't acting pregnant. Let's hope it isn't that! Dallas would be a horrible father. Maybe she's studying online, in secret, to be a nurse or something?"

"Really, Jenea? Deborah is not an overachiever!"

Jenea notices that her eBay sale has ended and the final bid for the glassware is three-hundred and fifty dollars. She smiles in her temporary contentedness. "Well, then, I don't know *what* she is doing!"

Deborah is plotting revenge.

She has found something online that will solve the problem of her abusive husband once and for all. It would be undetectable and easy to slip in one of his drinks. Her only challenge now would be getting a hold of it without Dallas knowing.

The front door lock clicks open and Deborah scrambles to close the internet browser before Dallas comes through the bedroom to the bathroom for a shower. She waits for the water to start running and then she strips and climbs into the tub with him. She feels a strong urge to please him, as he won't be around for much longer.

Though Deborah is ready for things to change now, she can't act until Sunday, which is two days away.

Jenea and Marcy notice nothing out of the ordinary on the last few days of the week. Even the fighting has slowed in the house between them.

*

On Sunday, things take a dramatic turn.

Jenea anticipates Marcy's question and answers it as soon as she picks up the call. "He's in the bed. Sleeping maybe?"

They are, of course, talking about Dallas, but today is different, as they have just watched Deborah drive his truck away.

"Where's she going?" Marcy asked. "She never leaves the house."

"If she knew what was good for her, she wouldn't come back."

"She's stuck on Dallas. She's coming back."

"Should we follow her? We could take my van." The van sits in the driveway gathering mold and helicopter seeds from the tree in the yard. One of the tires is nearly all the way flat.

"No, we should stay and keep an eye on him."

Deborah is picking up the bottle that will change her future.

She knows she must return quickly. If her husband wakes to find her gone, she won't be able to return without suffering a brutal beating. His favorite football team is also playing later this afternoon. He has set an alarm to catch the game. She has an hour and a half and he is a heavy sleeper. The shop is easy to find, but it takes some work to convince the shopkeeper that *she* is the one who called about the powder. Once purchased, she conceals the small bottle in her purse with her tampons. Dallas never looks in the "woman things" pocket. She makes it back home with twenty minutes to spare. Enough time to binge eat a candy bar she bought, brush her teeth, and calm down.

Marcy has turned on Jeopardy and is waiting for her phone to ring. When it does, she answers it and looks out the front window to see that Dallas' truck is back in the driveway of the house.

"She's back!" Jenea tells Marcy. "And Dallas is still asleep."

"I'm dying to know where she went. Do you think there's another man?"

"No. She's not dressed up or anything."

"Well, we'll find out soon enough."

Deborah is playing it cool.

Much like she has tried to for her entire relationship with Dallas. He is a bomb with a short fuse and somehow most everything she does burns that fuse quickly.

Twenty minutes after she arrived back home, Dallas' alarm goes off. He transfers his still tired body to the couch and turns on the game. He does not greet his wife or give her any shit. He waits for her to bring him a beer and the chips he always eats when he watches sports.

"Where's Dallas? Can you see him?" Jenea asks Marcy.
"He's in the living room. What about Deborah?"
"She's in the bedroom, pacing."

"Deb! Hey, Deb!" Dallas calls without taking his eyes from the football game on the living room television. "Bring me a beer."

"Now she's going to the kitchen. Hold on, I'm going to the dining room so I can see her again."
"Sounds like a calm day in the Orcutt household. I'll call you later."
"Wait! Don't hang up!" Jenea hides behind her dining room window curtain. "She's putting something in his beer!"
"Yes!" Marcy exclaimed. "That'll teach the motherfucker! What does it look like?"
"It's a powder and it's in a little, dark bottle. There's no way I could read the label. It has to be the thing she was reading about online."

Dallas is chugging his beer.
It tastes great to him. He notices nothing out of the ordinary. His team is up by ten points. His wife isn't nagging him. Life is good.

Marcy is watching him and waiting for him to die. She is sure he won't make it to dinner. Her own husband will be home soon. She hopes Dallas dies before Martin arrives. Jenea has come over to Marcy's house and sits by her side. She couldn't stand not being able to see into the Orcutt's living room.

Deborah is sitting in the dining room watching the back of Dallas' head. *Will he slump forward or fall to his side? Will he urinate, or worse, on the couch?*

An hour passes. The game ends. Dallas staggers to the bedroom and falls asleep.

That night, Jenea and Marcy can hardly sleep. They lie awake in their separate beds, in their separate houses, and daydream about the ambulance that should be parked in the driveway the next day. About the police who will arrive shortly after to ask Deborah some questions about her husband's untimely death.

"He watched the game and then went to bed," she would say with tears in her eyes. "When I woke up, he was cold as ice. He passed away while I was sleeping next to him."

"I'm sorry, ma'am," the officer might say. Or simply, "I see."

They are both mentally choosing their outfits, for they are sure to be on the news when it is discovered that their seemingly normal neighbor has poisoned her husband.

"They seemed so nice," Jenea would say.

"I made her a cake," Marcy would say. "It's so sad."

Maybe, they both hoped, they'd be pulled into court to testify about the abuse. Deborah would call them as witnesses. They had seen her black eye. They had heard the yelling.

*

The next morning, before Marcy is ready to rise, her phone rings. Her husband is still sleeping, so she sneaks out of bed and takes the call in the living room. It's Jenea.

"He's still alive," Jenea, who ended up moving from her bed to her couch earlier that morning, screams into the phone.

Marcy smacks her forehead. "Debbie, Debbie, Debbie. You should have used all the poison."

"Something's definitely different about him though," Jenea says. "He dropped his breakfast plate."

Marcy, once again, is pacing the living room. "And?"

"*She's* yelling at *him*, but he's just standing there and staring at her."

Marcy is saddened by this change. She enjoys the drama and

doesn't want to lose her daily entertainment or the possibility of television interviews and court appearances. "And now?"

"She demanded he leave the kitchen. He is walking across the broken porcelain and leaving the room."

"Can any kind of poison damage your brain?"

Jenea shrugs, even though Marcy can't see her. "I can Google it."

"No, don't do that. You don't want to be implicated if anything happens." Marcy has seen similar things happen on TV and if Jenea goes to jail, she'll have no friends.

"Good thinking, Marcy." Jenea sighs. "I was sure she'd be rid of him today."

"What was in that bottle?"

Deborah is just as confused as her neighbors. She followed the instructions the best she could. *Maybe beer deactivates the powder?* She won't be able to look it up again for another week without risking being caught.

She makes the decision to act now while his system is still sorting through the first dose.

"Do you want a beer with dinner, Dallas?" Deborah asks. Her husband does not respond. He sits stiffly at the table and stares straight forward into the kitchen, not because Deborah is in the kitchen, but because that is the way his body is facing.

Jenea is watching the strange scene unfold in the kitchen. Dallas has never been so still and patient. Deborah seems on edge. "I don't know by how much, but she just upped her game," Jenea says into her cell phone.

"What do you mean?" Marcy is trying to see into the dining room, but the curtains are only opened a crack and Dallas' head blocks any view there might be.

"She dumped a ton of that powder into his beer."

Marcy feels her heart rate quicken. "Today might be the day we see a man die."

"Well, she brought it to him, but he isn't drinking it."

"Drink up, Dallas." Deborah tries to sound firm, but she fears that he knows what she is doing to him and he'll hit her at any moment.

He takes a sip of the beer and sets it back down.

"The whole bottle!" She yells, pissed off that she has to be so specific in her demands.

He takes another sip.

Deborah takes a risk.

She sticks the beer bottle into her husband's slack mouth and forces his head back.

"Drink!" she commands.

And he does.

"Brave girl," Jenea says.

Marcy, who also glimpsed the force-feeding, responds "Yeah!"

Dallas is exhausted. He does not know why, nor does he take the time to think about it. He feels devotion to his wife and does as she wishes. Even if it means finding the energy to make love to her when he can barely control his limbs. They spend the evening together. It reminds Deborah of their honeymoon, when Dallas would do anything for her.

In the morning, Deborah is surprised to find that Dallas' cock is very hard, sending the sheet and quilt of the bed up in a small teepee. He hasn't had morning wood for years.

Things are finally changing for the better, she thinks as she climbs on top of him. The rest of his body is tense as well, but she knows just what to do to change that. She rides him.

Something is different about the fit or the function of his phallus, but she enjoys it anyway until Dallas opens his eyes and grabs her. He jerks violently, his member still inside of her.

Jenea hasn't been with a man in years and now she's feeling that old yearning as she watches the Orcutt's bang. "You won't even believe

71

what I am seeing right now!" she yells into the phone at Marcy.

"You always see the good stuff!" Marcy can hear the excitement in Jenea's voice and jealousy floods her. Marcy and Martin almost purchased the house Jenea moved into. She is kicking herself for not choosing it now.

"She's naked and on top of him," Jenea whispers.

"Ew! We aren't perverts! This line is for drama only!" Marcy is about to hang up the phone when she hears Jenea shriek.

"Oh my god!"

"What?" Marcy says, still into her cellphone in hopes that Jenea will pick up again. She climbs over the back of her couch and scrambles to the dining room window, but the curtains are closed across the way. "Jenea, tell me what you see! I'm blind over here!"

"His dick came off! She was...on him and it just pulled away from his body! It was stuck inside! She had to yank it out! He got angry and started attacking her! Omigod, omigod."

"How can that be?" Marcy has never heard of anyone's penis falling off without help from a blade and a crazed housewife. "Did she cut it off?"

Jenea doesn't answer, but instead continues narrating the scene as it unfolds. "She's in the kitchen and he's followed her! Now she's stabbing him in the chest with a knife!"

"This is it! This is it! We'll be famous!" Marcy can't decide whether she should stay on the phone or take a shower and do her makeup.

Deborah is confused.

"Do as I say! Dallas, I command you! Stop!" she screams at him. *Maybe I didn't give him enough of the powder? Maybe I gave him too much?* These questions run through her head as she flees the kitchen for the dining room. The table, as long as she can keep it between them, buys her some time.

On Dallas' stumbling lap around the table, his flailing arms catch on the curtains and tear them from the window, allowing Marcy an uninterrupted view of his naked, package-less form.

"Holy shit!" Marcy yells.

Jenea laughs into the phone. "I told you so!"

"He's going to kill her. We have to do something!" Marcy can see Deborah's face and the fear plastered there.

"Arm yourself and meet me outside."

Marcy grabs a frying pan and Jenea, her garden shovel, and they meet in front of the house. They ring the doorbell.

"She's not gonna answer," Jenea says. "She's busy being chased by a dickless maniac!"

"We should let ourselves in then." Marcy turns the handle and the door swings inward.

Deborah and Dallas aren't in the dining room anymore.

In the kitchen, the flowers Jenea gave them have wilted in the vase.

In the bedroom, on the floor between the nightstand and the bed, a bloody, owner-less penis.

In Deborah's purse, tucked beside her tampons in side pocket, is a small bottle of odorless powder labeled "Poudrer De NeuroTox".

Jenea took three years of French in high school. She reads the instructions on the back of the bottle. "I tsp. per day, maximum."

"She overdosed him. He died and came back."

A scream comes from the bathroom just off the bedroom.

Deborah is hiding in the shower. Dallas is clawing at the sliding door.

"Okay, I'm going to open it! Get ready!" Jenea reaches for the handle of the bathroom door.

Marcy has never been so excited in her life. Her heart is beating faster than the day she married Martin. She regrips the frying pan with her sweaty hands and says "ready."

Jenea turns the handle and pushes the door in. "Debbie, we're here to save you!"

Dallas snarls and rushes the women, who are already swinging their makeshift weapons wildly in anticipation of his charge.

Blow after blow of frying pan and garden shovel fall onto Dallas' head. His nude and decaying form finally lies still.

Marcy leaves the room to politely vomit elsewhere.

"I've seen you two. In the windows." Deborah steps carefully out of the shower. She doesn't want blood on her shoes.

Jenea feels her face flush. "Why didn't you close the curtains?"

"I knew that one day I would need your help."

Dallas grunts and begins to stir again. Jenea brings the shovel blade down across his neck, wiggling it back and forth until it finds a path through the flesh and bone to the linoleum of the bathroom floor. Marcy returns with three opened beers in her hands.

"Boy, you were right about that!" Jenea smiles.

And with no blood on my hands, you're both murderers who will help me bury his body, Deborah thinks. It had been her plan all along. She was done being a victim.

Deborah is in control.

Marcy presses a cold beer to her sweaty brow. "Who wants cake?"

ALL THE COLORS

"I'm sorry, ma'am. You can't go in there," he said to me. I didn't know who *he* was, only that he blocked the heavy door leading into the parking garage. A trench coat engulfed him. It was meant to suggest officiality, but, due to the grease stains near the pocket hems, it screamed tragedy and "please wash me" instead.

I was wearing the one pair of heels that didn't really fit my feet- too snug around the toes- and already running late for work. I was the picture of impatience.

"My car is in there," I said.

"Not anymore, it isn't." He shook his head and offered no explanation. I shifted my weight onto my left foot.

"What do you mean, it isn't in there? I parked it there last night!"

"A lot can happen in a night ma'am."

"What type of things happen in a secure parking garage? I need to get to work." I was beyond agitated. He wasn't doing anything by the door other than blocking my way through it. I stepped closer to the frame and nearly had my hand on the handle when he hit it away.

"Do not touch the door, ma'am. You won't like what happens if you do."

"Are you threatening me? In my own building?"

"No," he said with a laugh. "I'm sorry, no. The door has been behaving strangely."

How can a door behave *at all?* I wondered. "And you know this how?"

"We took a reading."

I looked around the small hallway, but could only see *one* man between myself and the door. "We?" I asked.

"Marv isn't here anymore. He went through the door." The trench coat wearing man sounded sad and a bit defeated. That made me happy.

"What kind of reading did you and this Marv take?"

"This one," the man said as he pulled out a small, black device. I'd never seen something quite like it, except maybe a very fancy garage door opener. It whirred and the screen lit up when he placed it near the door. "You see? The door is very cold."

"'The door is very cold.'" I repeated. "That isn't abnormal! It's always cold! We're in the basement! Let me through!"

Again I stepped closer, but he folded his arms across his chest and rammed into me like a football player, nearly knocking me to the ground. My shoes were threatening to cut off the circulation to my toes.

He straightened his tie, which drew my attention to it. It was covered in tiny SpongeBob Squarepants drawings. I pulled out my cellphone and said a silent prayer that it would get reception in the basement. "I'm calling Marlene."

"The building manager? Go ahead. You won't reach her." He smiled, happy to know something I didn't.

"Let me guess, she went through the door?"

He nodded.

"She was the first. We received a call from her from the other side. It was garbled, but we were able to find the address and get here shortly after she was pulled away."

"Pulled away? Well, what do you think is on the other side then, other than Marv and Marlene? And where did my car go? And how did Marlene know to call *you*?"

The man removed another device from his pocket. It turned out to be a cell phone. "Marv was able to send this picture before I lost contact with him."

The image on the small screen was mostly indiscernible. There were bright colors, a dark blob and the bumper of a car.

"That dark blob does look a bit concerning," I said, trying to not appear like a complete idiot.

"No that's Marv's thumb, he isn't very good at taking pictures."

I looked at the picture again. "Right. Well, there are much too many colors for the parking garage. It's only grey cement in there."

"Exactly! **Too** many colors. *All* the colors. It's a rainbow."

"So there's a rainbow in the garage and because of it I can't go to work?" I laughed as I asked, but it didn't bother him. He was still dead serious. I was about to pass out from the pain in my toes. I pulled my high heels off and stuck them in my bag.

"The *end* of a rainbow, is my theory. I don't know how it got in. It's highly unusual."

"Aren't rainbows just reflection and refraction of light on water?"

"Sometimes, but not all of the time. It's a misconception. They are very dangerous and can come about for other reasons. You should never seek to find the end of one."

Pots of gold and leprechauns flashed through my mind. "What happens if I go in?"

"You'll be pulled to the other end of it. It's in constant motion and this end happens to be the one pulling things away. We should consider ourselves lucky for that."

I didn't feel lucky at all. I felt late for work and slightly lunatic. "Then we just head to the other end and get Marv and Marlene and my car and we can get back to reality!"

"It's not that easy. The other end could be in another world, another time, another dimension. The only way to know is to ride the thing."

"That doesn't sound too dangerous. Rainbow Bright did it all the time."

"She's a cartoon, ma'am, and it only goes one way."

"The end could be down the street."

"That is unlikely. Odds I wouldn't bet on. Near impossible."

"Can we go outside and get a better look at it? Maybe we could see the end if we head to the roof?"

"I've been to the roof. The view's no good."

If I still had a job, my boss wouldn't easily let my tardiness slide. "Well, what is your recommended course of action?" I yelled the question.

"Rainbows don't last forever. It will dissipate soon." He pulled out a business card and handed it to me. "Write down your number, take a bus to work, and I'll call you if anything changes."

The front of the card read *Herb and Marv's Mystery & Mayhem Mullers*. The logo, a man stroking his beard, deep in thought.

Their tagline?

Hmmmm...

Last Night While You Were Sleeping

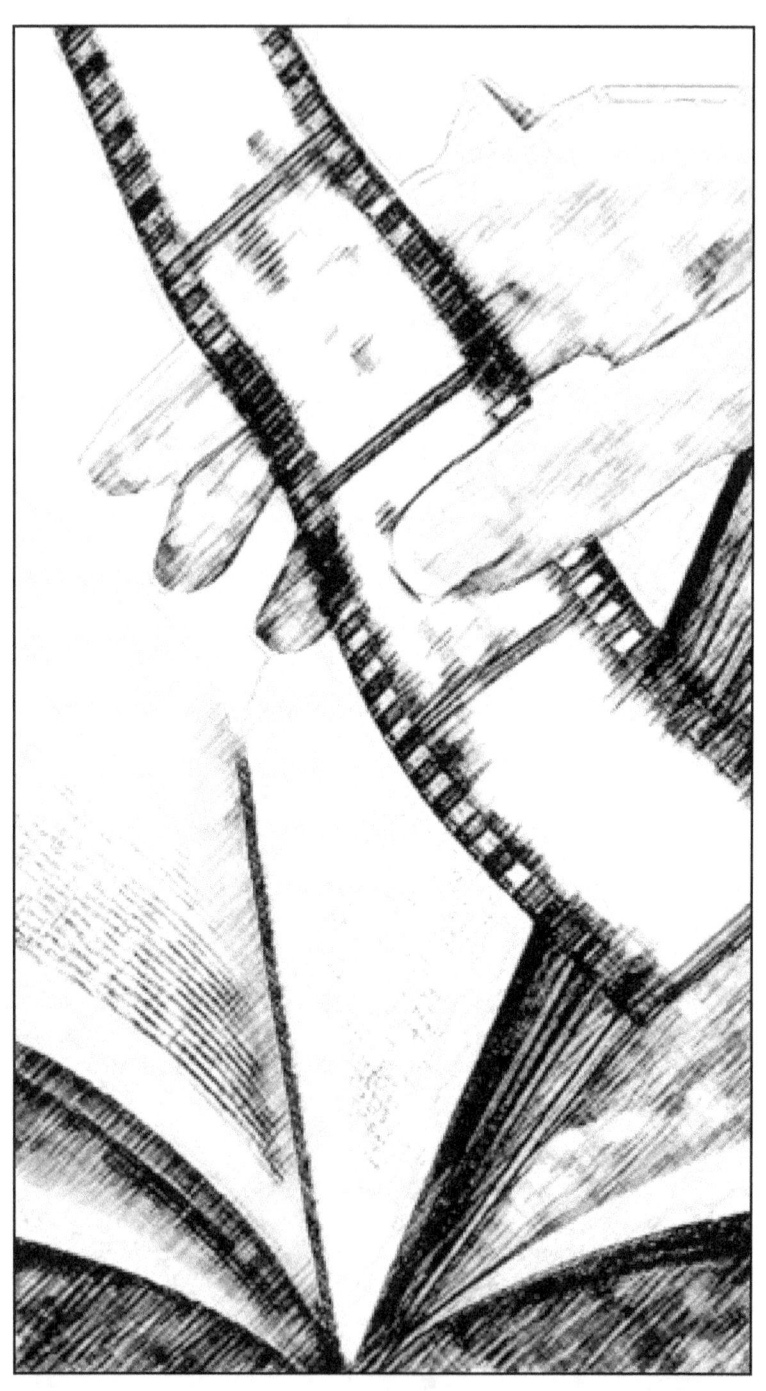

ART BY JERI BRACKETT

NEGATIVE

There was nothing special about pages one hundred seventy and one hundred seventy one in the worn copy of *Dreamland* that Chloe had checked out from the library, nothing she could see anyway. It was what lay between them, marking them that piqued her interest. She'd found other items tucked in books; love letters and shopping lists, pressed flowers and candy wrappers, but this had so much more dimension.

It was a negative strip, five frames tall, and it begged her to hold it up to the small reading light clamped to the paperback. She found a replacement bookmark-a hairband; it would have to do-and craned the neck of the light so that the bulb pointed up. The five frames were like a miniature novel. She eagerly peered into each little window of someone else's past.

Frame one - A grumpy-faced child rubbing one eye with a closed fist. The picture was taken so close to the child, Chloe could not tell if it was a boy or girl. The hair on the child's head was a mess of tangles. Chloe laughed as she recalled her own hair set in similar unintentional style that very morning.

Frame two - The same child, hair and attitude tamed, smiling behind a plate of Mickey Mouse-shaped pancakes. The child, now clearly identifiable as a girl, wears a plastic crown with indiscernible lettering across its front. The image reminds Chloe of one of her own memories. Her family, in a cabin at Lake Tahoe. They were staying with her mother's sister and her family. In the mornings, she enjoyed those same lovingly poured Mickey Mouse pancakes. In the afternoons, they stuck bacon in the water to fish for crawdads off the dock.

Frame three - No one is in the picture. A grouping of wrapped presents sit on a coffee table. Through the front window in the background, one can see a school bus dropping off a child. Chloe assumed it was the same little girl from the first and second frame. She gathered it was her birthday. Her birthdays were similar to this, only the photos taken contained a lot more people, more life.

Frame four - The same little girl, her cheeks full of air, about to blow out candles on a cake. *Happy Birthday, Claire!* the frosting exclaims in cursive, risen letters. Chloe thinks the girl is seven or eight, but there are thirteen candles on the cake and for her small size, she cannot trust their accuracy.

Frame five, an accidental photo. The world is upside down. Pieces of a broken beer bottle take up a third of the frame. The digital age meant a decrease in the lasting existence of such images. They are deleted from cameras and cell phones so no one can view the imperfection, the trivial. But here this one was, in all its fractured glory. Chloe tried to recall some of the photos she'd erased, but she could not.

In her dreams that night, Chloe fell into the frames and celebrated Claire's birthday with her. The pancakes were as delicious as she remembered them. The cake, even more so. She gave Claire a doll. In a round of Pin the Tail on the Donkey, Chloe accidentally bumped into an adult's forgotten beer and Claire's mother's camera, sending them both to the floor and capturing the final frame.

*

On her lunch break the following day, Chloe took the strip to the drugstore and asked them to print a double set of the five photos. After an hour, she viewed more clearly the little girl, her new friend, Claire.

Photo one - There she was. It's a morning photo of her waking up. Chloe could now discern her feminine features. Her delicate nose and girly lips. Her brilliant red hair. The scar between her eyebrows. Chloe remembers the day Claire fell while riding her bike. Ten stitches. How she was scared to ride her own bike after her best friend's accident.

Photo two - The plastic crown reads "Birthday Girl!" and the pancake syrup on the table is real, 100% maple syrup. Only the best for Claire on her special day.

Photo three - The wrapping paper is perfectly folded around her presents. The living room is spotless. Chloe can just make out a smile on Claire's face as she disembarks from the bus outside. Chloe was right behind her, ready for the after school party.

Photo four - Chloe remembers now why there were thirteen candles on the cake. They celebrated both of their birthdays together! Chloe turned six that year, but she was afraid of fire and so didn't help to blow out the candles.

Photo five - She remembers how the parents laughed afterwards and wondered if the camera had taken a picture. They wouldn't know until the film was developed. And then Claire's family's English Setter named Daisy came into the room and licked up the beer.

Chloe returned to the library and asked the librarian if anyone named Claire had checked out the book in the last year. He gave her a strange look, as though she was not to be trusted.

"We're old friends. I'm trying to find her," Chloe explained.

"Yes, she did," he replied slowly after typing on his computer, "but I can't tell you any more than that."

"That's fine. That's all I needed. Thanks!" Chloe was filled with joy. His answer confirmed two things: odds were good that Claire was still alive and living somewhere nearby.

The internet was extremely helpful in finding her. Chloe searched Facebook and found a smiling redhead with the same scar set between her brows. She looked so much like her younger self. Chloe was jealous of that. She always saw a stranger when she looked at her own childhood photos.

Chloe sent Claire a message, a lie. She would do anything to see her best friend again.

"We live in the same neighborhood. We met at the block

party a few summers back. I had such a fun time and wanted to reconnect."

Chloe eagerly awaited a response.

Claire responded two days later. "I'm sorry. I don't remember you!" But she accepted Chloe's friend request and left it at that. What harm could come from them being "friends"?

Chloe tore through Claire's photo albums and found other images from Claire's childhood. She took notes on Claire's favorite foods and music, and where she had vacationed. In one photo, she recognized a lending library, a small box in someone's yard that held books. It wasn't far from Chloe's house; she'd borrowed books from it before. The caption on the photo read "cute little library next door."

'Next door' was four blocks away. *Finally, I can see my friend again!*

Chloe looked at the birthday photos again. They had a date stamp. October 12th. It was just around the corner. *A reunion on her birthday!*

The walk took no time at all, as Chloe was speed walking as fast as possible. She'd stopped by the bakery for a cake and a grocery store, but forgot to select a birthday card. Her knocks fell heavy and urgent on the door. The camera strap dug into her neck.

"Claire?"

"Yes," Claire said through the smallest crack of her door ajar. "Can I help you?" "It's me, Chloe!"

"Chloe?" The name didn't register to Claire as anyone she knew or was expecting at her door.

"Happy Birthday!" Chloe yelled as she pushed her way into Claire's apartment.

She held a birthday cake with thirteen candles in it. The frosting read *Happy Birthday, Claire!* in the same heavy cursive frosting as it had thirty years before. The words *And Chloe* had been added beneath. "I hope you don't mind me barging in!"

Claire *did* mind. She didn't want visitors. She didn't know Chloe.

"It's me, from the block party and Facebook, remember?"

"Um...yeah?" She remembered her from the brief message on

Facebook, but not from before then. Seeing Chloe in person was doing nothing to jog her memory. "I saw it was your birthday, on Facebook. I live so close it would be wrong of me to not stop by!"

Claire tried in vain to recall if she'd actually listed her birthday. It didn't seem like something she would do. She hated her birthday.

Chloe set the cake down on Claire's dining table and started moving the piles of magazines and junk mail from around it. "I also brought some photos from one of your birthdays."

That's weird, Claire thought. "You haven't been to any of my birthdays."

Chloe laughed and removed one set of the photos from her purse. She laid them out around the cake. "I brought beer too. Even though we couldn't drink it then, I figured we can now, so why not? It's the Sapporo you like. The kind you drank in Japan."

Where did I leave my cell phone? Claire looked around the living room, but couldn't spot it. She wasn't yet sure if Chloe posed a threat, but it would be nice to have the police within arms reach if that changed. "We aren't friends. I don't know you. I don't know how you got those pictures."

"I was there! I already told you. Your mother gave me copies."

"My mother's been dead for a long time."

"Before that, she gave them to me before she died."

Had she been in the apartment? Did she break in when I was in Tokyo? Nothing had looked out of place to Claire. *I shouldn't have accepted her friend request.*

"I thought we could recreate the pictures! Have you seen those? When people try to remake photographs from their childhood?"

"No." Claire had seen them, but she didn't want to recreate anything. Her childhood was something she wanted to forget. She wanted Chloe out of her apartment.

Chloe approached her and tried to touch her head. Claire pulled away.

"We have to mess up your hair! You need to look like you just woke up." Chloe forcefully tangled Claire's hair, stuck her camera in her face, and took a photo. "Perfect! This one is great!"

Claire attempted to smooth out her hair. "I want you to leave."

"I don't have a good recipe for pancakes, so I bought this mix. All we have to do is add water! And I found a birthday crown at the dollar store. It's a pretty close match to the one in the second photo."

"You said your name was Chloe?"

"You know who I am, silly!" Chloe mixed the pancake batter. "My name's on the cake!"

"You need to leave, Chloe. I'll call the police." Claire's voice did not come out as steady as she planned.

"If you touch that fucking phone, I will kill you," Chloe muttered. "You don't want to die on your birthday, do you?" She smiled sweetly.

Claire wanted nothing more than to have the hot, heavy pan in her hands if she needed to defend herself. "I can help with the pancakes," she offered.

"I've got it. You can set the table. Once we recreate the photos and finish the party, I'll go home. Just like I did then."

No one was at Claire's seventh birthday party other than herself, her mother, and her father. Chloe most certainly was not there.

She set the table, making sure to put out the sharpest knives she had.

"The pancakes are ready! Put on the crown! I brought some of the good syrup too." Chloe lifted the camera to her face. "You need to smile. Look happy!"

"I'm not even hungry," Claire whined. "And I hate pancakes."

"You will smile and you will be happy! You don't have to fucking eat them!" Chloe screamed. She held the second photo up to Claire's face. "Do you need a reminder?"

Claire did her best to mimic the image. She gripped her knife and forced a smile.

Chloe took the photo. "We're going to skip the next one because we don't have a bus and I can't let you outside. I took a picture of some empty boxes wrapped as presents earlier. That will have to do. So now, it's time for the cake!"

Chloe moved the plate of uneaten pancakes to the kitchen sink and placed the cake in front of Claire.

"Now I'm not in this photo because I was scared of the fire. After some therapy, I got over that so we're going to be in this one together. Seven candles for you and six candles for me."

Claire shook her head. "There were thirteen candles because my dad was drunk. He couldn't remember how old I was! My mom didn't want to take the extra ones out because it would leave holes in the frosting! It had nothing to do with you!"

"That reminds me! I brought your dad's favorite beer too." Chloe pulled a Heineken out of her purse and set it on the dining room table.

Claire cringed. The bottle made her more nervous than Chloe herself. It represented her broken childhood and her mother's unhappiness.

Chloe set the auto timer and ran to Claire's side.

"We have to wait to blow out the candles until the photo is taken. Pretend like you're blowing."

The light on the camera would flash ten times before the picture was captured. After the eighth flash, Chloe's face hovering next to hers, Claire made a decision.

Now or never, she thought. She took the knife still gripped in her hand and brought it backwards toward Chloe's face. Chloe saw the approaching blade and grabbed Claire's wrist to stop the attack. With her other free hand, Chloe took the Heineken and smashed it on the table edge, breaking it in two and creating a jagged blade. She swung in a large arc and made contact with Claire's surprised face.

The birthday girl slumped over onto her cake and the candle flames began to lick her skin and hair.

"It broke well," Chloe said examining the bottle. "Looks just like the old photo!" She dropped it on the floor, kneeled in front of it, flipped the camera upside down and took a duplicate picture.

The smell of burning flesh filled the air. Chloe collected her things and closed the door to Claire's melting apartment. As she walked back to her car, she scanned through the pictures on her camera. They were perfect.

"Happy birthday to me," she sang.

In the distance, the smoke alarm began to sing too.

Last Night While You Were Sleeping

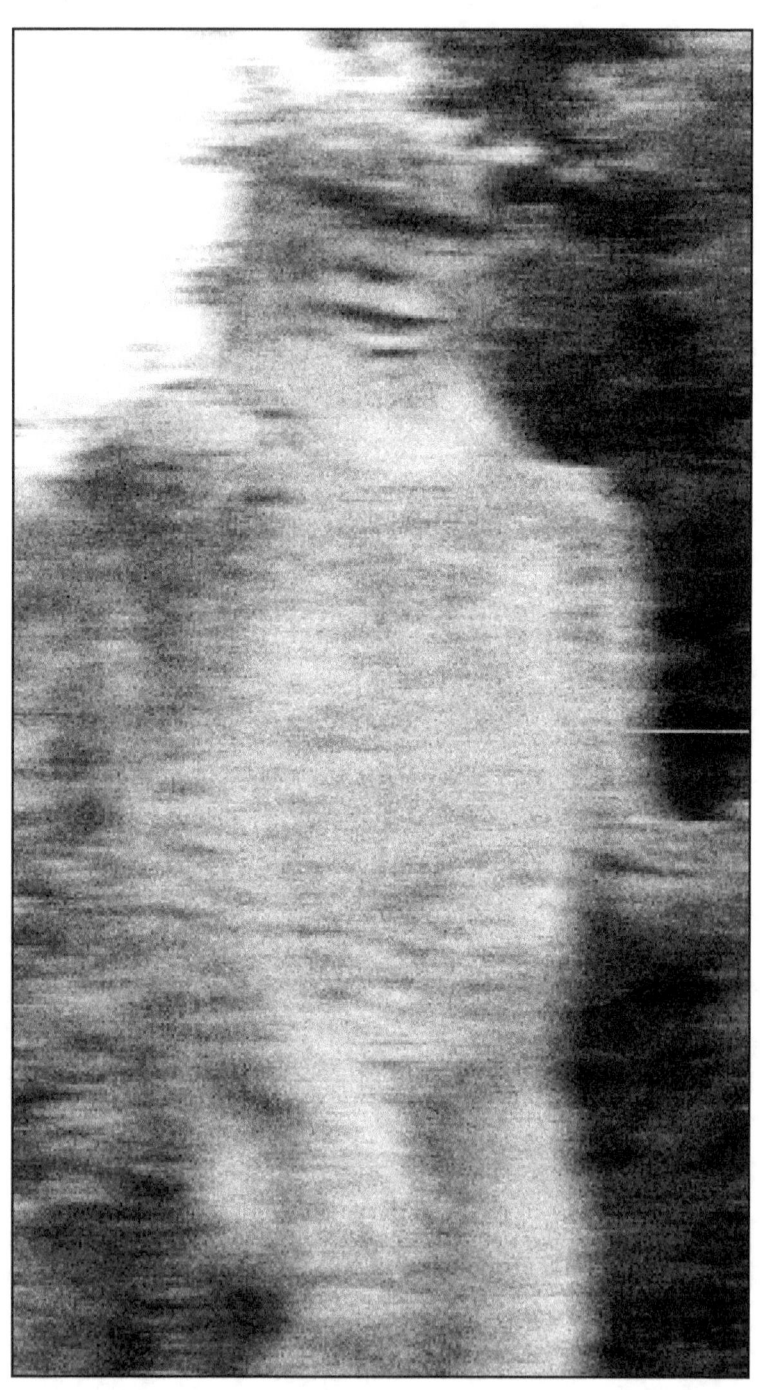

ART BY MICHELLE KILMER

BIGFOOT EXPLAINS IT ALL

The dispatch radio crackles.

"This is Officer Clayton. Let Sergeant Romano know that I'm coming in and I've got...company."

"Sure thing, honey," Cheryce replies. 'Company' usually means a prostitute found working the logging roads in short shorts and Timberlands, arms pockmarked with memories of syringes, legs with memories of mosquitoes.

He can hear Cheryce smacking gum around her mouth. "Cheryce, please tell him!"

She blows a bubble and pops it. "It's not like I ain't gonna do my job!"

This is the moment when, if she was doing her job, he would hear Cheryce yell to the Sergeant, whose office was just across the hall, but she wasn't. Officer Clayton has to give her something more, something gossipy. Then she will tell the Sergeant.

"It isn't another prostitute, either. Tell him I caught Bigfoot."

Cheryce squeals. *Thank God it isn't a dirty whore. I'd have to wipe the waiting room seats down and we're out of Handi Wipes*, she thinks. She adds wipes to the list of things the station needs. "Okay, I'll let him know we's about to be famous!"

"Cheryce, It's not like th-" he begins, but she has already dropped the connection.

*

When Officer Clayton pulls up to the station, Sergeant Romano is waiting in the parking lot because he thinks he's about to get lucky. He always came out to greet the hookers and he always had a hell of a time hiding his hard-on. This morning was no different. When he heard the name 'Bigfoot' from Cheryce he thought it was the street name for the mama of the mamas, the hooker in charge of the local prostitute club. The "club" being a loosely organized group of the local pimpless hoes; a band of trail worn women managing themselves under the guidance of the most seasoned of them all. But the club leader's name was actually Big Becky and she is not who has been arrested. The wad of cash he'd put in his pocket suddenly feels desperate. The bulge in his pants, wasted.

"What the shit, Clayton?" Sergeant Romano asks after looking in the backseat of Clayton's patrol car. His hard-on leaves as quickly as it appeared.

He'll have blue balls for the rest of the week, Officer Clayton thinks. "You should go inside," he says.

"You bring this here and now you're telling me what to do?" Sergeant Romano's face is red now. With the promise of pussy destroyed and orders being given from someone below him, he feels his masculinity is under heavy attack.

"He's nervous," Officer Clayton explains. "I don't want to spook him!"

"Fine! Put him in one of the interrogation rooms 'til we can sort out what to do."

Officer Clayton escorts the beast into the building. The handcuffs barely fit around its thick, hairy arms.

*

"Wow," Cheryce says as she joins the men in the small space adjacent to the interrogation room. She is looking through the one way glass at their captive. "He's kinda cute. Like a really big puppy."

"Cut it, Cheryce! Don't you have a phone to answer?" Sergeant Romano has little patience for her, or chatty women in general, but he keeps her on staff to break up the sausage festival that is the precinct otherwise.

"Nothing wrong with a little hair," she says with a smile. Officer Clayton blushes and the hair of his own chest rises. Even though

Cheryce likes to slack at work, Officer Clayton finds her playful attitude extremely attractive.

Sergeant Romano snaps two fingers in front of her face. "Don't tell a soul about this!"

"Sure thing, Sergeant," she says as she skips out of the room.

Officer Clayton watches Bigfoot for a while. "Do you think he's hungry?"

"Dunno. What do you suppose he eats?" Sergeant Romano asks.

"Maybe something from the snack machine?"

"Cheryce, get back in here!" Sergeant Romano yells out the door. He takes some of his designated hooker cash from his pocket and redesignates it. "Pick a few things from the machine and bring 'em back. And bring some coffee too."

Again Cheryce skips out.

"What are you thinking, sir?" Officer Clayton has no idea how to proceed. He's hoping the Sergeant might.

The Sergeant shrugs. "Well, we could be famous for debunking it."

Officer Clayton shakes his head. "No, there's no way he'll ever go on camera."

"He'll do what we say. Why'd you put him in there with the suit on?"

"He refused to take it off."

Sergeant Romano taps his foot quickly and repeatedly; something he does when he is impatient. "We have clothes he can wear. Did you offer him those?"

"It isn't about that, sir." Officer Clayton had some time on the drive over to talk to the man in the suit. It feels good to have more answers than his superior, even though Romano's toe tapping causes his nerves to fray.

"Well, then? Tell me what it's about!"

"I think he'll have to tell you himself."

"Why is he under the table?"

"He'll explain that too."

"Is this some kind of joke, you know, because I'm retiring?"

"I wish it was, sir. I wish I could tell you he's naked under the suit and going to start stripping in the box, but I can't."

Cheryce comes back with a handful of snacks and two coffees and follows Sergeant Romano into the room. She bends at her knees and sets some food down on the floor.

"Hi!" she says with a smile to the man in the suit beneath the table.

"Out!" Sergeant Romano snaps. He sits down in the chair opposite the chair that remains empty. "What's your name, son?" he asks the man.

"Bwian," the man says. His voice is slightly distorted by the mask and the mouthful of Fritos he is devouring through it.

"Brian?"

The apelike head nods. With one of his large hands, Brian points to the camera in the corner of the room. "Is that thing recording?"

"Yes. Of course. But we haven't decided if anyone's going to see it yet."

He pulls his arm back beneath the table. "As long as it's recording, the suit stays on and I stay under the table."

Romano laughs. "Brian, you can't be serious. We need to see your face."

"It's not gonna happen." He folds his arms over his massive, hair-covered chest in defiance.

Sergeant Romano leaves his chair and kneels near Brian. Sometimes it helps to be on the same level as the person you are speaking with. It helps with dogs and children, anyway. And Romano is considering Brian to be some strange mix of the two.

"Can't you just take it off for a minute?"

Brian turns away from the Sergeant. "That's all it takes."

"All it takes for what?"

He lifts up his mask enough to whisper "for the lens to take your soul."

Romano can't suppress a chuckle, which turns into a cough because Brian doesn't smell very good under the suit. "You think the camera's going to steal your soul?"

"Out there in the world, people are watching all the time. You're being recorded as you go to work, documented as you shop for groceries, captured as you mow the lawn. Slowly you lose yourself in the system and get caught up in being how they want you to be. You forget who you really are."

"So you escaped to the woods to live your life as an upright bear?" Romano asks.

Brian lets out a long sigh. "It's a cross between a bear and an abominable snowman."

"Abominable Bearman. That your furry name?"

He pulls his mask back over his face. "I'm not a Furry."

"Okay." Sergeant Romano now knows that Brian is a white male, approximately thirty years of age, and in desperate need of a shower and shave, but as law enforcement, he needs more. "Do you have any identification?"

Brian reaches into the depths of the suit and pulls out a library card from the one county library that no longer exists. His name is handwritten on it. There is no photo.

"One with a picture?"

He shakes his head. "Not since this was taken." He pulls out another card.

Romano examines it. It's a student ID card. "Brian Buckahenee," he reads. "This is from tenth grade."

"It's all I have. And my social security card."

"Voted most likely to live in the woods as a bear," Romano mumbles, thinking of high school and the silly things done there. He gives the cards back to Brian. "Why do you run from folks? It really makes people want to chase you more."

"The suit can't block all of the soul-stealing capabilities of handheld cameras. I have to stay out of the pictures and off the television."

Romano expected a wacky answer, but a failure of a soul-protecting fur suit was not one of them. "Right."

"And I don't like talking to people. As you can tell."

Since Brian *is* talking, albeit through a layer of fur, Romano throws in a question he's always wanted to know the answer to. "How do you explain the giant piles of shit?"

Brian doesn't respond immediately. It's a private question and something he's not comfortable speaking about. *But if I want out of here*, he thinks, *I need to do what they want.* He sighs. "The camp food messes with my stomach and I eat a lot, from all the running."

"Well, you've been causing quite a stir. Hikers have been catching glimpses of you. There's roadside gift shops selling anything and everything with your image on it. Even an espresso shop called Bigfoot Cafe."

Brian is happy that Romano doesn't want to speak more about his digestive situation, but he shakes his head. "Can't a man find any peace and anonymity in this world?"

Romano pulls several items from one of his jacket pockets. A pressed penny that claims the region as 'Bigfoot Country', an eraser head for a pencil in the shape of a mini Bigfoot, and a napkin with a coffee stain and the logo for Bigfoot Cafe on it. He pulls something larger from his other jacket pocket and sets it on the table. A Bigfoot bobblehead doll. "My personal favorite."

Brian reaches his large, hairy hands to the tabletop and touches each item one by one. "I didn't mean for this to happen. I didn't want this to happen."

"Kind of hard to keep a low profile when you're a gigantic, furry, running, anti-social man with unstable bowels."

Beneath the suit, Brian winces at himself being described in such an unsavory way. He looks up at the security camera. "Is it still recording?"

"Yes, and it's not going to stop."

"How long do I have to stay here?"

"Just a bit longer. You can leave once you take the mask off for the camera."

"It stays on."

Romano changes tactics, but doesn't think Brian will fall for it. "This is a new, non-soul-stealing camera. State of the art. You can come out from under the table."

"I've never heard of those."

"Well, that's what happens when you spend too much time in the woods. You lose touch. You aren't up to date on technology."

"You're sure it won't hurt me? Why didn't you tell me before?"

"I'm living, soul-filled proof that this particular camera will not steal your soul." Romano doesn't answer the second question and hopes Brian doesn't notice.

Brian grunts and gets up from under the table. He slowly sits in the chair.

"See, much better. Now we can talk man to...man."

They sit together in silence for a few minutes. Each one sizing the other up. Romano is tall, but not really when compared to the mammoth of a man across from him. He imagines the head of the suit adds some height to Brian as well. Brian isn't concerned about Romano, he even enjoys his company slightly. It's the camera he has issue with.

Brian picks at the burrs stuck in the long hairs of his suit. He places them in a row on the table, and organizes them by size, largest on the left. He also finds a bobby pin which, from the glitter that covers it, he recognizes as belonging to Nicole. Nicole is short and bearded, because she is really a man named Nick and Nick likes hairy men and glitter, a lot.

Romano watches him clean himself. "Where'd you get the suit?" he asks.

"I made it."

"All by yourself, man?"

This makes Brian self-conscious until he realizes it might be a compliment. Still, he's on the defense. "Nothing wrong with a man making things out of fabric."

Romano reaches across the table and tries to touch a piece of the synthetic hair, but Brian pulls his arm away. "I wouldn't call that fabric."

"You buy it at the fabric store. It's fabric."

More silence. Brian farts. Sergeant Romano distracts his olfactory system by smelling the steam climbing from the bitter cup of coffee in front of him. "Can I see your face now?"

Brian shakes his head. "Someone could be taking my picture through the glass."

"Officer Clayton doesn't even have pictures of his kids in his wallet and Cheryce is dumb as a box of rocks. She couldn't work a camera if her life depended on it." Romano silently hopes neither of his staff are listening. If they were, he would later play his comment off as strategy; a carefully laid plan to unmask the monster.

Again Brian shakes his head.

Sergeant Romano stands up. "I'll be right back."

In the viewing room, he and Officer Clayton are trying to devise a plan to get Brian out of the suit.

"We could bring in one of the broads and pay her to seduce him," Clayton suggests.

"I have a feeling he does it with the suit on. And how would we explain that expense on the budget?" Romano is not a stranger to hiding pleasure expenses, but witnesses change the equation.

Officer Clayton scratches his head. "We could sweat him out of it. Actually turn up the heat on him."

Sergeant Romano does not torture prisoners, but the more time he spends with Brian, the more his curiosity grows. "Do it."

The rise in temperature is imperceptible at first. Brian feels cozy and safe in his suit, but then a bead of sweat rolls down his chest. Another bursts from a pore on his forehead. He pulls up the mask to let in more air. The relief is temporary.

Cheryce has let herself back into the viewing room. "Do you remember when that skank Ellie stayed overnight in the holding cell? When she was so high she lost her shoes in the pond by the woodmill?"

"Yep." Officer Clayton remembers that night well. He chased Ellie in the dark, through the big machinery, and tackled her to bring her in.

"Well," Cheryce continued, "she stayed up all night long talking about a hairy mountain man who liked it rough, but was *real* nice and quiet otherwise. I thought it was just some trucker or logger."

"But it was Brian."

"Must have been."

In the room, Brian is faced with a difficult choice between death from heat exhaustion or death by soul-sucking security camera. He wants to move, to hide beneath the camera, but the heat weakens him. Sweat pools in the fingertips of his hair-covered gloves. Body odors grow more rank as the temperature inside the suit reaches sweltering levels.

He slowly lifts the mask. Long, moisture-heavy strands of hair cling to his face. His beard, a slow waterfall.

"Cut the heat, Clayton! I'm going in for the mask!"

Romano rushes into the room, nearly faints from the smell and snatches the Bigfoot mask from the table. Brian stands, but quickly sits again when Romano moves his right hand toward the holstered gun on his belt. His suit is not bulletproof; Kevlar was too expected.

"Calm down there, big boy. You'll get it back in a second."

Brian has no words, only fear. He watches as Romano holds the mask by a few of the head hairs.

"See, you're okay, right? Still got your soul in there and everything."

"It's a slow process, the draining."

With the mask still in hand, Romano is more in control of the situation. He continues the interrogation. "So, the woodland prostitutes have known all along who you are?"

Behind the glass, Officer Clayton shakes his head.

"They're good at keeping secrets," Brian says. "They're understanding. Brooke is a good listener."

"No son, they *pretend* to understand and Brooke is a meth head. In fact, I drove her down to detox at the rehab clinic just last week."

"Panda doesn't pretend!" Brian blurts out.

"Panda goes by the name 'Panda' and claims to speak 'Pandanese'. I'm fairly certain Panda's entire life is a lie."

With the mask off, Romano sees the hurt on Brian's face. Romano is attempting to hide his disgust that he's been sharing bedmates with the dirty beast in front of him.

Another officer has arrived at the station with, appropriately, a hooker in tow. It's Kruse, a fairly pretty blonde who doesn't need the money, as she is quick to admit, but has an insatiable addiction to sex. They walk by the interrogation room and Kruse peeks into the door's small window.

"Hey Brian!" she yells. Kruse is one of Brian's favorites. He enjoys the scent of her shampoo and how she obsessively applies chapstick. He thinks of her as clean. She likes that.

"He can't hear you," the officer says.

"He hears me in his heart," she says.

The officer rolls his eyes. "I'm sure he does."

Kruse attempts to backtrack to the windowed door. "Why is he in there? He hasn't done anything wrong."

The officer leads her down the hall. "Paying for sex is wrong. How many times do we have to tell you that?"

"Sergeant Romano might disagree." Kruse winks, but she doesn't have to. The entire department is aware of his interests.

In the interrogation room, Brian is ready to leave. "Do you have anymore questions for me? Because avoiding cameras isn't a crime. You can't keep me here."

Romano has more questions, but his mind is foggy from the lingering smell and heat. He sips his coffee and focuses. "Where are you staying?"

"I inherited a plot of land from my parents."

"You been paying the property taxes on that?"

Brian nods. "With profit from my Etsy shop."

Romano looks to the mirror, through it, to Officer Clayton. "What the hell is an Etsy shop?"

Officer Clayton doesn't know.

"It's like a crafts super mall, but online," Brian says with some reluctance. It could begin a long conversation he isn't interested in having. "The ladies helped me set it up. I sell handsewn plush cats. With the extra fur."

"You got a business license for that?"

Brian nods. "I'm a sole proprietor. I'm good with the government."

No other questions come to Romano's mind and even if another query found its way to the surface, the room is no longer hospitable to those needing clean oxygen.

"Stay here a sec," he says to Brian and then returns to the viewing room.

"That was tough. The whole room smells like ass."

Romano is taking deep breaths. Clayton is laughing hysterically. In the room, Brian is smoothing out the hair of his mask before putting it back on.

"Hard to find a laundromat in the woods that cleans hair suits, I suppose," Officer Clayton says.

"He's dirty under the suit too. He must be carrying all sorts of diseases from the hookers."

"Super strains!" Cheryce exclaims as she rejoins them.

"Cheryce, I'm gonna need you to wipe down the interrogation room with antibacterial wipes. Maybe bug bomb it too, just to be safe," Romano directs.

"We're out of wipes."

"Well, the bug bomb and some Febreze will have to do. Maybe find a fan to air it out or something?"

"Ugh!" Sometimes, Cheryce hates her job.

"So, what are we going to do with him?" Officer Clayton asks his superior.

Romano shrugs. "Let him go. He didn't do anything."

"Then what?"

"Well, we can keep the legend of Bigfoot alive or...we can tell the world about...*Brian.*"

SHADOW THEORY

A small man, smartly dressed and bespectacled, walked slowly to a podium at the center of the stage. Beside him, a poster listed his name, Professor Ervine Scodge and showed the cover of his one and only book, *Shadow Theory*. He tapped the microphone to check that it was on, cleared his throat, and began to speak.

"In our lives there is always a little bit of light. It's difficult to find pure darkness and I wouldn't recommend seeking it out. Horrible things live in it like assumptions and fears, death most certainly. But let's start by talking about the other end of the spectrum, bright white light. Obviously this can be just as dangerous as the dark, only in a different way. Even when we enter the tolerable levels, this class of light is still doing negative things to us psychologically."

Ervine signaled to a woman off stage and the lights in the auditorium were turned as bright as they would go. The crowd reacted in the expected way, covering their eyes, squinting, and generally becoming more self-conscious.

"I see many of you flinching, or rearranging your hair to hide the blemishes on your face. This light is terrible isn't it! Honest and unflattering. I bet you can see all of my wrinkles. Think, for instance, about those long, fluorescent bulbs hung above us in places of work and commercial spaces. The light they emit is not satisfactory for peaceful moments or sleeping. They are made to promote alertness and productivity, to display consumer goods and high-paced living, and to focus on everything around us. They, like "the man" above us in the corporate food chain, don't want to see us stop moving or making, or buying. These levels of light also make us self-conscious and doubtful of our good appearance. They encourage insecurity and make us more eager to please."

He signaled again and the lights were turned back down to a tolerable level. The crowd once more adjusted in their seats, but this time in a more relaxed manner.

"Now, this is the level most common to public spaces. It isn't flattering to everyone, but it will suit a large majority of complexions and egotistical sensitivities."

Ervine clicked on the projector and used a laser pen to point at the graph displayed on the pull down screen behind him. "Between here and here," he pointed to two points fairly close to one another, "this is where romance lives. Stop giggling! This isn't just physical love but a fine dinner with friends too. The level of light that makes everyone beautiful. When friends or family, even strangers, are having issues, I recommend this range most often. We are all lacking love and beauty, or at least enough appreciation of them."

Faces in the crowd looked to the woman controlling the light switch in expectation, but she didn't move to alter the lights.

"No demonstrations of that light level, I'm afraid. There will be no hanky panky on school grounds!" he quipped. "In my book, there's an entire chapter dedicated to it though, so you can take it home and fix your relationships!"

Laughter rippled through the room. Those lines were scripted, but Ervine delivered them naturally each time.

"Of course, the color temperature matters as well. We don't just have soft light, we have yellow, white, and even red hues. Any of you who have picked out interior paint at the hardware store know what I am talking about. I won't go more into this, because color temperature is much more about personal taste. My book is about the broader categories of light levels."

He sipped some water and continued.

"Darker still, we enter the realm of calm and relaxation. These are the sleeping levels. Many of us use nightlights for our children to achieve these dim levels of light. Dark enough to still quiet the daytime functions of the body, but light enough to close young eyes without fear. And us adults, weaned from the need for nighttime light sources, still have the benefit of the moon and stars, even when out in the wild."

Ervine signaled to his helper, but she wasn't paying attention. He cleared his throat into the microphone. "Next level, please."

She turned the lights down quickly, skipping the sensuous levels.

"Don't fall asleep on me. I'm going to finish the talk in this glorious lighting. After this level, we enter the pitch black. As I said before, this isn't somewhere you should go. That darkest of levels is responsible for more horror and depravity than I care to think about. It takes a very strong mind to overcome its power."

An uneventful question and answer segment followed his speech. Ervine managed to sell half of the books he'd packed into the auditorium. Back in his hotel room, specifically selected for its fading light switches, the professor relaxed. The day's talk went well, but his speaking tour hadn't gone without its hitches. His Wichita hotel room was poorly lit and made for disturbed dreams and an unsatisfying breakfast. The light affected his mood, and his mood affected his taste buds. It was a losing battle to find any enjoyment when the level was off. The crowd to which he spoke in Tallahassee had an overwhelming majority of hecklers who had made it difficult to get through the presentation without losing his temper. His assistant turned the lights down slowly, imperceptibly, and that helped to calm them.

He poured himself a glass of scotch and took the one chair in the room. The alcohol warmed his tired body and he fell asleep.

*

Hours later, a cold, wet feeling pulled him from sleep. The room was dimmer and he was tied to the chair. Before seeing the man, Ervine knew he was not alone.

"What will you do in this light?" the man asked him as the

105

space grew even darker. "Will you touch yourself? Will you ask me to dance?"

"You have it wrong, this isn't quite the romantic level," Ervine laughed. He could have cried too, from fear, but he was sensitive to the light and the level *did* have a calming effect. "Someone hasn't been paying attention." His head was heavy from the combination of drink and sleep.

His laughter angered the intruder. The room was plunged into total darkness in response.

Ervine looked for the glow of the alarm clock, but he couldn't locate it. The clock on the coffee pot had been covered as well. "Bring back the light at once!" he roared. His boyhood fears of the Boogeyman and Swamp Thing threatened to crawl out of the abyss that surrounded him. Or worse, the ghost of his ex-wife; a bossy and idiotic woman who only stifled his dreams to be an author when she was alive. Her sudden heart attack had been a godsend to Ervine, until the visions began.

As if the man knew what Ervine was thinking, he asked "what is hiding in this dark, professor?"

"I wouldn't want to assume anything," Ervine responded calmly. "It's only a hotel room. With a bed, a chair and table, and two men. Or, one man and one...boy. That is how I choose to see it." With his body bound to the chair, his thoughts were the only thing he had to defend himself.

"But you know there are other things out here, if your mind allows it." The man ran a finger along Ervine's right arm.

Keep a level head, Ervine thought. He was doing everything in his power to fight the thoughts the dark elicited from his mind. He clenched his teeth and hummed a happy song to himself. His daughter had insisted he hire a bodyguard and, when he hadn't, she did. But Ervine left that bulky man back in Richmond to chase nearly rich, almost southern women and drink iced tea. He was a boring meat head, some fifty years his junior. Ervine didn't trust the man to tie his own shoes. Now he regretted that decision and would gladly listen to the muscle man's useless ramblings about protein shakes and deadlifts if it meant he would survive the night.

The lights came up and the man turned the chair to face the bed. Ervine then saw someone else in the room. It was a woman, a stranger to him. She was slumped over herself on the edge of the bed.

"Who is she? How did she get here?"

The man caressed her thigh and then pushed her limp body backward onto the bed. "She is whatever the light tells her to be. But that really isn't true, is it?"

Ervine looked again at the woman. Bruises dotted her exposed skin and drool had gathered at the corners of her mouth. It was clear she needed medical attention.

"I don't follow," Ervine said.

"I did what you said. I found the perfect level of light, but she still didn't want me. Stupid bitch!"

Another one of these guys, Ervine thought. The crazies always found him. Though none of them had bound him to a chair before, or even found his hotel room for that matter.

"There are plenty of fish in the sea. Maybe you're a clown fish and she's looking for someone a bit more...serious."

"Serious? I'm deadly serious!" He pulled a knife from his pocket and showed Ervine the blade.

"Yes, I see that. But love takes more than lighting. It takes time."

The man ignored Ervine's lesson. "You did this to her, you know? Your 'shadow theory'." He bent down and looked directly into Ervine's eyes. "Yeah, I read your *fucking* book."

"You must have found a hidden chapter, because I most certainly do not condone using light to alter the lives of others! Or tying them up when light therapy doesn't work!"

The man scoffed and pocketed the knife. "You do it every time you give a speech. Fiddle with the lights, the people in the audience." He walked to the side table and removed the lamp shade from the bedside light, exposing the glowing, brilliant bulb. He then pulled the cord from behind the table and held the lamp to Ervine's face. The cord wasn't as long as he expected, so he dragged the chair, and Ervine, closer to the outlet.

Ervine then understood the burns on the woman.

The man pressed the scorching light bulb to Ervine's face and hands. Pain radiated through his body as his skin and peach fuzz shrank away from the heat.

"Please! Please stop! I don't torture or tease anyone! It's all temporary, a demonstration!"

The man shoved the bulb into Ervine's crotch and held it there for a moment until the scotch-made content of his bladder was urged out by pressure and warmth. "How does it feel to not have control of yourself?" He again held the bulb up to Ervine's face. "Can you see your flaws now?"

The tears came then. His daughter would never forgive him for firing the bodyguard. He would never forgive himself for leaving the book tour unfinished. His ex-wife's ghost would find and follow him in the afterlife. No one would know his brilliance.

"I'm a writer. A teacher. A man of light!"

"Not anymore you're not." The man sunk the blade into Ervine's eye. He slowly pulled it out, stabbed the woman on the bed for good measure, and then sent the room into pitch darkness once more.

Last Night While You Were Sleeping

ART BY MICHELLE KILMER

THE REASON WHY

Hear not a mournful wail,
instead a desperate mother's tale
of events that have unfolded
and have led me to assail

What's the cause of all my gloom?
Well, he took her from her room!
Then later placed her lifeless body
in a shallow, earthen tomb

I called out to her that night,
my bearer's body taut with fright,
and I screamed toward distant heavens
demanding rescue from my plight

No cavalry was sent,
no helping hand was ever lent,
and no God nor mortal soul could ever
make the man repent

Where has he left my child?
I searched the wood and fields, wild.
Hardly a rock was left unturned if
'neath her bones may've been piled

Dressed in a gown of white,
perhaps a frightening, ghastly sight,
but how else will she see me
in the middle of the night?

'Tis not a game made for the weak,
that wicked, endless hide and seek.
She'd been missing then for months
and the outcome looked so bleak

I crossed the ancient cemetery
where I knew she wasn't buried
and wandered to the spot that
would make me legendary

She was sleeping somewhere near,
oh, my darling little dear,
I'd been looking 'round forever
finally, I sensed her here

Here! by this bend of road
I found her precious body, stowed,
left to dirt and air and water
left to damage and corrode

Still and peaceful as she lie,
a tiny life just made to die,
I told her that I loved her,
but her form gave no reply

I surveyed the damage done
until my heart was overcome
when I saw she'd lost her shoes,
that she had suffered, she had run

Weakened at the knees
and thinking of soft-spoken pleas,
I fell beside her body
and I gave in to the freeze

Last Night While You Were Sleeping

In my soul there grew a rage,
a ceaseless fire, an unturnable page
and I, then, there, determined
the depth of war that I would rage

Pain and I stand 'side the road
forever doomed to not grow old
inviting travelers passing by
to come and join us in the cold

"Do you know my little girl?
she liked to read, and sing, and twirl!
Her skin was soft, like velvet,
her hair was set in curls

It's hard to tell with rotten sight,
but you look to be his height.
In fact, I'm certain it was you
inside her room that fateful night!"

For all the unmade memories
and all the ne'er sung lullabies,
please allow these mother's hands to
help the life drain from your eyes

I bid you heartily, sit still!
Slow your breath and tame your will!
The others' bones are lonely
they're waiting just beyond the hill

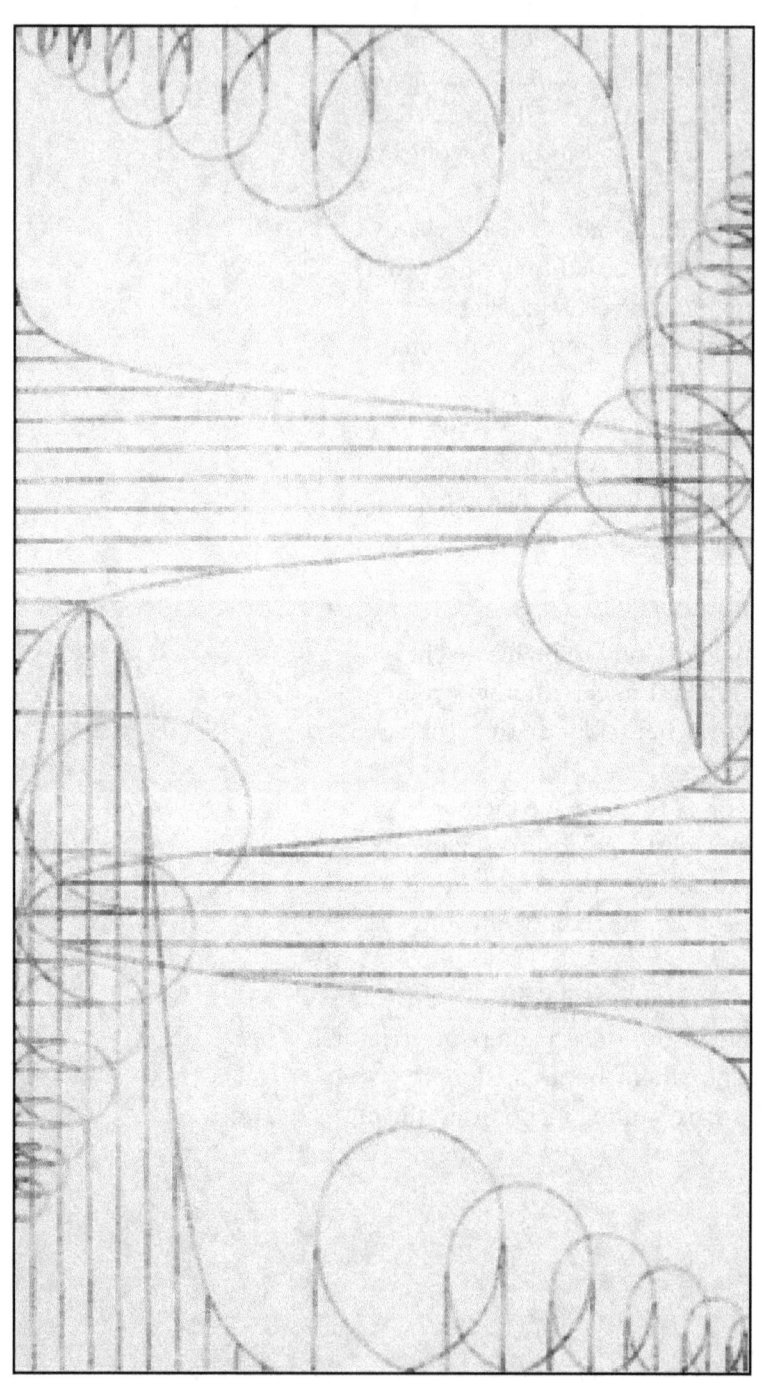

ART BY MICHELLE KILMER

DREAM LAND

It was meant to be the end of things, but to its riders, it would feel like a beginning. It was a rocket ship to a new plane of existence; the rainbow road to eternal rest. Exhilarating and exhalting. Death in three minutes and twenty seconds.

All this was well and good and math, physics, and biology suggested it to be one hundred percent effective. No one would ever live through it. Human trials had not been run, but that was only a matter of time. There was a waiting list that would fill the twenty-four passenger train more than eight times.

The problem was, Blake didn't want to die. He wasn't ready to go at all. The assisted suicide roller coaster was someone else's design; a solution to the problem of killing humanely. He was the only contractor willing to build it. And now he was paralyzed and locked into the damn thing, about to meet his maker.

He awoke in the seat with no memory of the night before. His head ached. He couldn't move anything, apart from his eyes.

How the fuck did I end up here?

Enemies of the machine were few, but bold. They were the pro lifers. Anti-abortion and therefore, anti-assisted suicide. They bombed clinics and served jail time. It wouldn't mean much to them to kill one more time in the name of life. But the site's outer wall was near unbreachable. *How did they get in?* There were fears about emotional teens breaking and entering to make choices they couldn't take back. Or thrill seekers who doubted the coaster's lethality.

Why didn't they just dismantle it? Or drive explosives into it? You should kill the executioner, not the maker of the guillotine or the unknowing weaver of the noose's rope!

He could just drag his fingertips along the waterproof fabric of the seat. It was waterproof because the ride made people lose their shit, literally. Every coaster kit, a packaged buy-and-build for contractors, would come with a hose. It would be *his* shit that someone would spray off the seats, *his* lifeless body trucked away to the on-site incinerator.

His chest could feel the compression of the metal bars that held him down. He'd chosen the shape, the finish, and the locking mechanism. He carefully selected it all a year ago, before construction started.

Sensation was slowly returning to his body, but not fast enough to afford him time to undo the harness and remove himself from the ride. He could hear the familiar hum as the machines started working. Even that hum had been altered, fine tuned and formulated to soothe. Soon, the seat would carry him up the drop tower some one thousand six-hundred seventy feet high before it dropped sharply and flew into a series of loops, the rails of each one painted a different bright color of the rainbow.

In his mind he was screaming. There might be others nearby who could help him, if only they could hear him. *As long as they aren't in on it.* But the sun hadn't even come up yet and the birds were only now starting to sing.

The cars were pulled up the lift with an incessant and heavy clinking noise. The engineers couldn't do anything about that sound, but it was nostalgic, at least; reminiscent of a traditional theme park ride. With each clink, his eyes blinked. He had two full minutes to stare at the sky, breathe the morning air, and make peace with his God. It might have been pleasant, had he not fear-urinated. Now the piss had puddled at the bend in the seat where the backrest met the seat cushion. It was climbing the dry threads of his shirt, soaking in and sending a chill up his spine.

He knew the course by heart and, even if the sappy music hadn't started playing, he would have known he was about to hit the crest and drop to ride the first loop.

The fall was like standing on tracks, watching a train rush at you. Part of Blake wished it would crash into the ground instead of spinning him upside down. But spin, he did.

After the first loop he reached greyout where colors didn't

matter anymore. The grass was no longer green nor the sky blue. His color vision was gone. His vomit, just one more colorless liquid coming out of him. Black out followed quickly. He'd been blacked out before. Blackout drunk, punched in the face by an enemy blacked out, but never no-turning-back-blacked-out. Never dead.

The additional five loops were precautionary; extra go rounds to make sure the g-forces had done their work and killed every passenger on the ride. Blake was brain dead after the second one.

The builders on his crew found Blake's body later that day, sitting peacefully at the end of the ride. There was no one else on site and further investigation and viewing of the security cameras determined that he'd drunkenly set the auto-timer for a test run, locked himself in, and passed out.

Whispered conversations suggested he was suicidal, but no note was ever found. No one knew that Blake suffered from sleep paralysis, especially after heavy drinking. Blake had been too hungover and confused to remember that fact about himself. The good news was the coaster worked. There was little visible trauma to his body, save for some vomit on his face and shirt and the urine now dried on his pants, but the coroner decided that had been due to the alcohol in his system. He died with a smile on his face. He was the champagne bottle to christen the ship before its first sailing; the test run that proved the viability of the ride as a swift killing machine. He was also the first to test the crematory fires. There was enough bad publicity around the assisted suicide ride so the company hid his death.

Dream Land opened the following month. Food trucks and picnic tables dotted the patch of land around it. A small chapel was built on site for mourning family members.

The first train of twenty-four pulled slowly up the drop hill.

A month after that, the contracting company was hired to start work on a second coaster- this time for a prison looking for alternatives to death by lethal injection.

ART BY KRISCINDA LEE EVERITT

AN ENTRY FROM SATAN'S JOURNAL

June 6th, evening. Tried writing Haiku earlier. Fuck that shit. A pedophile from Japan turned me onto it. I'm surprised too. I totally thought he was going to pressure me into watching a kiddie porn *anime* with him. I hate when they do that (and they almost ALWAYS do!). Anyway, I should have known better than to try Haiku. Pedophiles never have good ideas. Or maybe it's the Japanese? One of them taught me *Ikebana*, but as you can imagine, flowers are hard to come by in Hell. That hobby lasted about a minute.

For writing, I think I'll stick to my journal and the scarification I perform on the self-harmers who end up here. They come in with their suicide notes in hand, like a pink slip from life. So usually, I carve the entirety of their written woes into their backs, but yesterday I wrote my name in all caps on everyone, just for fun. See that? No rules. No counting syllables! None of that *nature* shit. Just ink, or blood. You would think I prefer the latter, but it's so hard to wash off!

The main problem with traditional journaling down here is that the pages always catch on fire. I've written, lost and re-written this entry alone three times so far. Maybe I should journal on the backs of the suicides? It would be a hell of a lot more meaningful than their suicide notes. Maybe not this entry, but the other (more meaningful) ones I've written. The wounds would last an eternity, heal every night, and reopen every morning. To re-read, all I'd have to do is line them up in order. Too much work?

Heard Bloody Mary was journaling too. Thank Hades! That woman really has a stick up her ass. I'll tell you what, she needs a lot more than to share her feelings with a blank page. I'm not the only one who thinks she needs a therapist. There's a few people down here who've met her in person and they can attest to her attitude. She's a big showman for the terror, but lately there isn't any passion in her eyes. She's a burned out bitch, that one.

I've been throwing around the idea of holding a weekly mixer, to increase "community" here in hell. Some of the demons think it's a horrible idea. They haven't said it to my face, but when they skip all the planning meetings, I know what they're thinking. Attendance has been poor to past events I've tried to organize and I'm thinking this is because there really is no incentive to come to the hottest part of the underworld (and literally, the hottest area, like 900-degrees-in-the-shade-hot).

A killer named Stevie wants to hold an open mic, but he has a creepy fetish for mouths and I can see right through his plan. Note to self: don't invite Stevie to the mixer.

Maybe invite Bloody Mary?

SUBMISSION

Brady hit send and then commenced freaking out. The first stop was the Sent folder, where he confirmed the email had actually left his computer. Then, he opened it to read and reread the words he chose. The cover letter, or email in this case, could be just as pivotal in securing his acceptance as the story itself. Were there any misspelled words? Any lines that read too egotistical or alternately, self-deprecating?

One misspelled word had snuck past the defenses. *Fuck*. That wasn't the word. "Fuck," he said it aloud the second time. 'Previously' does not have a 'd' in it. 'Previousdly' is *not* a word. Maybe they wouldn't notice it. Or they would and they'd trash his email without even downloading the submission. "Fuck!"

His first big decision. *Should I write them again with a corrected email to show that I strive for perfection and care about the language, or do I move on?*

He cracked open a can of Dr. Pepper and its carbonation soothed him. "Don't bother them, Brady," he said. "It will be fine."

There were other writers he'd befriended online who operated under the motto of "submit and forget." They hit send and moved on with their lives. They did the dishes, went to bed on time, and showed up at work, but Brady didn't work that like that. There was just no way for him to forget the work into which he'd poured himself.

He drained the soda and opened another. There was still work to be done. Now that the story was submitted, he would try to track its progress until he knew its fate for certain.

There were five tabs open in the web browser and he refreshed them every ten minutes when the small kitchen timer whined. Extra batteries, in case the constant use exhausted the cheaply made timing device, filled a drawer of his desk. He'd tried not using the timer in the past, but Buffy reruns sucked him in and he lost precious time following the feeds.

On the first tab, he scanned the publisher's Twitter feed. The updates weren't related to the submission call, only posts on famous author quotes and birthdays. When they did mention the call, it was only to invite more submissions. Not wanting the competition of his writer friends, he never shared those posts on his own social media pages. If they weren't yet aware of the call, they didn't *need* to know. He took every advantage he could get. It wasn't beneath him to wish for sudden deaths of the bigger players in the industry; the ones whose names filled many of the table of contents' and splashed victoriously across more covers than they deserved. He wanted to yell "save some for the little guy!" He wanted to see his name in chunky, stylized font, exciting any and all who laid eyes on it, enticing them to buy and read.

On the second tab, the publisher's Facebook page. The timeline there was filled with much of the same stuff as the publisher's Twitter page. Of course he made sure he liked the publisher's page before he submitted. He wanted to show dedication and vested interest. He liked trivial posts about grammar memes even though he couldn't stand them. He shared posts on editors and cover designers. Here, he got a better feel for his competition. They too stalked the feed like lions circling a wounded giraffe, hoping for a bite.

On the third tab was the publisher's rarely updated blog, but it could contain a hint about the anthology if he looked hard enough. The "great" submissions they were receiving. He read it like a J.K. Rowling or Anne Rice fan might pick up a genre-crossing piece by their beloved, just in case it referenced something from a world they already knew. Brady left a comment on a blog post that mentioned the submission call. "Just submitted! Hope you like it!"

He retyped variations of the phrase nine times before he

found the perfect mix; enthusiastic, but carefree. A lie, yes, but one would remain lost in the crowd if they didn't jump up and down sometimes, even if they hated jumping. And Brady did. After years of being mostly sedentary and sitting at his desk, his toes were no longer visible beneath his plump belly.

On the fourth tab was the Twitter account of the publishing company's owner. She only posted about cats and Brady was allergic. After reviewing her tweets for the last three years-*in which three anthologies had been released by her company*-he confirmed that she never mentioned anything work-related in this space. He closed the tab.

On the fifth tab, now upgraded to fourth, was the submission call itself. He reviewed it often and reread his story to make sure it fit each and every one of the specifications, from font size to word count to the naming convention of the file.

And on the new fifth tab, his email inbox, emptied to receive the good news.

An email popped up just as he was about to click to another tab. It was from the publisher!

Dear Brady,

Thank you for your submission. We look forward to reading your work.

Best,
Dark Hearts Press

A form letter. An automatic response. Canned. It wasn't what he was waiting for, but he enjoyed seeing the email in his inbox, so he left it there.

There was only one day left in his vacation bank at work and he had two long days to wait until the submission deadline. He'd used the rest of his allotted time off waiting to hear back about his Active Member application to the Horror Writer's Association back in August. He didn't get in. With more rejections than acceptances, his body of published work was too small and low-earning to qualify him. Now, he wished those days and Dr. Peppers weren't wasted. He could use them.

Brady had a good feeling about the story now sitting in the inbox of the publisher. The concept was original and the plot, unpredictable. His day off flew by in a blur of reloads, soda chugging, and pacing. Waiting was one of the only times he got any exercise, if the manic back and forth could be counted as such. Hope that his story had so impressed the editor, and would be accepted early, filled his heart, but his inbox sat empty on his evening off.

*

The next morning, a few hours past the start of his scheduled shift at work, the phone rang. Comfort coddled him on his couch, his new bed during the waiting period, causing him to ignore the rhythmic request for communication. His ancient answering machine recorded the message onto a small tape cassette.

"Brady, this is Harvey. We didn't see you at work today. I know you had Monday off, but you were due back today. Call me."

He chugged his breakfast, a soda, and coughed a few times in preparation for the call back. The phone rang once and then his manager, Harvey, picked up.

"Hello?"

"Hey," Brady said. A coughing fit followed and he threw in a fake sneeze for good measure. "I got something real bad. I'll need a couple more days. I'm sorry man."

"I'm sorry to hear that. You'll have to call around to find coverage for your shifts. I've got to get back to the sales floor."

The phone disconnected and Brady hiccuped. A real one brought on by his soda chugging. The Stereo Zone didn't need someone to cover his shift. There were always three extra workers standing around, kicking the floor and waiting for their lunch breaks. Unless it was Christmas, which it wasn't, they'd be fine.

Back in his computer chair, he began his day.

A sea of retweets filled the publisher's Twitter page. He waded through them, sinking deeper into the blue as he scrolled. On the publisher's Facebook page, Brady's hope hit the floor. There, a repost of the submission call ridiculed him, silently scorning his story for all to see.

It's so bad, they had to remind others to submit. Yours won't make the book, Brady.

He considered reporting the post as offensive, but his paranoia assured him such an offense would karmically return to him somehow.

On the third tab, a new blog post sent his heart into a fit, nearly destroying him. *Ten Mistakes Writers Make When Submitting to Anthologies* was the title. He read it *Ten Mistakes Brady Made When Submitting to Us*. He spent an hour reviewing each of the mistakes and scrutinizing his story to find them. He quadruple checked the tags at the end of the post for his name, the title of his piece, anything to confirm the post was directed at him. No fruit, rotten or otherwise, came from the exercise.

He skipped reviewing the submission call still open on the fourth tab. His eyes hurt. Words he knew to exist no longer sounded real. English was becoming a foreign language.

Brady hopped onto the fifth tab long enough to see no new email had arrived.

Then, the part he hated almost as much as waiting.

It was time to change his diaper. He'd been wearing it since Monday morning and his dinner the night before hadn't sat right with him. At some point during the night, he'd shit himself. Regular underwear had sufficed in the distant past, but his obsessive haunting of his computer screen did not allow for regular trips to the bathroom. It took too much time and worry to catch up on any posts he missed, especially on Twitter. So many characters, words that meant nothing to him or his goal. It was easier to relax and allow the shit and piss to leave his body and much healthier than attempting to suppress the urges.

He stood in the middle of his living room and pulled down his

Depends, exercising extreme caution when removing his legs from the holes, as the diaper was full. Once out, he reached for the baby wipes, but the email dinged from the fifth tab.

Brady waddled to the computer, leaving a trail of stink in the air and soft splats of shit on the carpet. He clicked on the tab to bring it on screen and was saddened to see it was junk.

Please Her! Be the Man You've Always Dreamed Of! Enlarge Your Penis Today!

"Shit on the carpet for *penis enlargement?*" He deleted the email with a few angry clicks of the mouse. "Motherfuckers!"

While he was at the computer, he refreshed the other tabs. Nothing new. Nothing worth reading. He walked back along the shit trail to the wipes, cleaned himself and the carpet, and pulled on a new diaper.

His email dinged again.

Meet Your Beautiful Chinese Bride Today!

He almost clicked on it. It would be nice to have someone else around; someone to cook for him. Someone to distract him from the waiting. Someone to wipe up the shit.

Thinking about his lovelife, or lack of it, depressed him. He opened a sixth tab on the computer and spent some time on Youtube with kittens, musicians who would never have record contracts, and poorly recorded clips of cartoons he grew up with. His mood lifted enough to brave checking the other tabs again.

Tab one's Twitter feed held a glimmer of hope.

Exciting anthology news from Dark Hearts Press coming later today! Watch our Facebook page for more details.

Brady tossed a frozen turkey pot pie into the microwave, set the timer for eleven minutes, and clicked to the second tab. His eyes wouldn't leave the screen until the status was posted. *The news could be about me!*

The phone rang. Brady *could* multi-task, but he knew who would be calling. The answering machine clicked on.

"Brady, it's Harvey again. No one came in for your shift. This isn't good. Call me back."

No excuse sounded good enough to undo the damage, but once he knew his story was accepted, he could call and explain that a fever knocked him out and he was unable to do more than sleep. A few apologies later, the fault would be forgiven and forgotten.

He stayed up all night to watch the clock tick past midnight. The deadline. He'd reached the end of his waiting. The email, the news he'd waited for would come at any moment. Though he tried to keep his eyes open, the springy hug of the couch allowed sleep to claim him.

*

When he awoke, his diaper again full, now chafing his inner thighs. He sat down at his desk to check the browser tabs. His ass cheeks squished the shit dangerously close to the available escape routes.

One recent tweet, an automatic post from the linked Facebook page, exclaimed that all authors had been emailed.

Sweat leaked from his palms. A twitch began below his left eye. The pounding of his heart was so intense he feared cardiac arrest. He considered jumping straight to the fifth tab and opening the email, but it was too soon. He needed time to prepare himself, maybe a fresh diaper. Breakfast, at least. Getting back up from the desk wasn't an option though. Knowing his fate rested just inches away, and the thick layer of shit caked to his ass, kept him glued in position.

Aware of the post it held, he skipped checking the Facebook page on the second tab.

The blog would be worthless as well. A table of contents list wouldn't be published until he and the others who were accepted agreed to terms and signed contracts.

The submission call too was no longer a source of information. If Dark Hearts Press was like most publishers, the page would now hold only a message that submissions were closed.

Now or never, I guess, Brady thought. He'd run out of tabs and excuses.

He hovered his mouse over the fifth tab, closed his eyes, and clicked. There, in the inbox, a single email. *Your Submission*, the subject line read. The two 'o's stared at him, emotionless, but powerful and penetrating. The moment he'd been waiting for was finally upon him. He opened it.

Dear Brady,

Thank you for your submission to our upcoming anthology. Unfortunately, it isn't what we are looking for. We wish you the best and hope your story finds a home.

Dark Hearts Press

He closed the tabs and shut down his computer like the publisher had shut down his dreams. Carelessly. Without thought.

Do you want to save before closing? a program asked him.

"Nothing worth fucking saving apparently!" he yelled.

The screen went dark.

The phone rang.

Brady picked it up just to have something to do, but he didn't speak. He breathed heavily, working up to a sob.

"Are you there, Brady? Is everything okay? I hope whatever is keeping you from doing your job is worth it. I have to let you go, man. You've missed too many days. Hello?"

Brady ended the call.

In the bathroom, he gingerly removed the soiled diaper, now stained with small spots of his blood. His story had failed, his work life was now as non-existent as his love life, and now his body was rebelling. He looked down at his cock. He could use that penis enlargement. He could use that beautiful Chinese bride.

He could use a lot of things he didn't have.

Brady cried as he wiped the shit from his body and spread the rash cream on his breaking skin. He clawed through the medicine cabinet, but found nothing for the pain in his heart.

ART BY RACHEL HANSEN

ORDER IN

A slip of white paper prints out of a small black box. The scratchy sound of the printing mechanism echoes through the large warehouse.

"Order out," a man named Paulino shouts. "One female, tall and blonde preferred."

A chuckle ripples through the small group of others working in the storage and shipping facility.

The PA system's speakers crackle on. "What have I said, Paulino?" the voice of Herrera, the shift supervisor, booms. "Read the fucking slips as they are!"

"How does he always hear me?" Paulino asks with a sigh. "One female, folks. One female."

"On it," a wiry worker named Tolman calls out. She runs to the large shelves that line the outer edge of the warehouse and selects a small box from one of the columns labeled 'F'. Back at her desk she opens the lid and a small, bright white sphere of light floats gently from the box. She smiles adoringly at it for a moment and then types the eight digit code from the order slip into a keypad. Next she flips a switch to activate a suctioning tube on her desk, and then she carefully guides the glowing orb toward the vacuum. When she is sure the orb is gone, she switches off the suction and goes back to what she was doing before the order came in, a crossword puzzle.

"Hmm, three letter word for 'exist'?"

"Are!" Bartlett, a word nerd, answers from his desk where he is reading a paperback.

Another white slip prints out. "Order in," Paulino yells. "Male."

"I got this one." Perry, a male employee covered in piercings and tattoos, turns on his station, types the number from the slip, and waits for the delivery. The orb comes through the tube and Perry is pleased to see that it's a partial one, split exactly down the middle. He opens a drawer in his desk and several other half and quarter orbs lazily float from its depths. Perry looks through them for another perfectly split half. He remembers one that came in last week, that he'd snagged from Tolman. When he finds it, he pulls a squished tube of superglue from a pocket of his cargo pants. Once the orb halves are joined, he smooths the seam with his dirty, glue-crusted fingers, places it in a box and onto a shelf in a column labeled 'M'.

A phone rings. *The* phone. The *only* phone in the whole place. It is up in the foreman's office and the workers know that if it rings, it is *never* good news.

"The bad news phone," Paulino remarks. He hardly named it that. It's just what it is.

"Fuck!" the foreman yells. He yells it loud enough that it breaks through the walls and bounces around in everyone's ears. There is a short pause and then the door of the office swings open. Herrera, a tall, burly man with a crew-cut and a pissed off look permanently etched on his face, comes out. He takes his time walking down the stairs to the first level of the depot. His slow pace ups the tension and the workers *should* feel tense. They know what the phone means.

"Shit," Paulino says just loud enough for the others to hear.

"Can't be good," Brewster mutters. "Can't be good."

Herrera walks to the middle of the warehouse and waits for the workers to shut down their tubes and line up. They know to line up when he is on the floor.

"Good afternoon Soul Depot Unit Thirty Seven," he barks. Herrera is very ex-military, time-wise, but he still acts as though he's in charge of an army company.

"Sir," they respond in unison. His pleasant greeting throws them off, but they can tell by the redness of his face and the throbbing vein in his forehead that the phone call was worse than usual. Things are about to go farther south than they ever have.

"I'm going to cut right to the chase. We've had seven fuck-ups this week alone." Herrera stares them down, waiting for any reaction to the news that they suck horribly at their jobs.

From the line, Paulino raises a hand. "To be fair, sir, five of those were computer error."

"Fair, Paulino?" You gave a happy couple a miscarriage instead of a healthy baby boy!"

"Again, it was the computer, sir. Not me." Paulino is a step below Herrera on the corporate ladder. It is his duty to run the floor when Herrera isn't standing on it. It is his job to make sure the computer is maintained by Kendrick, the technician on staff, and he has made sure of that for the past twenty years. So if the computer doesn't work, it's Kendrick's fault. Not his.

Herrera looks at the computer. It is no larger than a watermelon, as black as coal, and it sits at the front of the room. The computer maintains the connection between the living world and their world. It tracks life and death and assigns order numbers to send souls to the proper depots, or out of them.

"Computer looks fine to me," Herrera says after a less-than-thorough examination of the device. "Is anybody in the room going to take some responsibility for this poor record?"

A woman steps forward from the line. It is Brewster, an anal-retentive, clean worker who normally makes few mistakes. "One of those was my fault, sir. I lost my polishing cloth down the tube."

"You sent a piece of fabric into a body?" Herrera's face has reached a new shade of red.

"Not intentionally. And I reversed the tube flow almost immediately to retrieve it, but I may have damaged the body a little in doing that, sir."

"May have? A *little*? You sucked off what was to be the arm of a little girl! You altered her life forever!" Splotches of purple are now showing themselves on Herrera's face.

"I am aware of the consequences of my sloppiness and I'm

sorry. I leave my polishing cloth in my pocket now."

"Tell that to the little girl who was supposed to be a left-hander, but now has *no* left hand! This is real life people! We have a direct line to physical beings!"

Brewster hangs her head and steps back into line.

Herrera paces the floor for a moment, as though to process some of his rage. It does help bring his skin color somewhat closer to normal. "Anyone else have anything they'd like to say?"

Bartlett, the word nerd who is a loner and usually keeps to himself, steps forward. "Suda didn't turn off his tube and we came in one morning to find seven souls floating around and Eldridge types his codes wrong all the time. I've seen his error log. Sir!"

Herrera laughs and shakes his head. "I'm disappointed. Bashing on the night shift when they aren't here? You should be ashamed, Bartlett! And those are hardly damning offenses. What about yourselves?"

Bartlett steps back in line and again Brewster steps forward.

"Tolman dropped a soul the other day," she says as she points at Tolman, who stands beside her in line.

"How is that even possible, Tolman?" Herrera puts his head in his hands. "They float!"

Tolman shrugs. She can't remember what happened, only that one minute the orb was hovering happily and the next, it was sitting on the ground beneath her desk amongst the paperclips, rubber bands and dust bunnies. She blew it off and polished it extra before storing.

Herrera stands in front of Paulino. Too close to Paulino, if you ask him. "You're the floor supervisor. What do you have to say about all this?"

"Our numbers are better than Animal Division, sir." Paulino says quietly and with his eyes down to avoid meeting the penetrating gaze of his boss.

"Speaking of animals, someone here sent a human soul into a horse foal's body last month. You know who you are." Herrera moves to stand in front of Bartlett, in case he has forgotten.

Bartlett shakes his head. "The order number printed funny. We need new equipment."

"Your brain needs new equipment!" Herrera screams, spit hitting Bartlett's face. "You've all made mistakes as horrendous as the person beside you!"

Herrera paces again to cool off. He paces for five minutes without a word. The line of workers begins to shift on their feet.

"Sir, may I ask what the phone call was about?" Paulino doesn't really want to know and asking is like opening another can of worms, but he can't fix issues on the floor if he doesn't know what they are.

Herrera sighs. "Yes, thank you Paulino. I was getting to that. Fifteen years after the fact I'm getting a phone call telling me that, because of you screwups, Jimmy in New Mexico is looking down his pants and doesn't like what he sees. Says he's Jenny 'on the inside'."

"Classic mixup," Perry says with a chuckle.

"No, it isn't classic! It's *wrong*! We failed that soul! We put it in the wrong body and now its current life is a confused mess!"

"It's not like souls are color coded! It's a ball of white light!" Perry yells. "How the fuck am I supposed to know if it's a boy or a girl?"

"Calm down, Perry," Herrera, who still isn't calm himself, says. "All you need to do is read the labels on the shelves. In case you forgot, 'F' is for female and 'M' is for male. Two choices. It shouldn't be difficult!"

"It's not our fault, sir," Brewster says. "It's the stockers on the night shift. They aren't putting shit where it belongs."

"Don't call the souls shit, Brewster! Paulino, give me the timesheet." Herrera points at the clipboard hanging on a shelf post. "Who worked last night?"

Paulino leaves the line and brings it to him. "Looks like Suda and McClain, sir. Also Eldridge."

Herrera flips through some of the older timesheets, but gives up as they date back hundreds of thousands of years. "And what about fifteen years ago?"

"Essentially the same crew," Paulino replies.

"So first it's the computers and then it's the night crew from fifteen years ago. Who or what are you going to blame next?"

Tolman looks as though she is considering the question.

Perry is picking his nose.

Paulino is trying to remember the last time he saw Kendrick touch the computer. Or the last time he saw Kendrick at all.

Bartlett and Brewster are pushing a dust bunny back and forth with their feet.

Herrera wants to strangle all of them, but they are already dead.

"Look," he says. "None of you are new, so I shouldn't have to go over this again, but these issues warrant another training session."

Even Paulino groans.

Herrera picks up a discarded order slip from a trash can at the desk nearest to him and walks the line with it. "We have the motherfucking slips for a reason! A body dies, a soul comes in, the slip tells us if its a boy or a girl, the slip tells us if it's damaged, split or whole! We put it in a box and we put it where it's supposed to go! And for orders out, just reverse the fucking process!"

"He's swearing a lot more than I remember from the handbook," Tolman whispers to Bartlett.

"There's a handbook?" Perry can't recall ever seeing a manual.

"The slip is your bible," Herrera continues. "Do as it says, without question and perfectly!"

"Even when the numbers are wrong," Paulino says under his breath.

"Especially when the numbers are wrong!" Perry exclaims.

Herrera ignores the mindless chatter of his underlings. "Check the orb. Is it still circular? Is it white? Is it shiny? Is it whole? If the answer to any of these questions is no, you put that soul in the incinerator. This depot does not send out or store damaged souls! We take them out of circulation!"

"Seems easy enough," Tolman chirps.

"Shut up, Tolman!" Herrera snaps.

"How come I'm getting reprimanded when Perry wants to undermine the whole operation?" Tolman asks with a frown.

He offers no explanation and returns to delivering his lecture. "This isn't the Ghost Division either. You get a request for a soul, but with a seven digit order number, don't put the orb in the tube! Forward the order to the GD. We won't be held responsible for disembodied souls. Nor will we waste our stock on hauntings. That is not our department!"

"Again sir, to be fair," Paulino risks saying, "seven digits is very close to eight digits in length. Could the GD make their order numbers four digits long? That would be obvious at a glance."

"We aren't here to change procedure. We're here to follow it! And if I hear the word 'fair' in this room ever again, Paulino, I'll have you hiring your own replacement!"

Across the room from their lineup, the printer wakes up and prints another order. No one moves to read the order, not even Paulino."

"Don't let my sweet serenades keep you from doing your fucking *job*!"

Paulino jogs to the printer and reads the order. "Order in. One male. Perry, you take it."

"Can't, my tube is broken. The suction is poor," Perry says. It isn't broken, but Perry prefers standing around to working.

"Oh for fuck's sake," Herrera says as he smacks his forehead in disbelief. "Use another desk!"

Perry grudgingly chooses Brewster's desk, which irks Brewster because Perry leaves dried glue and boogers on everything he touches.

He types in the code, turns the vacuum tube on in reverse and waits for the soul to float to the top of it. He carefully guides it to a box and places it on a shelf labeled 'M'. When he is done he and Paulino return to the line, but as soon as they reach it, the printer whines a long, drawn out beeping sound as it prints another slip. Paulino runs back and reads off the order.

"Resuscitation on that last one. They need it back."

"You heard him, Perry, make it happen." Herrera is curious to see if he remembers where he put the soul on the shelf. "You better grab the right fucking box!"

Perry successfully picks the correct box and sends the orb inside of it back through the tube.

Herrera applauds their efforts, but no one can tell if he is being sarcastic. The claps are slow and rhythmic. "Now, see how smoothly things can work here?"

"But," Brewster squeaks.

"But what, Brewster? Say it!"

"Sometimes we run out."

"*Sometimes we run out*," Herrera mocks. "Then the body stays empty!"

"It's so tough seeing the mamas lose their babies though," Brewster says.

Herrera looks to the ceiling where ten large-screened televisions are mounted. They are filled with smaller images of humans being conceived, being born and dying. "Have you been watching the monitors again?"

Brewster looks up too. "Aren't we supposed to *monitor* our work?"

"Don't look at the goddamned monitors! Keep your head down, read the *fucking* slip, and do as it says."

She looks down at Herrera again. "Is it wrong to want to give them something to love? What if we have one soul and two bodies? A split soul can still live."

"Split souls are the root of all issues of the mind. A split soul makes a person incomplete and you doom them to suffer from depression and other mental conditions. Do you still think this is a gift?"

Brewster shakes her head. "No, I guess not."

"What about the split souls that come back to us? Should we be incinerating those?" Bartlett asks.

"Yes, of course!"

Bartlett smiles. "'Cause Perry likes to keep 'em in a drawer in his desk and splice 'em together."

"Perry, what fucked up place did you come from?" Herrera asks, though everyone is wondering.

"Detroit."

"Tell me, Perry. What happens when you stick two or more pieces of different souls together?" Herrera balls his hands into fists and presses them together to mimic a joining of two separate things. "Think about it!"

"Um," Perry says, but it's obvious he isn't trying to find the answer or that he'll never find it on his own even if he was looking.

"You get a person walking around hearing voices in their head. Someone who can't decide who to be, so they become multiple people. The souls do battle inside, with a dominate and several subordinate ones along for the ride."

"Like having built-in friends," Perry says with a smile.

"Or a one way ticket to the insane asylum," Paulino adds. He's seen crazy people on the monitors before. He knows the damage. It isn't pretty.

"Life is difficult enough for people. We don't need to throw in a wrench when they're just getting started. Do not split souls! Do not rejoin split souls! Fill the order or don't pack the body!"

An alarm goes off, setting the normally white overhead lights to a strobing red and blaring a whining sound throughout the facility. The workers cover their ears. Herrera looks around the room for Kendrick, the computer technician.

"Kendrick, change the paper!" he yells.

A crotchety old man emerges from a small door between two of the warehouse shelves. He is wearing large headphones to protect his fragile eardrums from the noise. His movements are slow.

"Hurry up, Kendrick!" Herrera demands. "For all we know there could be a midwife looking for a heartbeat and all she's hearing is the mother's!"

Kendrick speeds up the best he can. When he finally reaches

the printer, he opens it. Next he removes a large roll of printer paper from the cabinet beneath the computer. When the printer is reloaded, the alarm ceases and Kendrick hobbles back to his office behind the stacks.

The printer spits out another order.

"Order out." Paulino laughs. "There's a note on here. Mom wants blue eyes and the body is a girl. But I think all we have is a blue-eyed male."

"What do you think the answer is, Tolman?"

"Give her what she wants?" Tolman replies.

"And repeat the whole Jimmy/Jenny fiasco? No! No, no no! Give her a green-eyed, female, or a brown-eyed one! I don't care. Just make sure it's a female orb going into the body!" Herrera personally walks to a shelf labeled 'F' and selects a box sitting there. He grabs the order slip from Paulino and chooses a desk.

"Not that one, sir," Perry says quickly. "The tube's broken, remember?"

"For fuck's sake. I should have realized this was your desk. Look at the state of things." Herrera picks another desk, types in the code, turns on the vacuum tube, opens the box, and guides the floating orb in.

"Wow, that was beautiful," Tolman says.

Bartlett scoffs. "It's the same thing we do all day."

"But to see the boss at work. He's so graceful."

Herrera switches off the vacuum and turns back to the workers. "We aren't here to make dreams come true! We're here to avoid creating nightmares!"

"Yes, sir," they all reply.

He points to a giant, dust-covered banner that spans a wall on one end of the warehouse. It bears the Soul Depot logo and beneath it, the company's slogan. "Read the slogan! Out loud! What does it say?"

"SPEED QUALITY ACCURACY PERFECTION!" the group shouts together.

"Now!" Herrera screams. "Back to work!"

The group scatters and returns to their workstations. Herrera is already climbing the stairs back to his office.

Perry picks his other nostril and finds something good.

Brewster wipes down her desk for any Perry particles.

Tolman returns to her crossword puzzle. "Five letter word for 'skilled'?"

"Adept," Bartlett replies.

In the front of the room, the printer screeches.

"Order in," Paulino shouts as he rips the newest ticket from the printer. "Male."

"I'll take it," Brewster offers.

Upstairs the bad news phone rings again.

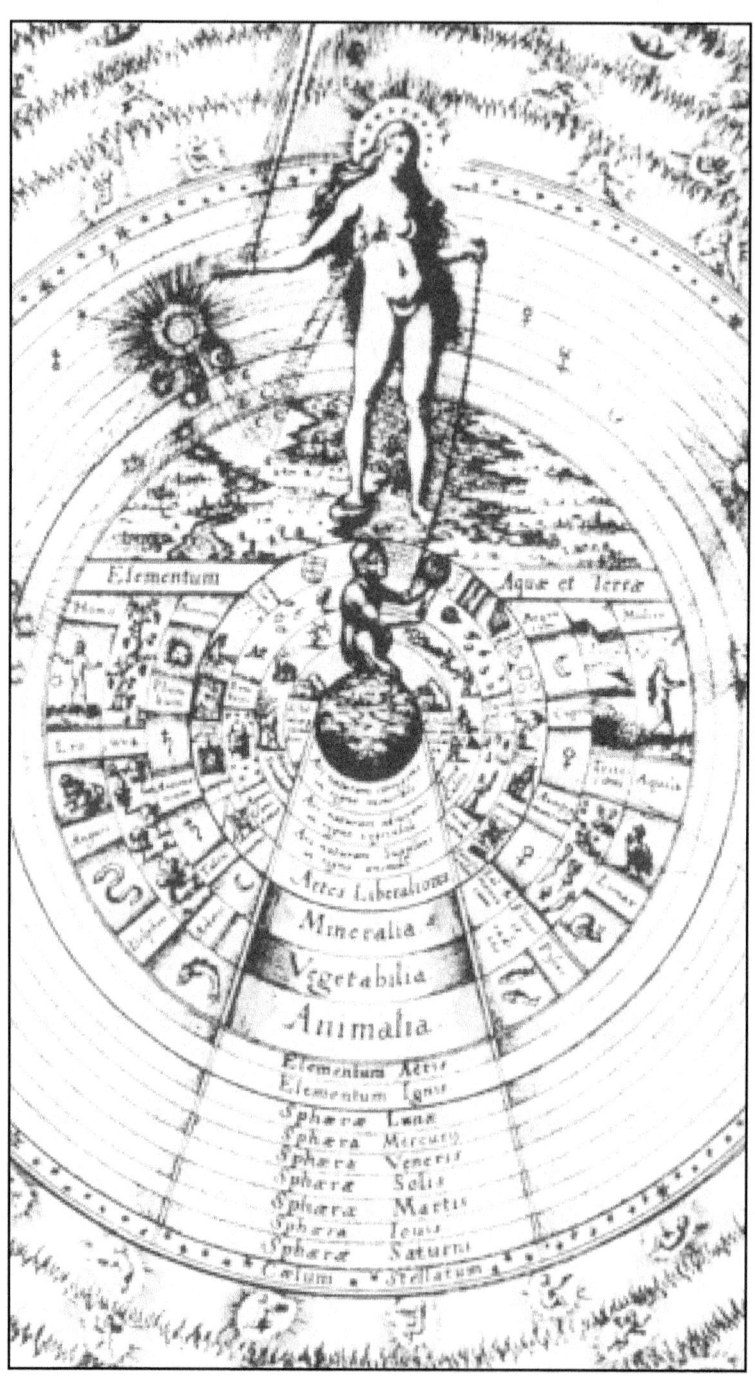

GREAT CHAIN OF BEING BY ROBERT FLUDD, 1617

GREAT CHAIN OF BEING

The steel pipe was on the plans. They should have been aware of its existence. Yet the underground drilling machine still chewed into the thing and set the crew a year behind schedule as the cutting teeth were repaired. Then they began again, but not twenty minutes into the rebooted operation, the mega drill hit something else.

"Fuck!" several workers yelled.

Hank, the Project Manager cringed at the strong word and the thought that the tunnel project could be delayed another year. "I triple checked! There's nothing else in the plans we need to watch out for." But doubt flooded his mind as the words came out.

"This drill ain't goin' any deeper. Sounded like a car crash. Metal on metal," the construction worker operating the drill replied.

Hank scratched his head. "Back it out, Casen. Let's take a look."

To humor his superior, Casen looked for a button or knob he knew did not exist. "You know this thing don't go in reverse!"

"Well, we're not digging another hole. Pull it out. I don't care anymore."

The construction crew removed the drill from the short tunnel with several chains and the largest vehicle they had on site. The removal was gentle, like pulling a plug from the bath.

Hank and Casen walked back into the tunnel and stood in the space the damaged drill had previously occupied. They stared up at a large, flat wall.

It, whatever *it* was, was as tall as the drill; some two and a half stories high and, though the drill had completed a few rotations, the metal-like surface was remarkably unscathed.

"How did this not show up on the ground surveys?" Hank asked. The question bounced around the tunnel and Casen ignored it. A question of his own concerned him more.

"What the fuck is it?"

Usually Hank insisted the crew watch their language, but the giant, seamless wall was so bizarre, the f-word hardly made him flinch. "Maybe a sewage tank?"

"Too big."

"And too strong. We'd be covered in excrement right now if it was a septic tank."

Casen wandered to one edge of the structure and then back to the other end, which was set in a shadow. In the dim light he could see a variation in the wall. He pulled out his keychain and shone the cheap flashlight that dangled from it into the black. "There's a door here! The drill broke the lock." He hefted the security device, now split in two pieces. "Kind of funny that the lock is the least sturdy part."

"Never seen a lock like this before. Looks old."

Casen laughed. "Are you kidding me? This is Northgate. There's no history in this place."

"Yeah. And it don't look any older than my grandma." Ed, another worker on the crew, had joined them in examining the broken lock.

"I say we open it. The drill is out of commission again. Why not figure out what caused it?"

"Right!" Casen agreed. A call to the university archaeology department was more in line with how Hank normally ran things on the job site. Not having to wait filled Casen with excitement.

The door obliged after some convincing with a crowbar. Its hinges moaned.

"Any volunteers?" Hank asked.

Casen, always eager and adventurous, walked inside. "I can't see anything," he reported. "but I can smell something. It's like rotting fruit. And there's a ticking noise."

"Like a bomb?" Hank yelled into the dark.

"No, more like a clock."

"Don't those sound the same?" Hank asked Ed.

"The ticking is faster and the smell is really strong now. Thick. I can almost touch it."

"Look, Casen, maybe you should come back out!" Hank and Ed stepped back to allow him a path out, but before Casen could respond or retreat, an explosion burst from somewhere deep within the structure. There was no flame or heat. It was more an expulsion of air than a fiery blast. A swift wind shot from the chamber door, knocking Hank and Ed on their asses. The scent of rotting fruit enveloped the entire job site.

"That could have been a lot worse!" A worker named Oliver yelled as he ran to help Hank and Ed off the ground.

The men and women dusted themselves off and got back to work doing anything they could before the time clock ran out for the day.

*

The next morning they returned to the jobsite and adopted the "act busy" state of being. The project manager was coming for a scheduled visit that was now an emergency one. No one could afford another costly setback. He would be looking for progress. The entire crew was on edge, worried they hadn't done enough since his last visit.

Rodney Pearl arrived at exactly nine a.m. His poor mood immediately worsened when he found the guard shack empty and the main gate unlocked. "Anyone could just walk i-what the *fuck*?"

The drill was in pieces, which he expected, but so were the other big machines; the backhoe, the cementer, and the mega crane all no longer the sum of their parts.

Casen approached sporting a grin. Rodney looked for nervousness in it, but saw only pure joy. *He should be nervous. He should be fucking terrified.*

The smile only left Casen's face when he gave Rodney an unexpected progress report.

"We're ahead of schedule on the disassembly and the removal team has been working through the night."

"Get the hell out of my way! Where's Hank?" Rodney pushed past Casen, who took it in stride.

"He's cleaning the box like you told him to!" Casen called after him.

Rodney journeyed through the mazelike stacks of machine pieces. Men and women on the work crew scurried about with focus as they sorted all manner of items into piles of matching metal, plastic, and rubber. He found his way to the tunnel's entry and there he found Hank.

The man looked worn out, yet he continued to scrub the dull box to an unreachable shine.

Rodney heard only a brief description of "the box" the night before. It was the size of a house, with a door on the front, but no other windows or openings that he could see.

"Hank!" Rodney yelled. Though the volume was unnecessary, he needed Hank to take him and the problem at hand seriously.

His subordinate snapped to attention as a soldier might in the presence of a higher ranking officer. Rodney took it as sarcasm. "Cut the crap and tell me what the hell is going on! It's a madhouse!"

"I know you told me to have it all polished before your arrival today. I apologize."

"I didn't tell you to polish shit! And I most definitely did *not* order the deconstruction of our largest and most expensive equipment! What is going on here?"

"The men had no choice but to take everything apart. It was the only way for them to catalog the pieces, as you requested last night."

"I wasn't here last night, Hank."

Hank shrugged. "Check the security cameras. I swear you were."

Rodney wove back through the sorted piles and to the construction site office, which was a white double tall trailer. He let himself in and quickly found the digital file from the previous night's shift. He watched his crew find the large box and then, the way in. A gust of wind escaping the box was visible on screen in ruffled shirts and hair.

What he saw next, he couldn't believe.

It was him, in the very clothes he was wearing off site yesterday, exiting from the open door of the box. He watched himself address the crew, who weren't disturbed or confused by the fact that they never saw him go into the box in the first place. Then, they began to disassemble the machinery. They worked well into the night; much later than their shifts required.

Rodney watched it over and over as he decided his next move. When he opened the door of the office, Casen was standing on the other side; the shit eating grin still on his face.

"You have *got* to see this, sir!"

Casen led him back through the piles, even larger than before, to the box. Rodney hung back, but Casen opened the door. The rest of the crew began to gather behind him, making escape impossible. The void was blacker than anything Rodney had ever seen. He imagined his face suddenly appearing in the middle and it sent shivers creeping over his entire body. He wanted nothing to do with the box and whatever form of him was inside.

"No, Casen. I'm heading home for the day. I'm not feeling well. Tell the others to put the machines back together."

Rodney turned to leave, but the workers formed a wall as impenetrable as the one the drill hit. Casen took him by the shoulders and spun him around to face the void once more. "Stand here and wait a sec."

Another burst of wind shot out from the doorway, hitting Rodney so hard he would have fallen backwards had Casen and the wall of people not been securing him in place.

Casen relaxed his grip and Rodney turned to face the crew. He gave a thumbs up to Hank, who was near the back of the crowd.

"Very nice work, everyone! We'll need more help for the reconstruction. As soon as you get all the parts separated, go home and bring your families back. You know what to do."

The crew nodded and doubled their disassembly speed.

"We should get the mayor here, to show him our progress," Hank suggested as he walked Rodney to the office trailer.

"Yes, I heard that too," Rodney replied. "I want you to look over the plans with Casen. Once you are confident with them, we can invite the mayor."

Rodney filed a report with the city that progress was being made despite the drill needing more repair. He spent the rest of the day watching over the workers and guiding them in machine disassembly.

Just before their shift was to end, Hank took Casen to the door of the box. "The plans are inside. Come with me. We'll get them together."

Casen, still grinning, grinned wider. It was elating to be such a valuable part of the new design.

Inside the structure, knowledge flooded their minds as the room illuminated. A long hallway pushed into the distance. The walls were covered in small, rectangular openings. Each one held a tube of paper. Hank walked with purpose to one of the storage holes. He removed a scroll and opened it to verify its text.

"There's a plan for everything on Earth in here. All the trees, rocks, leaves, animals, people. *Everything*."

"I know," Casen said, wide-eyed. "It told me too."

"This box makes things. It created the earth and was sealed when the job was done. Now that it's open again, it wants to continue creating things. But sometimes, you have to destroy before you can build anew."

Casen nodded. "And that's where we come in."

Any normal person would be impressed with Casen's ability to speak while still smiling so stupidly. Hank noticed nothing out of the ordinary. He too felt the joy. Smelling sweetly of fermenting fruit and wrapping around them lovingly, it was impossible to ignore.

They reviewed the plans together.

"We are building a bomb. The final one," Hank said as he rolled up the scroll.

Casen's face warped and twisted into a hole full of teeth and happiness. "I'll get the parts list out to the crew."

ART BY NICK GUCKER

FAIR HOUSING

Complaint Filed with the Department of Fair Housing
Bridge Trolls *vs.* City's Homeless Population

Complaint Summary
We are writing to complain regarding the unfair takeover, by the city's homeless, of all bridge under areas. The desired outcome of this complaint is an immediate investigation and the undertaking of any and all appropriate measures to eradicate this problem, some of which are noted at the end of this complaint.

Details of Complaint
We, the bridge trolls of Seattle, have been driven from our natural homes (and really the only life we know) by an ever-increasing number of humans without home. These so-called "homeless" individuals are much like an invading army and we have been made to feel powerless against them. If taking our homes were not crime enough, the homeless are also, to put it quite plainly, trashing the place! They discard all manner of items- food wrappers, dirty clothing, random bits and bobs- by tossing them on the side of the roads that run by the bridges. Bridge trolls, however, are notoriously organized, meticulous housekeepers. Indeed we are such skilled housekeepers, no one notices that we live (or used to live) under the bridges. As I type this I realize perhaps our cleanliness may have contributed to the usurpation of some of our homes, as they were so tidy they looked to be unoccupied. But this then begs the question, must we put out doormats to claim our space? Must we leave piles of our brightly-colored excrement

behind when we step out, so as not to be evicted?

Additional Notes

We've been here for hundreds of years and this fact alone should guarantee us residence. Heck, we were here before the overpasses were built and all we had to live under were piddly wooden things that creaked as wagons rolled over them! I shouldn't have to mention it, but there is even a monument built to us in Fremont. We were clearly here first and therefore, should be much more valued by the community. Must I remind you that we help control the rodent population as rats are our secondary preferred meal? Homeless individuals sometimes keep rats as pets! This is, again, unsanitary and non-beneficial to the community at large. We also *never* beg for money, as this is beneath us and we don't use the human monetary system.

Possible Interim and Long Term Solutions

The Bridge Troll Association (BTA) has met and discussed the situation and, apart from this formal complaint, we have identified and noted these possible solutions to work in conjunction with one another:

- Registration of all homeless individuals

- Development of website, similar to other real estate sites, specifically listing available bridge

- Laws surrounding unlawful usurpation of under bridge real estate

- Fit punishments including fines, community service, and deportation to other cities

Signed

Maalik, Khijazi, Vinjin, and Ttarmek, the BTA Board

Last Night While You Were Sleeping

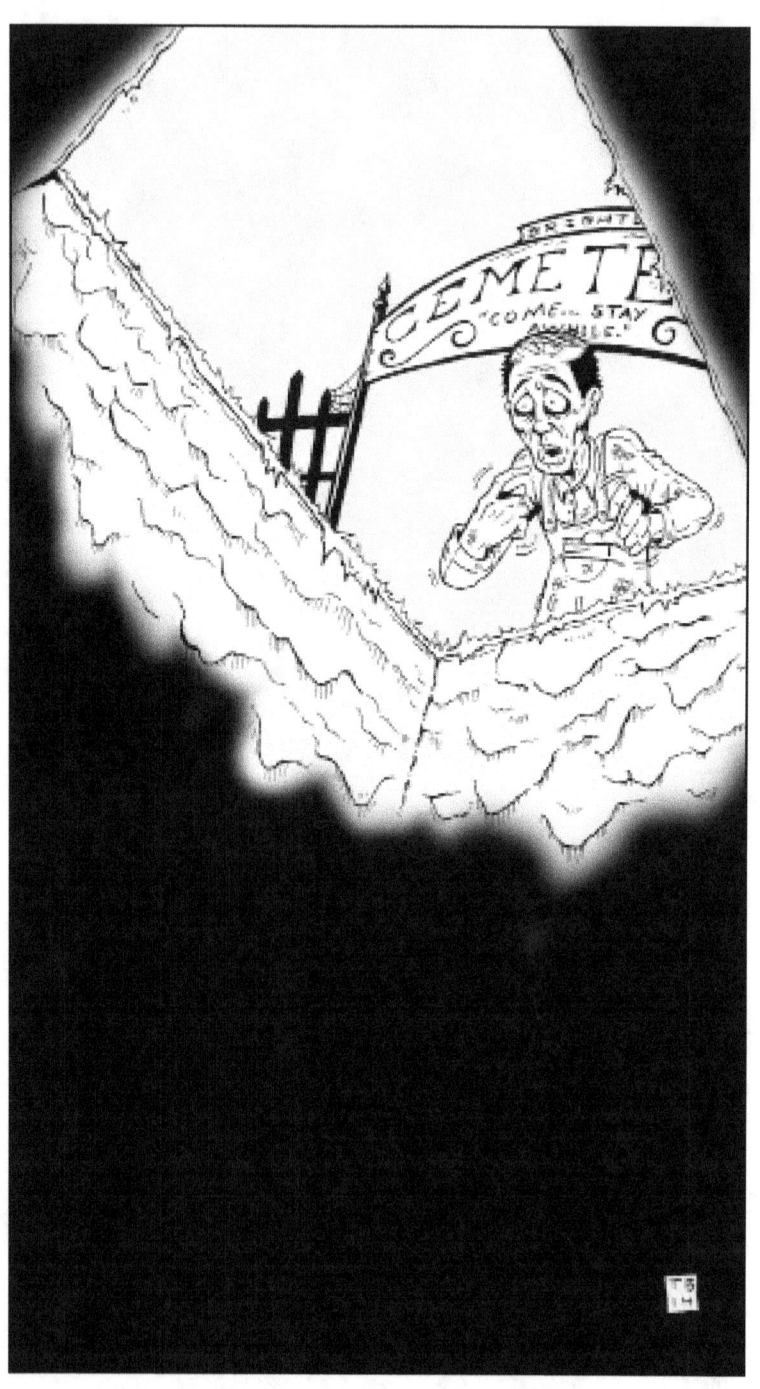

ART BY TRAVIS BUNDY

BYE BYE BRIGHTEN

Brighten, Washington was one of the last small towns in the overdeveloped West. Its residents had a long history in the manufacturing and farming industries. Hometown pride permeated Main Street, but things were slowing down in Brighten. Farmers struggled to stay in business against mega corporations and the manufacturing work was being outsourced to China. It was a sorrowful decline that had claimed many a small town. Brighten was not immune.

Main Street had the usual assortment of shops; a hairdresser, post office, grocery, seamstress, and a few others. And once you passed by those, the rambling houses began. Beyond the smatter of dwellings, Sleepy Hills Cemetery marked the town's end. The sign at its entrance read "Come...stay awhile!"

SUNDAY

Sunday morning, at first not particularly different than any other morning, Larry, the groundskeeper of Sleepy Hills, came across an odd sight. At the top of the highest hill, where the last pieces of unclaimed earth remained, a large collection of freshly dug graves greeted him. He hadn't even had his coffee yet, which may have been the problem. *This could be a hallucination brought on by caffeine withdrawals,* he thought. Lord knows he lived on the stuff. Larry counted them and recounted them and each time he came up with the same number: thirty-six.

The same number as the town's current population.

"Spooky," he said and walked back down to his office for his morning cup of joe. Thirty-six holes in the ground was strange, but

155

it wasn't yet anything worth mentioning to the rest of the town. He'd seen stranger things. Once, when a dairy farm still operated on the outskirts of Brighten, one of the cows gave birth to a two-headed calf. The calf survived, lived for six years, and provided some of the best milk the town had ever consumed. Dirt had to do more than move to raise his alarms.

*

Gil, the postal clerk, visited every door in town and then, just before dinner, he visited his wife's grave at Sleepy Hills. Brina had been gone for many years, but he still liked to talk to her about his day. Her grave lay near a fence at the back of the cemetery, in a shady valley beyond the tallest hill. Normally he went around the hill, but tonight he thought to take in the sunset before talking to his wife's headstone. When he came to the top of the rise, he nearly fell into one of the empty holes.

Larry was suddenly beside him, his arms crossed over his chest, a look of deep thought on his face. He offered no explanation for the many fresh graves, only a "good evenin', Gil."

"Someone could die falling into one of these!" Gil yelled with dramatic gesturing of his arms. He was out of breath from summiting the hill and this, coupled with his flailing arms, made him seem more exasperated than he actually was.

Larry grumbled. "I didn't put them there! They showed up this morning."

"Graves don't dig themselves, Larry."

"No footprints. No tools. The shed is still locked. I don't know what to tell you other than watch your step and say hi to Brina for me!"

*

Earlier that day, a baby was born to the hairdresser, Barbara. She flipped the Open sign over to Close, locked the front door, birthed the eight pound boy in the back of her shop, cleaned up, and then let the auto mechanic in for his buzz cut. Barbara named her new son Cutter. It was simultaneously the most creative and the least creative name she could have chosen, but it suited him nonetheless. She stayed up late into the night with her new son, thinking of all the exciting things they'd do together. It wasn't until almost sunrise that she realized she should have called the town doctor when the contractions started. She smiled at her silliness and fell asleep for a short time.

MONDAY

Agnes, the doctor who'd been so easily forgotten by Barbara, knew everything about everyone in Brighten. Phil Andersen, who ran one of the two used bookstores in town, was allergic to the trees that grew in his yard. She recommended he cut them down or move, whichever he could afford.

She knew that Nola, the occasional baker who worked from home crafting things to sell online, got terrible gas each time she ate berries. Agnes recommended she find other toppings for her morning granola or that she invest in some Beano, whichever she was willing to do.

Arden, the dedicated grocer of thirty five years, walked with a slight limp not because of a stint in the army that led to war injuries as others had assumed, but because one of his legs stopped growing before the other. She recommended he wear a special shoe to even him out or that he get surgery to lengthen the shorter one, whichever his insurance would cover. He still hadn't decided and continued to hobble between the aisles stocking the shelves.

Agnes could have been the town historian were it not for doctor-patient confidentiality. She knew of every death and of every birth within the town's limits. So, when Barbara came in with a baby boy in her arms instead of her belly, Agnes was surprised that news of the labor and birth had skipped her ears.

"Where'd this little guy come from?" Agnes stroked Cutter's cheek and smiled.

Barbara, a serious woman who didn't like to play games, pointed to her crotch and rolled her eyes. "You know damn well where he came from! Give him a look so I know he's healthy!"

Agnes sighed. Barbara wasn't her favorite patient in the town. "Let's see him then," she said as she took him from Barbara and laid him down on the scale.

*

At the same time Cutter was being poked and prodded by the doctor, Larry woke up and made his way down the street to Sleepy Hills for his shift. His curiosity pulled him to the hill, but he needed coffee in him before he examined the odd holes once more, assuming they were still there. When he reached the top, he could see that a new grave had been dug. It was much smaller than the rest.

*

A half hour later he was back in his office on the phone to Agnes. "Agnes, Larry here."

"Hi Larry. Make it quick, I've got another patient coming in."

"I have an odd question for you. Do we have any new babies in town?"

"Barbara was just in with her brand new boy, born last night. How'd you know?"

Larry was silent for a moment. "Interesting," he said and then dropped the receiver back into the cradle.

"Don't get yourself worked up now, Larry," he said. Stories of graveyard hauntings and curses filled his mind. He'd heard them firsthand from other groundskeepers at a national convention he attended long ago. "Land's just havin' a fit of some kind. It'll sort itself out."

*

Just before lunch, Gil started his shift delivering mail and fully intended to keep news of the cemetery holes to himself; gossip was against his nature. But when he dropped off a package at Good Eatin', a restaurant run by Edie Steuben, he couldn't help himself.

158

"Hey, Gil!' Edie rushed toward him to take the box out of his hands. "We go through napkins like there's black holes in the dispensers!"

"Speaking of black holes...have you heard about the graves at the cemetery?"

Mindy, a dark-haired twenty-something and the one waitress employed to work the lunch shift, stopped in her tracks. "Something's happening at the cemetery?"

"Don't let that tuna melt get cold!" Edie snapped. Mindy was into dark things and Edie knew if the Goth in her employ became distracted, she wouldn't get anything done for the rest of her shift.

"Hmph." Mindy set the plates down at their designated table with slightly more force than needed. She went about cleaning her tables closer to Gil and Edie in an effort to listen in.

Gil continued. "I saw them myself yesterday. One for all of us; at the top of the hill."

Edie was already pale, but now her skin was as pallid as Mindy's.

"Sinister," Mindy hissed; though not even the saltshaker she polished could hear her.

"I'm sure it's just a prank. Maybe the high school boys got together. End of year type joke." Edie wanted to believe this, but the high school boys got drunk and did easier things, like tipping cows or scrawling graffiti on the old billboards. They didn't dig holes, they chased them.

"Hopefully. Well, I've got to make some more deliveries. I'll see you soon!"

"Okay, Gil. Thanks."

Edie waited for Gil to leave before taking off her apron. "Mindy, watch the restaurant. We're out of zucchini." She walked the short block to the only grocery store in town and found Arden in the fruit section, struggling with a heavy box of cantaloupes.

"Here," she said, lifting one side of the box. "I'll help."

"Oh, hey there Edie! Thanks. They pack these boxes fuller every time, I swear."

Arden's hobble filled Edie with fear that the melons would

topple out of the box and bury her, which reminded her that she'd come for more than zucchinis.

"Have you seen the holes yet?" she asked over the box.

"Yep, yep. The aphids really are doing a number on the crops this year. We're lucky to get anything without a few holes in it."

Edie laughed. "I wish it were the bugs I was talking about."

"Are the potholes back on Main? They usually open up every winter."

Arden probably had ten other just as good hole-related guesses. "Gil told me someone's dug some graves on the cemetery hill. Enough for everyone."

"I definitely haven't seen those. I never make it out that way. Does Larry know anything about them?"

"Gil didn't say, but I reckon he's seen 'em."

"If you go, take a picture, will ya? There's no way my leg'll take me to the top."

"I'm not sure if I want to see them. It'll give me nightmares."

*

Word of the graves spread quickly to the remaining residents of Brighten and anyone who could make the trek to the end of town and up the cemetery hill did so that day. Larry hadn't witnessed such a crowd since the last mayor's funeral, when the entire town, as well as some out of town relatives, turned out.

*

Mike, known by the community as Mad Mike because he obsessed about aliens and always wore large headphones, unattached to anything, over his ears, bent down as inconspicuously as possible. He was there to view the holes like everyone else, but he also hoped to solve the mystery of them. A dirt sample would provide all the answers. The tiny vial didn't hold much soil and he still hadn't procured the right testing equipment, but he hoped to find traces of radiation or foreign material from the spacecraft he knew was responsible for the graves.

*

Both Agnes and Edie went home after work. Agnes thought too much about mortality as it was and Edie couldn't convince herself to waste a relaxing evening on what she saw as morbid tourism. Deep down, and like everyone else, they were scared, though neither would ever admit it.

*

Before the sun went down, Barbara, with Cutter finishing his nap in a sling across her front, huffed and puffed to the top of the hill. As strong as she considered herself, her post-labor, post-pregnancy body did not agree with her mind. She stopped three quarters from the top to nurse her son and she used the opportunity to catch her breath.

Larry joined her on the hillside. "You don't want to go up there, Barb."

She gently pried Cutter from her breast, causing Larry to avert his eyes, pulled her shirt down, and continued upwards. There were just some things she needed to see with her own eyes.

And then there were the things she could never unsee.

Like the night she walked in on her elderly parents having sex. The colors, the textures, forever etched into her memory. Or the time a malfunctioning dryer unit caused second degree burns on the scalp of one of her customers. That wasn't pretty at all. Neither of those sights compared to the tiny hole at the top of the hill. She set Cutter beside it for comparison.

"Larry, it's the same exact length."

He joined her at the graveside. "Coincidence," he replied while he searched for better words.

Barbara snatched Cutter back from the ground as though it threatened to take him there and then. "Do you know how fast babies grow?"

Larry didn't and so shrugged, but from the terror in her voice, he reckoned it was fast.

"He won't fit in this hole in a month! That is how fast!"

"Well, that's good! He just has to grow a little and it won't be a problem!" He hoped those were the right words.

"No, Larry! This means he's going to die and die *soon!*" Barbara burst into tears. "I just got him! How could anyone think of taking him away from me?"

"I think you should go home. Spend some time with him instead of worrying about losing him."

They walked together down the hill.

*

Mindy and her boyfriend Tod, the only other Goth in town, dressed in their macabre finest and walked to the base of the cemetery's hill that night.

"Come on, Talon." She called him by his Goth name. "Gil told Edie they were at the top."

Talon trudged along behind her. His lace up platforms weren't the best choice of footwear. If Mindy had mentioned they'd be hiking, he'd have fished out his old boots from the closet. The ones he wore squeaked as his ankles rotated and adjusted to the angle of the climb. Mindy's shoes, black stilettos that sunk into the soft earth, were no better, but she didn't mind suffering.

Caution tape, lazily draped by Larry between some of the larger trees, attempted to warn people about the holes. Mindy lifted it and they clambered under.

"Wicked!" Talon sat down on the edge of one of the graves, his legs hanging over into the darkness. Usually at funerals, they kept the holes covered up. He'd never seen how deep and dark they really were.

"This one's mine," Mindy said. She pointed to the grave on the left of the one that Talon was halfway in. They'd talked about a suicide pact in the past and alternately, about growing old together. It wasn't much of a stretch for her to dream of them being buried beside one another.

"Maybe," Talon daydreamed, "this is, like, Satan kind of calling us home."

Mindy lay on her stomach and looked down into her grave. "It does feel welcoming in there."

Talon tossed a pebble in front of his feet. It disappeared quickly into the black. "I feel like I could jump in and fall straight to Hell."

"Maybe tomorrow night?" Mindy stood up and left her future self a flower at the head of the grave. She grinned. "I want to sin with you a little more."

Talon chuckled and followed her back to town.

TUESDAY

"I want a refund." The words came resolutely out of the mouth of an elderly man whose back was so bent, he looked to be resting his chest atop his cane. Once upon a time, he was a spry janitor at the high school in the first big city outside of Brighten. Now he was dying from colon cancer and a general disdain for living. He wasn't able to make it to the top of the cemetery hill in person, but he heard from others that there was a grave there just for him.

"You know I can't do that, Marv." Larry often had morning headaches, but they usually didn't wear Depends, smell like mothballs, and reminisce about the '30s. "All contracts are final. The sign says as much."

There were several signs in Larry's office including *Don't Get Caught Without A Plot!*, *Reserved Parking for Hearses Only*, and *No Digging Without Permission*. The one which he was referring to said *Only Jesus Returned. No Returns, No Refunds!*

Marv straightened his back as much as he could. "The way I see it, hole's already dug. That's half the burial fee right there! And you can cancel my tombstone order too. No room between the rows for labeling the dead."

"No one is gettin' buried in those holes, Marv! Not you, not anyone! And even if you were, the policy still stands."

Marv stomped his cane. "I don't like this one bit. You've always been cheap, Larry."

"I run a business. Business make money, they don't give it away. Now, if you'll excuse me. I have to get back to running said business."

The dying man left without making any further demands. He simply didn't have the energy. What he'd do with a refund anyway, he didn't know.

*

The house no longer appeared child safe as Barbara considered it with new eyes. Each corner was a can opener for skulls. Every unsecured tchotchke a one way ticket for Cutter to the top of the cemetery hill.

She spent all of Tuesday packing anything hard or sharp into boxes and locking them in the attic.

*

Now that everyone knew about the graves, a town meeting was held to discuss them. The mayor, a greasy, portly man, attempted to calm the crowd. "Quiet now! We all have questions. Please form a line at the microphone."

The head of the microphone gave off a pungent odor of bad breath and corn chips. It had been repurposed for town hall when the karaoke bar had gone out of business. No one wanted to speak into it and those who did, didn't help.

"Is it true that there's one for each of us?" Nola asked. She wore a ratty crocheted vest over a hand-sewn pantsuit. Her baker's funk of yeast and sweat overpowered the microphone scent. "Because I'd like to be cremated."

"Me too," Arden said from the crowd. Others murmured in agreeance.

"And I've got a spot next to Brina," Gil said softly. "She's waiting for me."

"I want to be clear, no one in this town will end up in those holes on my watch! Next question." It was typical of the mayor to make bold statements without a plan to back them.

Nola sat down, leaving the stinky microphone open to Mad Mike.

"Maybe they're portals and they're only activated when we all stand in them and the aliens made them with a high-powered laser technology we've never even heard of and they'll take us to a new world or maybe one just like this one."

When Mad Mike stopped for a breath, Edie jumped up and tapped him on the shoulder. "Can I take a turn, Mikey?" she asked sweetly.

"Okay," he replied into the microphone.

Edie led him back to his seat before asking her own questions. "Are we all doomed to die here? What is going on?"

"Well, if you live anywhere long enough, you are bound to die there too!" Greer, the owner of the second used bookstore in town, said. Those around him chuckled.

Edie scoffed. "That isn't what I mean! Don't be a smart ass."

The mayor cleared his throat. "Like I said, not on my watch. We've come up with some ideas to keep the town safe."

"Like your plan to pay for the removal of the poisonous trees in my yard? Last I checked, they were still there, killing me slowly." Phil Andersen and his wife Maren sat near the back of the room. He already had a plan, regardless of anything the mayor or townspeople thought up.

"We can… we can talk about that tomorrow, Phil. We're here to discuss the holes. We'll start by filling them in."

A dusty looking man with calloused hands and coffee-stained teeth stood up and took off his baseball cap. He was a contractor and, all around, a good guy. "I could get one of my machines up there tomorrow."

"That's a good start, Benji," the mayor said. "Tomorrow, you said?"

"In the morning, if that doesn't conflict with anything on Larry's schedule."

Larry shook his head. "Nope, but you'll need to bring some dirt with you too. Don't know where it's all gotten to."

"Okay, BYOD. Bring your own dirt!" The mayor laughed, but no one else caught the joke. "And next, we'll organize a patrol to watch the hill at night, since that's when all the activity occurs."

Though the mayor paused a moment to allow for it, no one stood to volunteer for night watch.

"Finally, I'm setting curfew. It'll lift when this threat, whatever it is, is gone. No one outside between ten p.m. and five a.m."

"I have to start baking at three," Nola said.

"We'll make some exceptions for Nola and the patrol crew scheduled each night. If you aren't one of them, please stay at home."

*

After the meeting, Phil Andersen walked home on a mission.

"Pack your things," he told his wife as soon as they arrived.

"We don't have anywhere to go, Phil," Maren said.

"The trees are killing me, no one's buying books anymore, and those holes at the cemetery are freaking me out."

"This is just life telling you to slow down," she replied. "It has happened before."

"No, it's Brighten telling me to get *the fuck* out. Pack your things. I don't want to die here."

Maren did as her husband asked, guiding their three children on proper packing practices. They had plenty of boxes from book shipments and Greer let them use his old box van for the move.

Phil kissed his wife's forehead. "Greer said he could absorb some of our stock and that he'd hold a sale for us on the rest. He'll send us the money. We can stay with my parents in Issaquah until we find another place."

The Andersens left town that evening.

*

Mike pulled the cap from his telescope and wrapped his space blanket tighter around his body. The backyard of his parents' home was far enough from Main Street that the streetlamps didn't affect his stargazing. He'd once seen the Aurora Borealis and he knew the crater patterns on the moon by heart. Tonight though, he was looking for something else.

"If the spaceship came once, it will come again," he said into a small voice recorder.

A small flash of light crossed the sky and Mike held his breath. When nothing else happened he determined it was a shooting star. Excitement built in him, as though something huge was around the corner and he would be first to round the bend. Then, a strange mist floated in on the breeze. Mike sniffed the air, but could find nothing out of the ordinary about it.

*

A few doors down the mist crawled through an open window into Marv's bedroom. An oxygen mask lay on his bedside table next to a pamphlet for Sleepy Hills Cemetery. Marv wasn't in his bedroom, but down the hall on the floor, having never made it to bed.

WEDNESDAY

"Wake up, honey," Mike's mother said as she shook him. "You could have died out here."

"I...they...what happened?" Mike looked over his body for new marks. He checked his eyes in a small signal mirror he kept in his wallet. The whites were reddened, but not abnormal otherwise.

"You fell asleep on the deck and stayed out all night. If I had known you were out here, I would have brought you back in." She helped him stand up and walked him to the sliding glass door.

Mike stopped and turned to look at the sky. "The aliens."

"Did you see any in your telescope?"

"They did something with the fog. They coulda done anything they wanted with me."

"Mike, I told you not to talk about...probing."

*

Mindy had Talon up to a difficult task.

"Help me pick my funeral dress." Twenty dresses were carefully draped around the living room. Mindy walked from garment to garment, caressing the fabric and its adornments.

Talon sat in the middle of it all, watching Gothic metal music videos on his phone. "You look great in everything. You pick."

"Tod! Help me!"

"You know I hate when you call me that!" His voice held anger, but his eyes stayed glued to the screen.

"Tod would complain. Talon would get off his ass and know immediately which one I should lie dead in."

"The black one." He looked up at her. "Stop calling me Tod."

"*Tod*, they are *all* black."

He paused the video he was watching, set his phone down, and glanced half-heartedly at the fashion scattered about. "The one with the lace."

Mindy sighed. "That narrows it to ten."

"The one with the bow?" He was shooting in the dark and being the owner of only a handful of clothing items, Talon didn't understand why she needed so many options anyway.

"I don't own any bows. Like, at all."

"Okay, is there one that makes your boobs look good?"

Mindy nodded.

Talon retrieved his phone and pressed play. "That one."

*

The tracks of the big machines dug their teeth into the grass and pulled themselves up the cemetery hill. Benji rode lead in a backhoe.

"Whoa," he said as they arrived at the top of the hill as though he was slowing a galloping horse. "Whoa," he said again, in awe of the large patch of opened ground. It wasn't a mass grave, which was more unsettling. The walls of earth between each grave were two feet wide, enough room for a person to walk among them without falling in. No space had been left for grave markers or tombstones. This further terrified him.

"Alone and unknown," one of his men said.

"Look over here," another of the workers called out. "Looks like someone got a jump on us filling them in."

At the end of one of the rows, two large graves and three smaller ones had been refilled and grass seeds had been planted. The hair on Benji's arms stood up. A chill crawled up his spine and lingered on his neck, like a predator's breath beating down on its prey.

"Phil and his family left last night," he said.

"You think they didn't make it? Maybe they're in there?"

Benji bent down and touched the dirt. "I don't think so. It would feel different. Wrong to stand on or something."

"Pretty clear message to me," Larry said as he crested the hill with a mug of coffee in hand. "Get out or get in."

"That don't make sense," another worker said.

"Sure it does, you idiot. You leave, you live. You stay, well...it's your burial day."

"You didn't have to make it rhyme," Benji said.

Larry laughed. "But I did, didn't I! I still got it!"

Benji walked to the other end of the grave rows. "Here's another one that's been filled in."

"Hold on one sec. I've got a call to make." Larry walked back to the office and called Agnes.

"I don't want to hear anything more about the holes," she said before he could begin.

"Agnes, I need you to do me a favor."

"Depends what it is. I have a full schedule today. Something's spreading around town."

"It'll be quick. Can you check in on Marv during your lunch break?"

"I suppose. I think he has another month in him though."

"Just check, all right?"

Larry didn't return to the top of the hill. Instead, he waited by the phone.

*

Agnes knocked on the front door of Marv's rambler. In the yard the sprinklers were on. She could hear his television. No one came to the door, so she tried the knob. It was unlocked. "Marv?" she called out as she let herself in. The house, apart from smelling like mothballs and lasagna, was clean. She checked every room, but found no sign of Marv or of anything out of the ordinary. Before leaving, she turned off the television and sprinklers.

On her walk back to her office, she called Larry on her cell phone. "He wasn't home. I couldn't find him anywhere."

"Fuck! You're sure?"

"He's gone." Agnes feared for the dying man. He wasn't in good enough shape to climb the stairs to her office. Wherever he went, he'd have a difficult time of it.

"Okay, thanks."

"What's going on, Larry?" Agnes asked.

"Marv's pulled a fast one. I know it!" He hung up the phone and ran up the cemetery hill as quickly as his aging body could take him.

At the top, the workers had begun filling in holes and were taking a break for their own lunch.

"Dig this grave up!" Larry yelled, pointing to the one that had been filled overnight, separate from the five.

"We're here to fill 'em, not open them up again," Benji said between bites of his sandwich.

"It's my fucking cemetery!" Larry yelled. "Dig it up!"

After much grumbling and repacking of sack lunches, Benji's crew did as Larry directed. In the bottom of the coffinless grave, just as Larry expected, lay the body of a recognizable elderly man.

"Marv."

Benji gasped. "Oh my god. How'd he get in there?"

"He didn't bury himself! Somebody helped him do it!" Larry was pacing the length of the grave.

"Who would do something like that? Without a coffin? I mean, look at him. He's covered in dirt. It's so disrespectful."

"I'll tell you what's disrespectful! Sneaking into a grave after I specifically told him not to!"

"Dead people don't sneak, Larry. You ought to calm down."

"Get his body out of that hole!" Larry screamed and stormed back down the hill.

"Never seen that side of Larry before," one of the workers said.

"Help me get Marv," Benji said. "Then we can finish lunch."

*

By that evening, the holes were filled and the hill was looking closer to its old self. Marv's body had been autopsied and his death determined as natural after the results pointed to a heart attack.

A watch crew, consisting of Talon, Benji, and Arden (provided he didn't need to climb the hill), was arranged to patrol the cemetery that night.

"Seems silly guarding dirt," Arden said as the sun set.

Talon was sad to see the graves filled. He missed his void. Mindy offered to spend the night at the cemetery with him, but Talon wanted the men's respect. He wouldn't get that with his girlfriend fawning over him.

Nearing ten o'clock, Arden and Talon began to yawn. Benji hit a wrench on the side of the backhoe. The noise shocked them to attention, as he hoped it would. But it was only temporary and soon he watched their heads begin to nod.

"We have to stay alert. Someone is responsible for those holes, someone has dirt on their hands!" Benji yelled, but the men were already asleep.

He fought his own exhaustion as he grumbled to himself about sleeping in shifts and teamwork. Then, the same mist that Mike witnessed on Tuesday rolled over the burial acreage. Benji's tired mind told him it was a hallucination. He breathed it in and fell asleep.

THURSDAY

In the early morning hours, a light rain fell on the guard crew, waking them. Benji yawned, stretched, and wiped off some of the water beads that had collected on his jacket. "I don't know what happened. I guess I passed out," he said.

"Yeah, I've never slept so well in my life!" Talon exclaimed, though his back was sore from the hard ground and he, having no waterproof clothing, was soaked to the bone.

As soon as Arden opened his eyes he noticed a difference in their makeshift camp at the base of the cemetery hill. "The machines are gone."

Benji laughed. "What do you mean, gone?" He turned to face the backhoe, or where it should have been. It *was* gone. "How does a machine that big get away without waking us?"

The trio searched the lower section of the cemetery. No sign of the missing construction equipment could be found. As the search ended, Mad Mike walked through the main gate. He was there for a backup sample of the dirt. A precautionary measure and another excuse to examine the holes further.

"Does your...butt hurt?" he asked, his eyes down, but expectant.

"Why the fuck would my ass hurt?" Benji asked in reply. He knew the answer as soon as the words came out. "No, Mike, no. There was no probing last night. Of any kind."

Talon laughed. Arden cleared his throat. Mike hung his head further; not for the lack of probing, but because there were too many people around the graves for him to sneak another sample.

"I guess we should check the holes before going home for the day," Benji suggested.

"I have to stay down here. Can't get to the top." Arden was sore and not willing to showcase his disability in a failed attempt to summit the small peak.

"I'll come," Talon offered. Hope that the holes had reopened was all the energy he needed to reach the top.

Benji and Talon climbed the hill. Talon's heart jumped at the top, while Benji's sank.

The graves had been redug, the extra dirt removed to some unknown location.

"Fuck this shit." Benji sighed. "Time to see the mayor."

"I'll catch up," Talon said. He didn't mean that at all. He wanted to spend time with his grave.

*

For the fifth day in a row, Nola slept through her alarm clock and walked angrily into a dust-covered bakery.

"Dang it!" She whipped a kitchen towel across the tops of the day-old loaves, sending the fine powder into the air. "What a waste! Where in the world is this stuff coming from?"

The clean up cut into her baking time, which then cut into her crafting and TV time. She picked up the broom and got to work.

"And why isn't the rest of the town covered in this crap?"

*

No book from the library held the answers Barbara needed to read. Cutter's color was off and he cried more than she knew how to address. A breast, a bottle, a burp, a brand new diaper, nothing soothed her newborn. To make matters worse, Agnes took Thursdays off.

*

Mike shoved his microphone aside and laid his head down on the desk in his room. He'd been trying for an hour to get his Ham radio to work as it had a week prior, which was perfectly. If aliens were visiting the earth, others would be talking about their experiences. But no matter what he did to his setup, all it did in response was squawk and screech at him. Never had the box malfunctioned.

His only other thought was that the alien technology hovering above Brighten might be interfering with the signals.

*

Everywhere Mindy looked, she saw the holes. The shape of the napkin dispensers, the tables, and the parking spots of the restaurant reminded her about the other rectangles. The more interesting oblong shapes.

How such a void could speak to her, haunt her, she wasn't sure, but the impression it made was deep and inescapable.

*

Scents of body odor and old bologna clung to the walls of the mayor's office. Crusts from a mostly-finished sandwich sat abandoned on a paper plate on his desk.

"What can I do you for?" The mayor gestured for them to sit, but neither accepted. More holes than upholstery covered the chairs and what fabric could be seen was dotted with stains.

"There's got to be something more we can do about the holes; about the entire cemetery situation!"

The mayor shifted in his chair. It groaned more than the missing bulldozer when Benji skipped performing maintenance on it. "About those holes. I have a question."

Benji nodded.

"Have you seen one that's...a bit...wider? You know, *my* size?"

The mayor's question annoyed Benji. It was not his task to report on the size, shape, or quality of the holes. He didn't even want to talk about them. He wanted them gone. "I can't be sure. There's so many. I wasn't paying attention to size when I filled them."

"Next time you're up there, would you mind looking?"

"Sir, all due respect, I'm not going to do that. We filled the holes yesterday and today they are back. The dirt is gone. The weirder thing is that all the big equipment is too. The backhoe, the bulldozer, anything bigger than a sedan, basically. I don't know how someone could've stolen them. Keys stayed on me all night. No tracks leading away or anything. It's like they vanished into thin air."

The mayor laughed, causing his extra chins to tremor. "Benji, that's impossible."

"And thirty-some-odd perfectly dug graves appearing overnight isn't? I'm a reasonable man, but this is something else."

"Give me some time to think on it. I'm sure we can come up with another solution. In the mean time, you're in charge of picking the watch crew for tonight."

It was typical for the mayor to put things off for another day.

*

Larry felt a panic attack coming on. The cemetery had always been his domain. He knew each plot, each headstone, and every bouquet to be expected during a year's time. Now, the land was beyond his control. It was an ivy plant overtaking, as it would a brick building, the lives of the people of Brighten; choking them, suffocating them by its own design.

The land had always taken the dirt back willingly and now it preferred to sit open like many large wounds, unwilling to heal. And though death was good for business, he couldn't fathom thirty plus bodies at once. It would be a massacre. A tragedy unlike anything the town had seen.

*

Benji left the mayor's office and spent the afternoon rounding up a new watch crew for that night's shift. He visited Greer's bookstore first.

"Greer, we need you on watch today," Benji said from the front door. Greer wasn't visible, but if the door was unlocked, Benji knew that he was somewhere amid the rows of literature.

A cat named Reams emerged from the stacks and wrapped himself around one of Benji's legs, begging to be pet. Benji ignored him. "Greer?"

"Can't," Greer replied from somewhere in Science Fiction. "I'm too busy sorting through Phil's books. It's gonna take me two months."

It was the answer Benji expected, but one he wasn't willing to accept. "Something's going on in this town and we all need to pitch in to figure it out! It won't kill you to come camp out for a night at the cemetery."

"Who else'll be there?"

"Who would you like? I haven't asked anyone else yet."

Greer answered quickly. "Nola and Edie."

Reams the cat gave up and retreated back to a dusty corner of the shop.

"Nola will have to bake and she's too timid. I bet Edie will say yes though."

"Fine. I can be there around eight."

*

Benji was able to easily recruit both Edie and Gil to join Greer that night. Edie needed a change of pace from running the restaurant and Gil, like Greer, would spend any time he could around Edie.

*

Every Thursday after dinner for the previous thirty-five years, Arden left Brighten for Blainedale and the grocery store there. His success as a grocer and his customer's happiness with his prices required up-to-date knowledge on the sales and selection of his closest competitor. Arden hobbled through the aisles of the Super Shop and Save with a pad and paper, looking for orange tags and markdowns, and noting new products that hadn't been shopped to his smaller store. He didn't find much, except maybe the two-for-one tampons.

That'll be a hit, he thought as he jotted it down.

Arden always purchased one item from the store as a thank you and to not arouse too much suspicion around his activities. He walked confidently to the checkout lanes and perused the magazines and candy bars there. The gossip didn't suit him. His dentures couldn't handle the sticky sweets. Sometimes he bought a randomly selected paperback novel and then promptly donated it to one of the two bookstores in Brighten. On this Thursday, a supplementary rack had been added and shiny, laminated, cleanly folded maps stuck up, beckoning him to take one home.

"New maps," the cashier replied when he saw Arden examining them.

"Nothing's changed in the last ten years. What's new about

'em?"

The cashier shrugged. "Beats me. The box was delivered this morning, so I put them out."

"I'll take one." He winced at the cost of $10.99, gave the cashier a twenty, collected his change, and retreated to his truck.

He worked the map open in the cab and scrutinized the northern corner of the print for the familiar roadways and dot of his hometown.

They were nowhere to be found.

"New maps, my ass! It's misprinted!" Arden threw it, still open, into the passenger seat and drove back to Brighten. "How do you miss an entire town?"

*

"Is it always this cold at the cemetery?" Edie asked as she pulled her sweater tighter around her body. She was trying to keep her eyes off the gravestones in the distance. Her tired mind would surely place shadows around them.

"I've got an extra blanket if you need one," Gil replied. His mind wandered to sharing the blanket with her.

Greer rolled his eyes. If Benji had told Greer that Gil would be along for the night, he would have refused. They'd been competing for Edie for years, though Edie, too consumed by owning a business, had never bitten on either line.

Though the importance of staying awake and on guard had been stressed to each of them, Gil, from delivering mail, Edie, from standing on her feet all day, and Greer, from sorting through the Andersen's huge book stock, were in deep sleep before the mist climbed inside their lungs.

FRIDAY

"We need to check on the holes," Gil said as they all shook the cold from their bodies.

Edie shook her head. "I don't want to see them."

"Well, we fell asleep when we weren't supposed to. I'd like to be able to say we climbed the hill."

"Come on, Edie. Aren't you a little curious?" Greer hoped she was. It would mean more time with her.

"No. I'm not at all. They remind me of a creepy story I read once."

Greer saw the opportunity to impress Edie and jumped on it. "Tell me the plot and I'll try to guess the title."

"You won't ever guess it. It's more obscure than I care to admit having read."

"Be a sport. You can explain it while Gil looks at the holes for us."

"Whatever," Gil said. "I have to start my mail shift soon." He sighed and started the climb.

Edie cleared her throat and swallowed more of her morning breath-tasting spit than she cared for. "In the story, there's an earthquake and it causes a mountain to shift, exposing a new face of it. Hundreds or maybe thousands of people-shaped holes dot the surface. Each one looks different, individual, like we are."

"That is terrifying. Thank god our holes aren't shaped like people."

"But you've never heard of it, right?" Edie smiled. She liked stumping others. It made her feel special.

Greer racked his brain harder than he ever had, but nothing came to mind. "I'm sorry, I haven't."

"The Enigma of Amigara Fault by Junji Ito." Edie blushed slightly. No one knew she was interested in Japan or comics. This may have been the first time she mentioned it aloud.

"He writes comics. Those aren't really stories!"

"It's still a story!" Edie yelled louder than necessary, wanting to claim a true victory in his game.

"And the holes are still there," Gil, who had just returned to the base of the hill, said.

"What happened to the people?" Greer asked Edie, ignoring Gil.

Edie had never forgotten the end of the story, but she refused to tell it. "Nothing good. Nothing good at all."

*

A phlegmy chest cold spread like wildfire through Brighten on Friday. Agnes, the only medical professional in town, was handing out Sucrets and recommendations of bed rest, but she could do little for the paranoia.

"His color isn't right!" Barbara said. She was holding baby Cutter up for Agnes to see. "He's fixin' to crawl into that grave of his."

"He won't crawl for months!"

"You know what I mean!"

"That grave isn't for him." Agnes had said that line many times over, with only slight variation depending on whom she was speaking to.

"How could you possibly know that?"

"I'm the doctor! He's a healthy baby. Nothing is going to take him out. He's above average in all the measurements."

"It's just as long as Cutter is. You can't tell me that's coincidence!"

"No, but I can tell you to take your boy home and to stay the hell away from the cemetery! Doctor's orders!"

*

Even Mindy brought herself in. She coughed as Agnes listened to her lungs and heart.

"I'm not like, dying, am I? I mean, that would be okay. I'm not scared. But you have to tell me so I can tell Talon. He'll be miserable without me."

"Talon's always miserable, Mindy. I don't know why you hang out with him." Having treated Mindy since she was a child, Agnes felt like an aunt or older sister to the girl and often spoke her mind around her.

"It's called *love*. So, am I dying?"

"You will be if you don't stop smoking. And don't lie! I can smell it on you."

179

"I only smoke when I'm' stressed. And when I'm sad. And when I'm partying."

"Which leaves what? Sleeping?"

Mindy's eyes grew suddenly worried as an idea popped up in her mind. "You'd tell me if Talon were dying, right? Even if he told you not to?"

"You know I can't talk about my patients."

"But, it's *love*, remember? I'd need to know."

"Marry him and then maybe I'll change my mind."

*

"Agnes, can you diagnose me on the phone?" Larry croaked on the other end of the line.

"Are you calling me from the cemetery? You shouldn't be working if you sound like that." In Agnes' opinion, the entire town required bedrest.

"Don't worry. I'm not really working. Just sitting here trying to figure out those holes."

"Stress won't help you get better, Larry. You need rest. I'd like for you to stop by my office later if you can. I can give you something for your throat."

Larry hung up on her without saying more. He had things in a liquor cabinet at home for his throat. He didn't need a doctor to tell him how to administer them either.

*

The mayor, whose health was already in jeopardy due to his obesity, requested that Agnes visit him at his office. His worried town wouldn't benefit from seeing him visiting the doctor's office. Agnes didn't like the mayor or his office. She especially didn't want to sit in the room for any length of time when she knew he had been filling it with sickness. But it was her duty to care for all of the townspeople, including the ones she didn't like.

His coughs carried beyond the door and down the hallway. Agnes pulled the straps of a medical mask over her ears and knocked on the door.

"Come in!" the mayor said before entering another long coughing fit.

She immediately distrusted the quality and effectiveness of the mask as the smells of his office- bologna, farts, and stomach sickness- managed to waft between the closely woven fibers and into her nostrils.

"You sound horrible!"

When a ball of phlegm broke free, he spit it into the trashcan beside him and wiped his face on his jacket sleeve. "I know. I need whatever you have. Everyone's getting antsy about the holes. If we have another town meeting about them, I need to be well again."

"If we have another town meeting, the rest of the room will sound the same as you. I don't know what's floating around Brighten, but I can't think of many who haven't caught it."

"Heck doc, I'd take anything if it meant I'd at least get my appetite back."

His cholesterol levels came to her mind. The man could use the break from the solids he put into his body. "Go home. Eat some soup. I'll write you a prescription for a strong expectorant."

*

"Are you sure this is all you have for me?" Nola asked Gil as he gave her a small pile of envelopes. She pointed to the mail truck. "There isn't a big box in the back?"

"It's pretty empty in there. No big boxes."

"Darn it!" Nola paced. "I ordered a new mixer. It should have come by now. Nothing is going right these days!"

"I'm sorry. You might need to contact the seller. Make sure it was sent."

*

Nola wasn't the only customer that morning to complain about missing mail. Edie didn't receive an order of replacement plates for the restaurant. The mayor was expecting important documents to get Brighten on a list of historical places, but they never arrived.

During his lunch break, Gil looked through the remainder of undelivered mail. On most days the stack would be filled with out of town post from friends and family beyond Brighten's borders, but today it was oddly all local.

*

Things weren't looking up for Mike either. The soil sample he'd so expertly collected had disappeared. This only further confirmed his suspicions that aliens were invading the town. Or already had.

*

Arden practiced writing BRIGHTEN over and over until he felt he could match the lettering on the map. With his steadiest hand, he added his town back to it.

*

Saturday is the perfect day for a sidewalk sale, Greer thought on Friday night. He dusted off a rickety folding table, wrote a sign that read 'Everything on this table must go! $1.00 books!', and stayed up picking the worst volumes from his newly acquired stock.

*

No watch crew was organized that night. Benji tried his hardest to gather a team, but after more than thirty "sorry, I'm sick" type responses, he gave up.

SATURDAY

Main Street was usually a bustling thoroughfare on a weekend day, but Saturday, it was empty. Greer sat on a stool next to the sale table, under the awning of Phil Andersen's locked shop. The sign he'd painstakingly written flapped in a gentle breeze.

Edie sat alone in Good Eatin' for several hours. When no one came in for lunch, she turned off the ovens, closed the doors, and went home.

*

She knew that motherhood wasn't going to be easy and that postpartum depression was a real thing, but when Barbara added the graves into the mix, she was nearly convinced Cutter would come to harm by her own hands. It wouldn't be the sharp corners of the world or falling decor. She would be his death.

The newborn cried from his crib. Barbara cried in her living room, wanting to comfort her child, but knowing not how.

*

Mindy and Talon were holed up in Mindy's apartment, wasting ink pen cartridges as they drew countless solid black rectangles. Their obsession with the holes had reached a fever pitch.

"We should get tattoos of our graves," Mindy suggested after a long silence broken only by scribbling.

"That's a lot of ink," Talon replied without looking up from his equally ink-saturated piece of paper. "It'll hurt a lot more than your skull one."

Mindy looked at the inside of her left wrist. Jack Skellington stared up at her and smiled in all his bony, line art greatness. Talon was right, it would hurt a lot more.

Talon stopped drawing. "I have an idea. It might be too morbid."

Mindy laughed. "The queen of darkness can handle it."

"I was thinking we could get some sleeping bags and sleep in the holes over night."

"Not tonight though. I work tomorrow. Maybe Sunday night?"

She stroked his hair, coughed, and rejoined him in drawing the blackness.

*

Agnes was home sick, having finally succumbed to the respiratory illness for which she was treating the rest of the town. The phone rang incessantly and Agnes was just as persistent in ignoring it.

*

With the chaos in the graveyard and the frog in his throat, Larry switched from coffee to whiskey and moved his office from the cemetery grounds to his home. More specifically, his couch. Even if he wanted to return to his duties, the amount of alcohol with which he was self-medicating would no longer allow him to walk straight.

*

Nola cried into her baking. The thought of ending up in the graveyard, rotting in a hole was more than she could bear. Cremation was the *only* option in her opinion. The pot she used to hold the yeast would double as her urn upon her death. She liked recipes, plans, and exact known outcomes. The holes kept her lights on at night and came to represent everything she hated. She'd sooner kill herself than allow someone else to dictate her death.

*

Gil delivered the mail, avoided the cemetery, which hurt because Brina was there, and played solitaire in his boxer shorts for the remainder of the day.

*

The watch crew for that night was supposed to be Larry and Mike. However, Benji was unable to reach Larry and everyone else was still sick, so he was once again roped into the task. He could already imagine the topic of discussion as he and Mike watched pointlessly over the plots. It would be a long night.

Excitement kept Mike's thin body warm against the night air. The possibility that he might see an alien would surely help to hold up his eyelids beyond his bedtime.

"Look what I got." Benji held up a gas mask. "Military grade."

"For the fog?" Mike guessed.

"You've seen it too?"

"It put me to sleep. Anything coulda happened after that."

It would be considered silly by any resident of Brighten, other than Mike himself and maybe his mother, to put any stock in a word he spoke, but Benji wanted to believe they were making some kind of progress in the formless fight against the graves.

"I feel good about tonight, Mike. We are gonna figure this out together, okay?"

Mike nodded. "I already have a plan. You wear the mask. Hide and watch what happens to me. Make sure they don't see you."

"Okay, okay. That's good."

"But if they take off my pants, you have to promise to look away."

Benji laughed. "Of course."

*

Shortly after eleven that night, a mist fell over the town, pulled in through window-set air conditioning units and inhaled by the residents of Brighten. Benji watched as Mike steadied his body, breathed in the strange fog, and collapsed.

"I knew it!" Benji yelled through the thick rubber of the mask. He wasn't too worried about Mike, or the rest of the town for that matter, as they'd just carry on the next day as they had been.

But then a figure approached him in the dark. He was difficult to see through the mask, but Benji thought it was a man in a three-piece suit, who also happened to be wearing a gas mask. He dare not remove the mask for fear of passing out, but it was impossible to have intelligent conversation with it on. Instead, Benji held up his hands in a surrender-type move. The suited man pulled something from inside his jacket. Its head glowed a beautiful electric blue in the dark night.

"Shit." Benji turned to run, but it was too late. The Taser's hungry metal wires hit him and he was down.

The man unbuttoned his suit jacket. It was time for the dirty work. He knelt beside Benji and removed his gas mask, helping him to breathe in the fumes.

SUNDAY

Exactly one week after the holes appeared, the townspeople of Brighten didn't wake up. Cutter wasn't in his crib, he wasn't even crying anymore and he fit perfectly into his hole. Agnes no longer had to tell anyone to avoid the holes or to cover their mouths when they sneezed. Larry the groundskeeper was out of a job, as there was no more room in the cemetery to fill. Mindy was buried next to Talon, though not in the dress or graves they'd selected. Arden's short leg hadn't kept him from reaching the new height. There had been a larger hole for the wider-than-tall mayor. The decomposition process worked away at Nola's body; her urn sat still full of yeast in her bakery.

MONDAY

On Monday, the day after the disappearance of thirty-one people from Brighten, a sign went up at the opposite end of Main Street.

"Ghost Town", it read.

Two men in suits stood side by side, staring at the sign. The taller of the two held Mad Mike's vial of dirt. Arden's altered map had been refolded and tucked beneath an arm of the shorter of the two.

"Explain it to me again?" the shorter man asked.

"Brighten wasn't contributing to the national economy anymore, not really anyway. It was a dying town living on government life support. We pulled the plug. We...made it dead."

"Simple as that?"

"Simple as that. No real ghosts, no aliens, no cults or serial killers. Just a government agency tasked with clean up. It'll save a lot of money. Much cheaper than relocation procedures as well."

"Why'd you keep the dirt? Can anyone trace the gas?"

The Tall Suited Man held the vial up and inspected it mockingly. "Nah, untraceable. It's a souvenir. Like a keychain, but more meaningful."

"What about the pets?"

"Shot outside of town and left as carrion."

"Bye bye Brighten."

The Tall Suited Man turned, putting the former town at his back, and began to walk down the road. "Yes, bye bye Brighten."

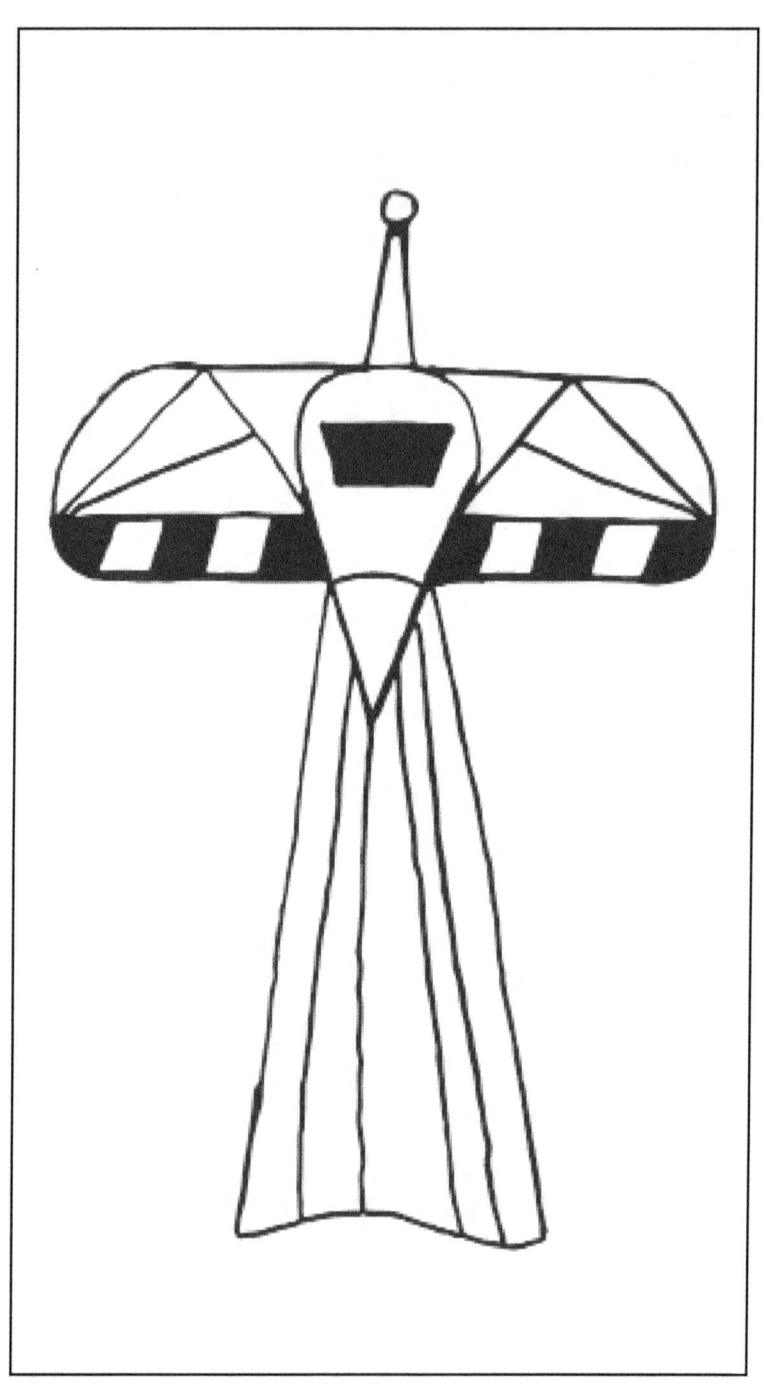

ART BY TOM KERNS

ERIS OF EARTH

"You're weird!" the little boy yelled. He sat across from her in the sandbox and was building a sand castle that he planned to destroy with his toy fire truck.

In her corner of the box, eight-year-old Eris was using a stick to draw sets of perfectly concentric circles. Her lips were stained green from lunch. It wasn't the first time she'd been called 'weird', or any other name with a similar meaning. She was actually surprised the boy hadn't abandoned his side of the sandbox when she arrived to play. Normally other kids gave her plenty of room to be alone.

"Eris, dinner!" her mother, Effie, called from their trailer, which was just behind the playground.

"See ya later," Eris said to the boy, but he ignored her as he crashed his toy fire truck into a pile of sand. She shrugged, admired her sand drawing one last time, and went home.

Inside the trailer she heard a tiny jingle growing louder. It was a small bell on the collar of her pet ferret Dash, who was running to welcome her.

"Hi, Dash!"

Hello, Eris, she heard him respond as he leapt into her arms. It wasn't a voice anyone else could hear. It was in her head. This was another reason the other children didn't like her. The birds on the playground talked to her during recess at school. She could hear the busy ants that skittered about in the cracks of the cement sidewalks that surrounded the classroom buildings. And her pet ferret told her stories to help her fall asleep while her mother was working at night.

Dinner was macaroni and cheese. The regular, store-bought, boxed kind that came with a packet of powder to make the sauce, except Eris' was green.

"It's not green enough!" Eris whined.

Her mother opened the cabinet above the stove and selected a small bottle of green food coloring. "Only a couple more drops."

"It's narcissism," her grandmother Evelyn croaked from her hide-a-bed in the living room.

Eris' eyes were a brilliant green and Evelyn had once caught her staring into a mirror at her own reflection. Eris had liked green before that moment, but Evelyn was convinced her obsession started when she saw her own eyes for the first time.

"That's not the reason why, mother," Effie said.

Eris just liked green and so she squeezed the bottle until it was empty. After copious amounts of stirring, she was satisfied with the dark green color her meal had become. The heaping spoonful she ate even tasted green to her. "Yum!"

Me too, Dash said to her from the floor. She looked down to see him sitting on his haunches, begging like a dog.

"Mom, can Dash eat the noodles?"

"I don't think he'll like them," she replied.

"He says he wants to try some," Eris said. She already had a small spoonful ready for him.

"Well, you tell him I tried to save him from the *ooblin garmina*."

Ooblin garmina meant 'green slime', at least that's what her mother had told her once.

Eris wasn't the only strange girl in her family; not the first to be ostracized or ridiculed. Her mother claimed to have been abducted by aliens not once, but on seven separate occasions. No one talked to her anymore, especially since she sprinkled her sentences with words from an alien tongue she claimed to have picked up on her many trips "to the outer worlds". The only job she could hold down was a graveyard shift as a gas station attendant and that was because she didn't have to talk to people and they didn't have to talk to her.

Dash did a happy dance on the floor after swallowing the cheesy, green noodles.

"He likes the slime!" Eris screamed with glee. "He ate it this time!"

"Careful with the rhyming, you'll end up like *brugansa*," Effie warned.

Brugansa meant 'grandmother' and Eris' grandmother Evelyn was a poet. This wasn't odd at all, but she was also addicted to painkillers and those highs made her usually complex written words devolve into snide, four-line rhymes. She often fell asleep while writing and would wake up with ink on her face and drool on her journal. Evelyn never left the trailer. Eris couldn't remember the last time her grandmother had gotten out of bed, actually.

Evelyn, hopped up on Percocet, then began to recite a stanza of a new poem she'd written.

"My coffin has two guests, I'll never have my rest, and I can smell the rotting feces of the brown, four-legged pests." She cackled, amused by her own wit.

Effie smiled. Her mother was published in several literary journals and had won an award for a poem detailing the plight of midwestern farmers struggling to survive against big corporations.

But that was a long time ago, before Evelyn found out that painkillers could take her worries away. She couldn't even remember the poor farmers now. Half the time she didn't recognize Effie or Eris.

She's talking about me, Dash said to Eris from the floor. *I'm not a pest.*

"You are not a pest at all! You're my best friend." Eris finished her food, picked up Dash and slung him over her shoulder. She took him to her bedroom and placed him on top of her bed.

*

The three generations of Everetts lived together in the trailer, which was made of wood. Her mother could have afforded a fancier Airstream, but the metal made it difficult for "visitors to communicate" and Effie was sure they'd return to Earth again someday.

*

The phone rang, causing Effie and Evelyn to jump. The elder's drug-addled brain was paranoid and thought it might be the police. Effie had to remind herself to answer with human words since the aliens never called on the telephone. "Hello?"

"Yes, Ms. Everett, hello," a man's voice said through the receiver. "This is Principal Matthews, from the elementary. I'd like to talk to you about Eris."

"Okay?" Effie hadn't held a conversation in sometime and she was finding it very difficult to remember the protocols. *Should I sound concerned? Or interested?*

The principal led the conversation for her. "Your daughter isn't following the art lessons."

"That can't be. She brings art home almost every day. I can't see the door of the fridge." Effie looked in admiration at the drawings. They were piled so high, the magnets were straining to keep a connection to the metal.

"She's making art. It just isn't the kind of art she is supposed to be making," the principal explained.

"For example?" Effie looked again at the art she had saved. She couldn't see much wrong with it. It wasn't offensive and it certainly showed effort.

"Yesterday they were to glue macaroni down in the shape of their house. Eris filled the paper with noodles. She said it was a field."

Effie laughed. "Well, there's a field across the street."

"But she doesn't live there. It isn't a house."

"No, of course not. She lives here at home with me, but sometimes she plays in the field."

There was a pause. Effie couldn't even hear the principal's breath, as though he'd taken the receiver away from his face.

"And," he began. There was another pause. "And this has

nothing to do with, how shall I say this, with your *experiences*?"

"She doesn't know anything about that," Effie lied. "We don't discuss the *anvertislies* in the house. Ever."

"The...*what*?"

"The aliens," Effie explained. She heard the teacher swallow hard and clear his throat. This kind of reaction was why she'd used *anvertislies* instead. It was temporarily palatable, unlike the word *alien*.

"Well, please let Eris know that she needs to follow the assignment directions better and listen to her teachers. If they ask for a house, she better give them a house!"

Effie put the phone back on the receiver and returned to washing the dinner dishes. There wasn't a point in telling her daughter to shape up. Eris had always been different and Effie hadn't helped that situation. She'd hung a mobile of planets and UFOs above Eris' crib. She'd sung her lullabies in a language from another planet. Eris' after school cartoons were documentaries on crop circles and their trailer had more alien knickknacks than the Area 51 Museum. Effie's favorite being the cross-stitched and framed piece of art above her kitchen sink that read in perfect threaded letters:

Look to the skies
There are no secrets there
Only truth

Reading it then, Effie resolved to keep going as they always had, at least until that was no longer possible.

In her room, Eris laid on her bed and stared out the window. Across the street from the trailer park the large, grassy field stretched farther than Eris knew. She'd never been to the end of it and her mother claimed it was the very field she was taken from, long before Eris was born and they'd moved into the park.

Turn off the light, Dash said. *You have school in the morning.*

Eris did as Dash requested and gave into her dreams. In them she lay in the field looking up at the stars, daring them to come and greet her.

*

The next day there was a new girl in class. During lunch she looked just as out of place and lonely as Eris did, so Eris extended her hand. "Hi, I'm Eris."

"Don't touch her!" another girl shouted across the lunch room. She gave no further explanation, but the empty warning was enough to scare the new girl away.

Eris sat alone to eat, as she always did. She pulled out her lunch. A cup of lime green Jello, four slices of pickle, two sticks of celery, four broccoli florets, a pile of Brussels sprouts, and a glass bottle of milk with green food coloring added to it. The other children stared, which they always did. Most of them wouldn't touch the vegetables she was fond of eating, but the fact that everything was green was more interesting to them.

A boy, younger than she by a year or two, built the nerve to approach her. "Why is everything green?" he asked. Even Eris' dress, socks and shoes were various shades of emerald.

"Green is my favorite," Eris explained. "I don't like the other colors."

He looked at her food again and then at her for a few seconds more. "You're strange," he said before running back to his friends.

"Thanks," Eris said, but she wasn't sure it was a compliment.

*

Later, back in class, she screamed when a classmate named Ethan squished a spider that was crossing his desk.

"Eris, what's wrong?" her teacher asked.

"He was just taking a shortcut!" Eris yelled. "He was trying to make it home for dinner!"

"You don't know that!" Ethan yelled back. He picked up the gnarled remains of the arachnid and threw it at her. "And if you *can* talk to him, tell him I'm *not* sorry."

Ethan was sent to the principal. Not for killing the spider, but for throwing it at Eris.

Eris thought of running the spider to the nurse, but it mumbled its last words while stuck in her hair.

*

The bus ride home felt longer than usual. Eris was counting her tear drops, which she half expected to come out green, as they fell onto her dress. The spider family was no doubt wondering what had befallen its patriarch and Eris couldn't locate them to break the bad news. The new girl was giggling with her new friends in the seats behind her. All in all, it had been a horrible day.

*

What's wrong? Dash was following Eris around the trailer, but she wasn't paying him any mind.

Evelyn followed Eris too, with her eyes and words.

"The weirdo child is sad, and the pest's becoming mad. For once life in the trailer isn't nearly half as bad."

"He was already dead! It was no use!" Eris screamed.

I'm not a pest! Dash yelled, which only made things worse since only she could hear his anger.

Effie awoke to the turmoil and cursed that she hadn't made it to her alarm clock. She dressed and started dinner, pesto pasta and green beans, and sat with Eris at the dining room table.

"What are you drawing?" she asked. It looked like little clumps of grass, but she didn't want to assume as she'd been wrong before.

"The spider family," Eris responded. Her voice trembled and she fought hard to keep any more tears from falling.

Effie could see the spiders now with their green legs sticking out in all directions. "They look sad."

Eris nodded and then looked into her mother's eyes. "Mom, someone at school called me 'strange'. Is that bad?"

Effie considered how best to answer the question. She knew what the other child meant and it *was* bad. "Strange is just another word for special and they don't even know how special you really are!"

"If they won't talk to me, how will they ever know?"

"Oh, they'll know," Effie said. She hugged her daughter close. She was special and, when no one believed Effie's stories, it hurt most because Eris was proof. She was a gift.

"The comfort that we take in the lies our mothers make will quickly crumble when we're old enough to know that it's all fake." Evelyn said from somewhere beneath her quilt.

"Damn it, mom! Shut up! Enough with the mean poems!" Effie left the table and yanked open a drawer in the kitchen that held her mother's pain medicine. She threw a new bottle of Percocet onto her mother's bed. "Take one, take seven. I don't care."

Evelyn's ink-stained hand reached for the bottle and disappeared with it under the covers.

*

Over dinner, Effie tried to turn the conversation to a happier topic.

"Are you excited for your ninth *ponjijam?*"

Ponjijam meant birthday and Eris couldn't say that she was excited for it. A birthday party wasn't much fun when you had no friends to invite. In her entire eight years, only two people had ever attended a celebration of her life, and they were both currently in the wooden trailer with her.

"I think your father has something very special planned for your birthday. I've had these . . . feelings. He's been trying to communicate something to me." Effie smiled.

Eris wasn't sure if she believed her mother as she had never met the man.

Some of the other children in the trailer park made fun of her for not having a dad, but she wasn't the only one. Others were missing dads as well, but they were in places like jail, 'in that other bitch's house', or dead. Eris didn't know where her dad was and her mom didn't know either.

*

That night she had dreams about the man she'd never met. He was tall, friendly, and strong, and he made everything better.

*

In the morning a small, wet nose prodded her cheek.

Happy Birthday, Eris, Dash said.

Eris didn't want it to be her birthday, so she turned over in bed and tried to go back to sleep where her father was. Just as she was retreating back to dreamland, her mother burst into her room.

"Wake up, kiddo! Happy Birthday!" She shook Eris, clearly more excited about the date than Eris was.

Eris opened her eyes and saw that her mother had laid out a new green dress for her to wear. She put it on and stumbled down the hall toward the kitchen. Strung up on the wall above the television was the 'Happy Birthday' banner her mother hung every year. It was worse for the wear and somehow had gotten wet in storage. Each letter was now covered in hundreds of black mold spores. It made Eris even sadder.

"Today is the day!" Effie grinned bigger than Eris had ever seen. She could see the fillings in her mother's teeth. And when she opened her mouth to start singing, Eris saw a black mark at the back of her mother's throat, like a tattoo. She'd never seen it before.

In the middle of the dining room table was a round cake. Everything on it was green, from the fondant and frosting, to the candles and the filling that was yet to be exposed. She sat at the table and smelled it. Somehow it even smelled green.

"Cake for breakfast?" Eris asked.

"Of course. Today's a special day!"

"But I want my Apple Jacks," Eris complained.

Normally Effie would have separated a bowl of just the green, apple-flavored cereal rings for her daughter, but there wasn't time for that this morning. "We need to do this quick!"

School, Eris thought, *should be canceled for my birthday.*

Effie went to the hide-a-bed and prodded her mother. "Evelyn, sing with me!"

"Oh holy night, the stars are brightly shining!" the old woman yelled.

"Not just any song! The birthday song!"

"Whose birthday is it?" Evelyn sat up and looked around the room. It could have been hers and she wouldn't have remembered.

"Your granddaughter's. You watched me hang the sign."

Evelyn furrowed her brow. "How long have I had a granddaughter?"

"Nine years, today!"

Evelyn took to her journal and began madly scribbling something in it, but she showed no further interest in discussing or singing to her granddaughter.

"Happy birthday to you!" Effie sang alone.

The town's tornado warning siren started blaring. There had only been one other tornado to threaten their town during Eris' lifetime, but she was an infant and had no recollection of it.

Effie sang louder. "Happy birthday to you!"

A booming *whooshing* noise rattled the trailer. Dash stood against Eris' leg.

Pick me up, he requested. Eris placed him in her lap. Together they watched the flames of the nine birthday candles flit and dance in a breeze that filled the trailer. She didn't like that the flames were yellow, but her mother couldn't change the color of fire.

One strong gust came whipping under the gap beneath the front door and blew out the candles for her.

I hope you got your wish in, Dash said.

The trailer was vibrating and jostling back and forth.

"Happy birthday, dear Eris!" Effie was holding onto the kitchen countertop for balance as she sang. Her knuckles were white, but she was smiling.

"Shouldn't we go to the shelter, Mom?" Eris asked.

"Happy birthday to you!" Effie finished. She served a slice to Eris and one to Evelyn in bed.

"Mom?" she asked again.

"Just eat your cake, honey! Everything will be *rustochi*!"

Rustochi meant fine, but Eris could hear the world being torn apart outside. She could hear screaming and explosions, followed by more screaming. She wasn't particularly scared. There wasn't much in the world that she would miss if it all disappeared. But she could hear the animals' frightened cries; their confusion. And dying on her birthday was not something Eris wanted to do.

It was Effie's plan to stay in the trailer until the noise died down; at least until Eris finished a slice of the cake. But then the wooden frame caught fire and the heat and smoke became too stifling.

"Outside!" she ordered.

Eris put Dash into her satchel. Then she tried to wake her grandmother, who was passed out on her bed with the plate of cake still on her lap.

"We have to leave her, Eris. She won't be able to keep up." There was more to it than that, but Effie had little time to explain that Evelyn's life had already been lived, that her legs no longer worked, having atrophied in bed, that inside Evelyn wanted to die.

"Goodbye grandma," Eris said and then kissed Evelyn's forehead.

She took her mother's hand and they ran down the path that led through the playground. The monkey bars and spider's web, both made of metal, had been melted into mangled shapes.

In the sandbox, the firetruck, the one belonging to the boy who called her "weird", was now just a pile of red goo sitting atop the sand.

Eris stared. "Wow!"

"Don't stop!" her mother shouted. "Get to the field!"

Eris looked to the field and saw that it wasn't empty anymore. Five giant, green spaceships, each one larger than ten of the trailers, had just landed. It wasn't a tornado, it was an invasion.

"*Ooblin*!" she shouted, because green really was her favorite color.

Her mother pulled her toward the ships. "We have to find your *vanda*!"

Vanda meant father, but Eris wasn't sure how she could help to find him. She had no idea what he looked like and she was certain that no father of hers would be exiting a spaceship. *Maybe they'd given him a ride?* she wondered.

"There!" Effie yelled over the din of exploding trailer homes behind them. She pointed to a being, a green alien, who had just stepped from a doorway on the side of one of the ships. "I knew he was coming!"

Her father, he wasn't a man after all. Not human anyway.

He was tall.

The being approached them and Eris' mother ran to it, but it held up a hand, causing her to stop in her tracks. Next, it raised her body from the ground and somehow managed to force her mouth open, all without touching her. The being was looking for something.

Don't be afraid, Eris, Dash said from the satchel. *He's checking for the mark.*

How does Dash know about the mark? Eris thought.

When the being was satisfied by what it saw, it lowered Effie to the ground and pulled her in for a quick embrace. "My love."

He was friendly.

"Eris," her mother called, "be polite and introduce yourself."

It's all right, Dash said, sensing her trepidation.

She took a deep breath.

"Eris, of Earth," she said, extending a small hand and hoping someone would finally shake it back. "Pleased to meet you!"

The being laughed and shook it. "I know who you are! You should know me too! Has your mother told you nothing?"

"Daddy?" Eris guessed.

"It's time to go home, young one."

She looked around her. A rabbit was hopping by. The hare was a mother and Eris could hear her worried thoughts about her babies tucked in a den beneath the field. "What about the animals?"

"They'll be okay. It's only the end of time for the humans," the being said. "And all their...stuff."

"But I'm human." Eris pointed to herself.

"You are *not* human, Eris. You are special."

Special is another word for strange. Special isn't anything good, Eris thought.

"I know what you're thinking, but you really are *something else*. Dash can explain."

He's right, Dash said. *You are a gem among rocks, a sun among stardust, a princess among peons.*

Eris' eyes opened wide. "A princess? A *real* princess?"

"A real one," her mother said. "I wanted to tell you, but you wouldn't believe me. You are a gift. A precious miracle. You'll see when we get home."

"But where's home?" Eris asked. It used to be behind her. Maybe Dash knew, or her mother. Definitely her father must know, since it was partially his fault that their old home had burned to the ground.

He scooped her up into his arms and held her close. As a family, they walked to the spacecraft.

He was strong.

And he made everything better.

"Home, Eris, is an entire planet named after *you*."

ART BY JAMES LACROIX

LAST NIGHT WHILE YOU WERE SLEEPING

last year when she was crying
you didn't lend an ear,
never once thought you of trying
to help her face her fears
so
last year while you were sleeping
she crawled out of the bed
to seek a quiet spot for weeping
and a bag that fit her head

last month when she was cutting
you made her hide the scar
instead of helping her to climb
out of her stifling bell jar
so
last month when you were sleeping
she stroked the kitchen knives
imagined the shallow valleys
deepening
and the ending of her life

last month when she was teaching
herself to tie a noose
you didn't see that she was reaching
because her ends were coming loose
so
last month while you were sleeping
she thought of taking all her pills
in her hand, a pile, *heaping*
but was it enough to kill?

last week when she was quiet
you didn't ask her why, but
cries for help aren't always riots,
sometimes the happy want to die

so
last week while you were sleeping
she sat on the window's edge
thought of ending it, of leaping
but had no strength to leave the ledge

last night while you were sleeping
slipped she, 'neath waves of blue
she felt the water filling, seeping,
drowning the pain that had accrued
and
last night when she was dying
you awoke and listened in
but you went back to your sleeping,
'twas but a temporary din

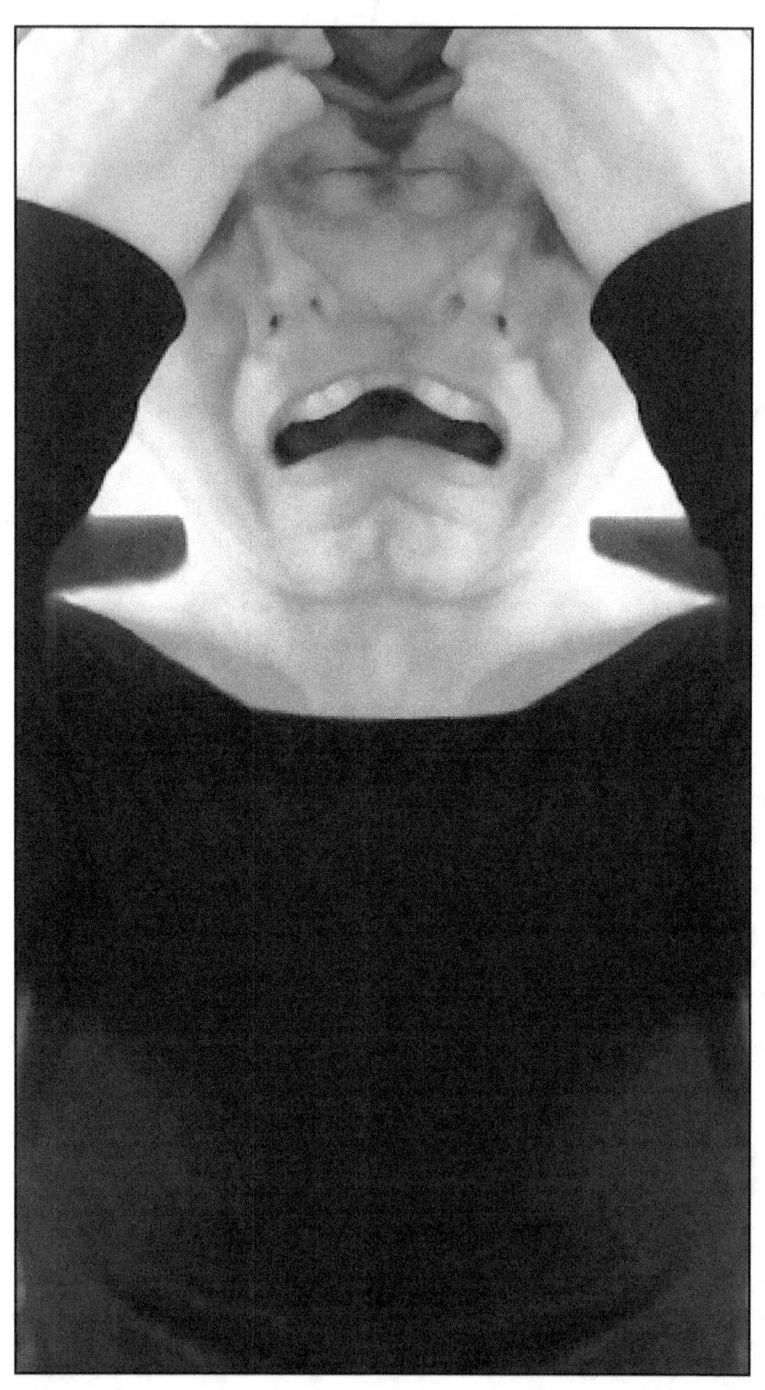

ART BY MICHELLE KILMER

STEVEN [MIRIELLE 2]

MINA

It took a week for her to get used to her reflection. She was beautiful still, perhaps more beautiful than she formerly was, but seeing Mirielle looking back at her was looking into the face of a ghost, a stranger.

It took a month to clean Steven's kitchen, to make it livable for herself. Hand scrubbing the piles of food trays was an exercise in emotional restraint. She was trying to be strong now, and accepting of what had become of her life. She trashed everything that was stuck to the fridge, everything but the mementos Steven had kept of the women who had died. Mina rearranged the plane ticket to Tokyo, the photo of Bahati, a lock of Ana's hair, and a menu from the cafe at which she herself had worked in Italy, into a rectangular memorial.

Mina found her passport in a desk drawer, but that face was no longer hers. Traveling back to Italy would be impossible until she could sort out that situation. She'd found her freedom from Steven, but she was still a prisoner. Even grocery shopping was off limits. Money wasn't the problem. Steven had massive amounts of passive income coming in every month from a few science books he'd written and was selling on Amazon. His credit card info was saved on any number of his online accounts, and his passwords to those also saved. The nearest town was a small one and she was bound to be recognized for who she wasn't. An old friend of Mirielle's most certainly would see her and faint or worse, approach her.

It wasn't an unfounded fear. When her first online order,

a book on psychology, was delivered to the house, the delivery woman greeted her warmly and called her by name.

"Mirielle! Been awhile! How are you?"

Dead, Mina thought. She smiled and said she was well. It was all a lie, down to her signature on the delivery slip. She'd had to practice Mirielle's elaborate scrawl in preparation for scrutinous eyes. The four additional letters always gave her trouble.

Steven hadn't been right about everything. Though she gained Mirielle's looks, Mina did not get any of Steven's lost wife's emotions or memories. Mirielle's soul was still floating in the ether somewhere, hopefully unaware of the events that had unfolded.

Aside from cleaning, Mina spent her days going through boxes of Mirielle and Steven's shared history. When she came across their wedding photo, her heart ached. Mirielle's dress was beautiful. Steven held her closely, but gently. His eyes were different, full of love instead of the monstrous pain that had consumed and changed him. He looked normal and completely sane. In every card, 'Forever Yours' was scribbled in both his and her writing.

She found photo albums, movie ticket stubs, hospital bills, and dinner receipts. Steven had kept everything as if in preparation for the inevitable day he would lose his true love.

*

Sometimes she could still feel the other women, hear them. Sometimes it wasn't only her inside the new body.

REN

Having remnants of Ren wasn't so bad. A week after Mina left the bunk room, she woke up and, before breakfast, completed Ren's entire calisthenics routine from memory. And, she *liked* it. There was comfort in the familiar and exercise always brightened one's mood. The exercise benefited her in other ways too. She felt in full control of her new body now. This body held more weight at the hips than her old one. Her butt was bigger now too, less flat, more firm. She'd have to work to keep it that way.

When Mina slept, her dreams were exciting as well. She'd always wanted to travel to Japan, and through Ren's third eye, she got to. Her sleeping legs traveled down many an alleyway and her sightless eyes saw Tokyo in all of its glory.

On a whim she tried to use a pair of chopsticks she found in the kitchen, but was saddened to find that Ren's grace and muscle memory weren't shared with her hands.

There was a downside to Ren's company. She cried, a lot. And occasionally she asked Mina to end her life to spare them all from further suffering.

ANA

Ana appeared often. Mina, normally quite level headed, could feel Ana's unique rage bubble up over the smallest of things. When she burnt toast, Ana arrived screaming and cursing. *Motherfucker! Fucking cocksucker!*

She complained often of missing the weather in Mexico, missing her husband, her dog, everything she couldn't have.

Ana, Mina could live without, but she knew that wasn't an option. Her hatred and her backbone would be needed on the path which Mina was about to embark.

BAHATI

Mina first knew Bahati was still a part of her when, while scouring the closet for clothes she actually wanted to wear, she got a whiff of Steven's cologne. It was a smell she normally hated; one that induced nausea on several occasions, but this day it was wonderful. She sought the scent and found it still clung to one of Steven's unlaundered shirts draped forgotten over a hanger. Mina buried her face in the fabric and took deep inhalations.

It would be so good to have him here with us. The thought crept into her brain.

"Stop!" Mina yelled at herself. She stuffed the shirt behind a trunk. "There is no *us!*"

He chose us. He wanted us.

"No, he wanted *her!*"

He loved me. I know he did.

"Bahati? Are you really *all* still here?" Mina wasn't sure if that made her happy or more depressed. Some company in the big, empty house wouldn't hurt, but she had finally begun to appreciate being alone.

*

Because of Bahati, Mina wanted to see Steven and hold him. A small part of Mina felt bad for what she had done to him. Lucky for her, Steven wasn't dead. He'd only lost consciousness that day. And he'd been disoriented in the room for five weeks, eating his meals and calling out for *her*.

INTRODUCTIONS

"Steven," she said. His name, the first word she spoke to him since she strangled him, felt foreign. She wanted it to stay that way. He was a monster she knew enough about.

It had been quick work to hose down the room and after fiddling with the mechanisms, she opened the walls back up. The two sets of bunk beds were once again pushed up against one of the walls. It looked just as it had when Ren first arrived.

Mina tried to channel Bahati and sound loving as she spoke into the microphone, but it was difficult to see Steven's face on the monitors. "Honey, wake up."

His eyes fluttered open and he grabbed at his throat for a moment. It was something he did often upon waking and when he realized he was still alive, he cried.

"It was all a bad dream," he said aloud. He looked to the camera. "Mirielle, let me out of here."

In the control room, Mina sighed. "I can't yet, Steven. You need to be isolated. The doctor has confirmed that you are *very* sick."

"But I feel fine. I want to see you."

"You are still contagious and my immune system is weak. I'm

sorry."

Again, Steven cried. Every moment he wasn't holding his wife felt like an eternity. She was so close to him, but untouchable. "We're meant to be together!"

"And we will be. Please be patient."

Steven was unaware of how limited his time was. He had no fear of the situation. He felt no danger. He touched the walls without trying to move them, stared into the camera unconcerned that he was being monitored, and knocked on the door as though she would simply open it for him.

Mina had all the time in the world.

CYCLES

The pastels of the baby book stood out amongst the dark leather of the other photo albums. She flipped through it, admiring the carefully lettered updates of Mirielle's first pregnancy. The pages counted down to the due date, a Christmas many years ago. Ultrasound images, nursery plans, and cravings, it was all there.

Mina looked down at her new body and tried to imagine how it might wear a pregnancy. She turned another page and a photo of Mirielle, standing sideways with her hands atop her expanding belly, gave her a better visual than she could ever conjure. Mirielle was glowing. Mina felt the joy bursting from the image.

When her page turning brought her to the second trimester, something was noticeably different. The entries were messier, more frantic. Mirielle was admitted to the hospital for abdominal pain and bleeding.

And then the entries stopped. No birthing suite photos, no happy couple, no new baby. The pages were slightly altered. The countdown had been scribbled out. And on the final page, where it once read *Welcome, Baby!*, it now read, in what Mina recognized as Steven's handwriting, *R.I.P. Baby Sophia*.

The tears flowing down her face weren't a surprise. Mina understood the pain and grief of a miscarriage. She'd suffered one as a young adult. The loss still haunted her.

She closed the book and considered returning it to the pile. *It would be too much to use this against him. I'm not that wicked*, she thought.

Ana spoke up almost immediately. *He took me from my honeymoon, from my husband! I had a family planned! He stole that from me!*

Mina could hear Ren crying. She imagined that if some kind of soul-cutting blade existed to sever her connection to this world, Ren would find and use it without a second thought. Bahati was singing in her native language what Mina assumed was a lullaby.

Just then she remembered something Steven said to her while they were still in Italy, before the damage.

"You'd make a great mother someday."

It warmed her at the time. His eyes meant it. But he was seeing Mirielle in her when the words came out. It was part of the deception. He never intended to have a family with her. Ever.

*

"For my next act," Mina said to herself with a laugh, "we're having a baby!"

She looked through Mirielle's clothes once more.

The outfit should say youthful, but serious, Ana suggested.

"Healthy, but uncomfortable," Mina added.

She found a stifling mock turtleneck and yelled at Bahati to stop singing.

Why do you need an outfit if you aren't going into the room to see him? Bahati sneered.

"I have to play the character. The others understand."

*

"Steven," Mirielle's voice called out to him.

"Where are you, what day is it?" He rubbed his eyes and searched the room for his wife.

"I'm heading out," she said. "I have an ultrasound appointment. I'm going to see our baby."

Steven leapt from the bunk. "Sophia!" Had he somehow

forgotten about the appointment? "Why didn't you wake me earlier? I want to be there."

"There's no time, Steven. I'm leaving now and besides, you're sick. I'll have them print one of those pictures."

"But, I feel fine! Let me come." He ran full force at the door, nearly dislocating his shoulder. "I have to be there!"

"I can't risk making the baby sick. Stay here and rest."

Of course, Mina wasn't going to any appointments, or leaving the house for that matter. She stayed in the monitoring room for the remainder of the day, watching Steven comfort and rock an imaginary baby. It was the most tragic and beautiful thing she'd ever seen; a man so committed to a lie. It seemed she only had to mention or hint at something from his past and he would latch onto it with a death grip.

*

That night, in separate rooms, with doors, and locks, and walls between them, Mina's and Steven's minds couldn't move on from the thought of the child.

A dream, closer to a nightmare, took hold of Mina. In it, Sophia was real. Growing inside of her and bringing her closer to Steven as she stretched and deformed Mina's already foreign shape.

Steven lay awake, staring at the bottom of the top bunk, envisioning what their child would look like as she grew up. She would have Mirielle's nose and her blue eyes. His height would make her a knockout when she was done growing. She'd have Mirielle's sweet disposition, but his stubbornness would surely make an appearance. He fell asleep happily, with family on his mind.

PERSPECTIVE

In another room of the house, Mina found boxes full of old notes and printer sheets full of highlighted research dating back to the year that Mirielle died. It seemed that from the moment he lost her, Steven became obsessed with finding a way to replace her, or better yet, bring her back. Again she felt the strength of his love and Bahati welled up inside of her, daring her to open the room and free the monster.

Let him out. Let him love you.

"How could I ever love someone so selfish?" Mina asked in reply, but Bahati offered no reply.

All of the boxes were labeled *Mirielle*, but a stack in one corner of the room had Steven's name scrawled across the cardboard. Mina pulled one down and dumped its contents on the floor in front of her. Maps, emails, and photographs of several men from different online profiles covered the carpet.

"They look so much like him." Mina sat in awe of the likeness. She'd experienced it firsthand, but to see it a second time was incredible. "He found his doppelgängers too."

Motherfucker, Ana said. *When or where does this man stop?*

It made sense that he would keep tabs on them. Steven was the type of man to consider all routes, all possibilities, and all endings. Though, he hadn't foreseen that Mirielle was impossible to bring back, but only because his love so blinded him.

She read all she could on each man. There was Thom, a writer from the U.K., Benito the Argentinean winemaker, Hui, a businessman from China, and Baako, a West African tribesman. They were all living completely different lives across the globe with no idea that a madman had been spying on them, following their every move. Should she warn them? If Steven made it out of this alive, they would surely be next.

A chill came over Mina. He'd done the same for her and the other women. Somewhere in the stacks of boxes was everything he had discovered about them. Their digital footprint had been traced and examined, scrutinized and obsessed over.

*

Mina watched Steven pace the room, again rocking the invisible baby. He wasn't putting the "baby" down for anything. She searched the internet for an audio snippet of an infant crying and played it on repeat.

"Shhh, shhh," Steven said to the tiny and fragile Sophia. "Daddy doesn't know how to help you. Mommy should be home any minute. She'll know what to do."

"Mommy's never coming home," Mina mumbled and raised the volume of the wailing.

"Sophia, please stop crying," Steven begged. He rocked the baby faster. Back and forth, back and forth.

His arms grew tired and the shrill screams of his child cut his ear drums like tiny knives. Without thinking, and at his wit's end, he threw his baby girl to the floor.

Mina flinched. The child was a figment, something she couldn't see, but it was all too easy to imagine Steven harming a life out of frustration. She stopped the audio track and watched him scoop a big armful of nothing off the ground.

*

That night, Steven called out for Mirielle endlessly, asking her to feed the baby and change it. Sophia wasn't crying anymore and that concerned him. She was too silent for a newborn.

When Mina finally fell asleep, she relived the union in painful detail. Only this time the men, Steven's doppelgängers, had been imprisoned with the women and sixteen arms and legs, and eight heads, fought to join into some recognizable form. Steven and Mirielle stood at one end of the room, smiling and holding hands, watching the fruit of their love grow into a wonderful monstrosity.

ROOTS

After reviewing the years of hospital bills she found, Mina had another idea. According to the documents, Mirielle had died after an unsuccessful fight against uterine cancer. It was the very reason her body could no longer support the life of baby Sophia. It was another sad part of their history and chemo causes hair loss. Steven had taken their hair from them in the past. She couldn't pass up the opportunity to take his.

She searched the bathroom cabinets for the hair removal

cream. Steven, unaware how long the merging process would take, had stocked up on giant tubs of it. She stripped off her clothes and stood in the shower with an opened tub in her hands. The smell was sickening and pieces of her and the other women's hair still stuck to the sides. She stuffed small wads of toilet paper in her nostrils and pressed forward, smearing the cream over her hair and rubbing it down to the roots.

"Ah!" she screamed. The white goo burned much more than expected. She had been too unconscious the last time it was applied to remember the pain. The cool water of the shower soothed her aching skin and she smiled as her hair rinsed off into a small pile at the drain.

Her fair skin looked sickly without the golden-brown locks to support it. It was the effect she was going for.

She gassed the room and stood over Steven until she found the courage to touch him in order to smear the cream on his body. Shudder after shudder rocked her body as she removed every last hair. He was repulsive. When she was removing the hair between his legs, Bahati surged forward from within and forced Mina's hand to grip his flaccid penis.

I want him, Bahati said.

Mina fought back from inside with all the strength she could muster, prying the fingers from him. "Too bad. He's mine to do with what I please and it *isn't* that."

She tied him to one of the bunk beds and waited for him to wake.

First, he smiled at her; a large but brief smile. Then, he noticed how different she looked and how immobile he was. "What happened to your hair? Why am I tied up?"

Because you're an asshole, Ana said.

"You don't remember anything?" Mina asked.

Steven cried. "I've been forgetting a lot lately."

She held up a hand mirror so he could see himself. "Look."

He ran a hand over his hairless head. "What happened to *my* hair?"

"It's the house Steven. It has made us very sick. Our hair fell out. The insulation or the paint or something. It did something to your mind. You went crazy and you hit me."

"I'm so sorry! I would never hurt you!" Mirielle didn't look well at all, as though she was very near death. The look was familiar to him, but he couldn't place it. His thoughts jumped to Sophia. Surely such a sick body could not support the growth of a child. "The baby?" he asked.

Mina was surprised Steven still thought the baby was inside of her, since he'd been rocking her in his arms and mind just the day before. "Gone." A smile pulled at her facial muscles. To hide it, she dropped her face into her hands as though she was crying.

"No!" he screamed. "No!" The child, an ultimate physical expression of their love, was everything to him. The future wouldn't be the same without his little girl in his arms.

She left the room quickly. He was a gullible man, perhaps because he trusted Mirielle wholeheartedly.

*

When Steven awoke next he was free from the bunk. He flipped the floor pillows, turned over the mattresses, and pulled the bunks from the wall, looking for his lost child. He knelt before a God he'd never spoken to and prayed for the return of the baby.

Mina listened and was happy that for once he screamed a different name than Mirielle's.

LAYERS

Mina searched the house high and low for her suitcase, but she couldn't find it. *Steven must have thrown it away*, she thought. He kept little from the women's previous lives; just another part of his conversion process. A complete stripping of the soul. Though Mirielle's clothes fit her body, they weren't Mina's style. She found duplicates of some of her favorite pieces from Italy online and instantly felt more human when they arrived and she could pull them over her head again.

In her quest for garments, Mina learned more about the tragic relationship that was Steven and Mirielle. Tucked beneath a pair of high heels in a shoebox, she found love letters to Mirielle, but they weren't from Steven.

Good for her, Ana said.

What a bitch! Bahati hissed. *I'd treat him better!*

The man, only identified by the letter 'D', begged her to be with him; to leave her secluded life with Steven and run away with him. He claimed Steven didn't love her, but rather, obsessed over her like a madman. *It's different*, he explained, *he doesn't* care *for you. He keeps you. But I care.*

Steven either didn't know about the letters, or the love affair, or he had conveniently erased it from his mind as he was so capable of.

On Steven's side of the closet, which she mostly avoided, another box beckoned her to look inside. It was labeled *Harmen*. The name was not unfamiliar. Mina read it several times before; on old letters and on the wedding invitation. *You are cordially invited to the union of Horn and Harmen.* It was Mirielle's last name.

The contents of the box shouldn't have surprised her. The photos, emails, and notes were typical Steven-esque research. But it wasn't her doppelgängers, or his, it was Mirielle's family.

When Mirielle died, Steven stalked them.

The most recent email was from about five years prior and from a woman named Lauren.

She's dead, Steven! Gone! Leave us alone! We're in as much pain as you, if not more. Please don't come around the house anymore. My mom is frightened.

"How sad. He terrorized her family too." Mina closed the box. The love letters, she could probably find a use for those, but she vowed to never open the box labeled *Harmen* again.

They should have shot him, Ren said.

"Yes, they should have."

PROXIMITY

Though her plan was not to affect Steven physically, especially as there was no one easily accessible for him to merge with and Mina couldn't kill four innocent men for revenge on one man, she *was* looking forward to moving the walls. He needed to know what it felt like to be trapped in a shrinking world with no hope of escape.

Where Steven moved them gradually, Mina went the more drastic route.

"Mirielle?" Steven called to her one morning. "I must be losing my mind."

Mina watched him feel the walls, deep in thought.

"The room, it was bigger yesterday." He could only get out of the bunk bed and turn around in place in front of it. It was now the size of a closet.

"No," Mina said over the speakers, her voice filling the small space as though she was an omnipotent force. "You're still sick. You must have a fever. It hasn't changed."

"I feel fine. I'm not hot or anything."

Feeling the urge to exercise her power, Mina upped the heat of the room until his skin shone with sweat.

"Maybe," he said as he wiped his forehead and lay down on his bed, "you're right. I do feel a little warm."

After only a day, the plan backfired. Steven was a pacer, a wanderer, and when he no longer had the room to work out his thoughts through movement, he turned to masturbation. Before then, he must have saved it for later in the night, when Mina was no longer watching, not that he knew that. But now he did it all the time.

Disgusting, Ren said.

We should be in there pleasuring him, Bahati pouted.

Gas the fucker every time his hand travels south, Ana demanded. *How unfair that he could have such an escape!*

SPEECH

"Look at the camera, Steven! Say hi and welcome home!" Mirielle's voice was happy and full of life when Steven had brought her to their new house. She filmed Steven as he gave her a tour.

Mina was feeding the audio into Steven's prison, just as she'd done with the shrieking baby. A home movie collection which had been gathering dust in the den was her latest ammunition find. The DVDs and videotapes dated back to the 80's and contained the most intimate of moments from the Horn and Harmen history, including a luckily grainy sex tape that Mina stopped watching as soon as she realized what it was. Enough content was recorded that she could play video after video for him to hear, 24/7, for the rest of the next two years. If nothing previous had irreparably damaged his soul, that surely would.

"We are not staying here that long," Ana said.

"Shhh," Mina said aloud to quiet her. "Steven's saying something."

In the monitor room, Steven was reciting the words of the past from memory. He knew every syllable of the conversations, every bit of laughter, every sigh.

"And here's the kitchen." Steven's voice from a time long past seemed to echo. "You'll love it here."

He is so smart, Bahati said with a sigh.

He's a fucking lunatic! Ana spat back. *Can someone shut this woman up?*

Mina ignored them, not wishing to ask for silence a second time.

"This will be the baby's room." In the video, Steven points to a door that Mina recognizes. It's the door to the room in which she was trapped. The door that holds Steven captive.

"How many babies will we have?" Mirielle asks sweetly.

"As many as we want!" Steven smiles and then leans behind the camera to kiss his new wife.

In the room, Steven jumped to his feet and began yelling. "The baby, the baby, the baby! Mirielle! The room isn't ready for the baby!"

REFLECTIONS

Steven stood in front of the mirror, examining his face and body. He didn't feel sick and his body certainly didn't look sick. His hair was growing back. Doubt crept into his mind.

Something was different about her.

The walls had moved, he knew it to be true. He began to look for a way out of the tiny room, a weakness that could allow for escape.

*

Mina too looked at her reflection. She was changing again; not physically, but psychologically. The sadness she'd been looking to escape had turned to madness, insanity. Bloodthirst bubbled in the pit of her stomach.

How long are we going to do this? Ren asked. *I don't want to be in this house anymore.*

I don't want to leave, Bahati replied.

You don't have that choice you stupid cunt! Ana shot back.

"Please, stop fighting. We've only been here for a few months."

Where will we go when this is over? Ren asked.

"I don't know. We can't go far, not yet anyway."

Mexico, Ana whispered. *The beaches are beautiful.*

Japan, Ren whispered. *We could walk those streets you dream about.*

I like it here! Bahati yelled. *This is where I'm meant to be!*

"Anywhere but here," Mina said. "End of conversation."

TOUCH

Stop feeding him! Ana screamed. *Let him starve!*

"I want you out of my head." Mina mumbled it so as not to wake Steven. Chains bound him to a chair at the kitchen table; the same chains that had held her and the other women as the union began months ago.

It's time, she thinks. *Let him see you.*

Let him touch you, Bahati added.

"He'll never touch me again!" Mina shrieked.

219

Steven awoke with a start. "What are the chains for?"

"There're some things we need to talk about. You aren't going to like them very much. I had to make sure you couldn't hurt me," she explains. *More*, she thinks.

"I would never hurt you."

Mina laughed, but cut it short. Staying in character as Mirielle was more difficult than she expected. "You've been doing things you shouldn't have. You've hurt people." Mina fought hard to make it sound impersonal, like she wasn't talking about herself.

"I would never harm a soul, honey. I don't know what you're talking about. You've kept me locked in a room! How could I have hurt anyone?" Steven stretched an arm out to hold her hand, but she pulled hers farther away. "It's really hard to not touch you."

She pushed her chair out and walked the long way around the table to the fridge, far from any reach Steven might have. She carefully removed each of the four mementos, trophies, that Steven had kept to remember his twisted escapade. She laid them out on the table in the same rectangular shape as she'd arranged them on the fridge.

"Tell me about these."

Mina searched his expression for any sign of recognition, but confusion covered it instead. "I don't know where any of these things came from! I've never seen them in my life!" He picked up Ren's plane ticket and examined it. "You'd know if I went to Japan!"

She tore it from his hands, thinking of poor Ren as she did. They had all suffered, but Ren was stuck in the room for years. She'd been driven to multiple suicide attempts. "Don't touch her things!"

"I'm so confused, Mirielle. Please tell me what's going on!"

She looked directly into his eyes. "You've been seeing other women. Admit it."

"How could you ever think something like that? I can't live without you! Don't you love me?"

"Love can never return from such a complete death. We've

grown apart, Steven. Can't you feel it?"

"No, I can't! I'm chained to a chair for starters! I can't *feel* anything I want to! Why are you saying such silly things?"

Mina set the love letters from "D" on the table. "I've found someone else too."

Steven read them.

"Someone else? I don't believe it. Mirielle, please, listen to me?"

Mina watched his face change from crazed to sweet and loving. It was a look she'd seen before, many times. On the camera as he listened to her voice, in the photo albums when he had the real Mirielle, and right before she strangled him on the day the union was complete.

He loves you, Bahati said. *Can't you see it?*

Don't trust him, Ana roared.

Ren whispered, *He isn't worth all this. We need to get out of here.*

"Mirielle," Steven cooed. His singsong voice sickened Mina, burned her to the core. The more she heard the name, the more it became her. Vomit threatened to burst from her gut.

Mina slammed a fist on the table. "I thought I had you tucked away, like the others, where you couldn't hurt me...I was so *fucking* wrong!"

"Who are you talking about? What others? I don't understand."

"Ren, Ana, Bahati, *me*! You killed us all!"

He shook his head. "The illness, the loss of the baby, it has your mind mixed up, Mirielle. I can help you."

"I don't need your help. You've *helped* enough!"

"I want to be with you. Why won't you have me?" Steven sobbed. "I am built to love you."

"Then God is one screwed up individual." Mina collected the mementos and returned them to the fridge. She heated soup and set a bowl of it in front of him. "You'll eat your dinner here and then I'm putting you back in the room."

"Just let me touch you!" Steven cried out. "You'll feel it too!"

*

Steven fell asleep thinking of his beautiful wife. At the table earlier, he could smell the scent of her skin. He imagined holding her close and the way her fingernails felt as they dragged down his back. When he was finally free of the room and the chains, she would have to try very hard to keep him off of her.

It felt right to be next to her and he couldn't imagine anyone else taking that place.

THE UNION

Exhaustion took hold of Mina. Playing mind games, it turned out, was an all-consuming mental exercise that hurt *her* more, it seemed, than Steven. She wanted to stop, but it didn't yet feel right. Determined to press on, she sought motivation to continue the war.

Back in the monitoring room, Mina looked in on Steven. He had fallen asleep in a corner with the floor pillows piled atop his body.

If only he could stop loving her, everything would be easier.

You could try loving him, Bahati suggested.

"Impossible," Mina said aloud. "Do I have to remind you why?"

It was finally time to confront the very thing she'd been through; her captivity and merging with the other women had all been captured on tape. The DVDs were neatly organized in labeled boxes. Ren had her own box, perhaps since she was alone in the room before the other women arrived. Mina avoided watching them out of fear of seeing the suicide attempts.

She dug through another box and found the stack of DVDs that included her name on the label. Her nerves sent her teeth chattering. A bag of popcorn felt like an insult to the gravity of the entire situation, but her hands required something to keep them busy and her teeth needed something to bite down on.

She pressed play.

The opening scene, one in which Ren, Ana, and Bahati collapsed where they stood, raised the hair on her arms and neck.

The gas worked quickly, sending them to the floor like machines suddenly losing power, as though their plugs were pulled. She'd seen it over and over with Steven, but she hated him and he deserved to lose his spark. Watching the women fall reminded her of their helplessness.

Then, her arrival. Steven carried her limp and hairless form into the center of the room, removed the hair of the other women, and left them to reawaken.

She fast forwarded the recording, watching the changes occur in high speed and only pausing when Steven entered the room. He caressed them, stared at their changing bodies, cried over them. He touched himself and lost himself over them and then cleaned up the mess to hide the violation.

Mina vomited popcorn bits on the floor of the monitoring room.

Ana screamed inside Mina's head.

Kill me! Ren cried out. *Let me die!*

Bahati said nothing, but Mina could feel the love for Steven, the love that Bahati held, leave her heart.

He has to go! Ana snapped. *As long as he is alive, he will search for you, for us! He will try to replace her. If you want to truly live, you must get rid of him!*

I agree, Ren said. *Steven found all of us. He will never stop looking for what he lost. He must be stopped.*

She no longer needed to see the union.

"To have and to hold, from this day forward," Mirielle's voice recited over the speakers. Steven held himself, remembering their wedding day, and wishing more than ever that he could hold his wife again.

MIRIELLE

It was a fluke that Mina found Mirielle's burial plot. She wasn't even looking for it as she assumed the woman had been cremated or buried elsewhere. In an unmarked black album, she discovered a collection of photographs that marked the day of her funeral.

Mina recognized the backyard immediately. The tall white fence and the small plot of grass. Mirielle had been buried in her own garden. Few were in attendance. Relatives or coworkers? Mina couldn't discern.

She had been looking for an end to Steven's story and with this discovery she found it. He was the greatest thing to happen to Mirielle and the most horrible to Mina. It was necessary; his removal from the monstrous pedestal on which he sat. He was only a man.

And men are mortal, all four women said together.

*

She stayed in the backyard all night long, sweating and digging, and sobbing over what she had become. When the shovel hit wood, Mina laughed. She was right.

The real Mirielle was found.

Next, the part she was dreading. The grotesqueness of her experience, and the other women as well, had strengthened her gut, but a rotting corpse was an entirely different situation. She prepared for squirming things and horrible smells, but when she pried the lid of the coffin up, only a wisp of dust came out. A bare skeleton dressed in disintegrating burial clothes barely filled the box.

Mina noticed a small piece of cloth in the dirt next to the coffin. She tugged on it and a bony hand popped out of its grave.

"Another body?" Mina asked aloud. No energy remained in her body to figure out who it could be. She put the corpse out of her mind and the dirt back in the hole.

With the grave recovered, she brought Mirielle's bones inside. Mina ran the gas and dragged Steven from the room.

*

When Steven awoke he was chained to his bed in his real bedroom and he smelled smoke. *Maybe Mirielle is burning breakfast again?*

After she untied him, he would pretend to enjoy the blackened food; that's what lovers did.

On the mirror of the dresser across the bedroom, a lipstick painted message said "Forever Yours" and above it, an arrow directed him to look up. So he did.

Mirielle's corpse was attached to the ceiling and the empty sockets of her skull stared down at him.

Steven sobbed. "What have you done to yourself?" He tugged on his restraints, but she had secured them tightly. "Why would you do this to me, Mirielle? Let me go! I love you!"

Out of the corner of his eye, the flames jumped into view at the bedroom door. It was then he realized the house was burning down around them.

"What happened to us?" He searched her skinless face for any answer to kill the pain inside. "We were connected! Why have you abandoned me?"

As Steven struggled and then burned, Mina drove away in his truck.

*

A fire was a highly visible death and something it would be difficult to travel away from without drawing suspicion. She could already see the smoke cloud in the rearview mirror. It wasn't about evidence. Her fingerprints were tied to a woman long dead. When she thought about Steven and all he had done, it wasn't only him that needed to go. The house was full of love and hate in their most pure and potent forms. It all had to burn with him.

The sun shone brightly, forcing her to search for sunglasses. She reached into the glovebox and blindly felt around. Maps and receipts filled the space, but no sunglasses. Mina felt a pile of papers rubberbanded together. She pulled to the side of the road to examine them. The stack contained passports and driver's licenses.

On the identification, four faces stared back at her. She recognized them. It was Steven's doppelgängers: Thom, Benito, Hui, and Baako.

The other body in the grave! Ana exclaimed. *Those poor men!*

Mina's jaw dropped. There was no limit to Steven's selfish evil. "He kidnapped them before us. He tracked them and trapped them. He moved the walls. He forced them together, just like us!"

He knew the union would work. He'd already done it once before, Ren said.

"And in doing so, he made sure no one could do the same to him."

Mina pulled back onto the road. The distance glimmered and played with her eyes. It was in motion, ever-changing. The future could be anything she wanted it to be. She was no longer prisoner to the room, her old life, anyone's idea of her.

You can be anyone, Bahati said. *Please, be someone, for us.*

The freedom to reinvent, Steven had given her that.

SUPPLEMENTARY CONTENT

OBACHAN

About the Ghost

Japan has a plethora of yokai (ghosts) and stories to go with them. The story of Miyu and her grandmother was inspired by the tales of the Ubume, a female spirit who asks passersby to hold a child for her. She then disappears and as the people walk, the child becomes heavier and heavier until they realize it is a not a child at all, but a rock. In other stories, she either offers candy to children or seeks to purchase it for her own child. I combined both of these ideas into Obachan.

Glossary of Japanese Words

Bento - a single portion, home-packed meal, usually in a compartmentalized box. Bento boxes are also sold at train stations in Japan. Some mothers make cute characters out of the food to make it fun and appealing to their children. These are called *kyaraben*, or character bento

Koi - A type of fish, ornamental variety of common carp

Kuzuyu - A thick, sweet, hot beverage made from adding kudzu flour to hot water

Mochi - a cake made out of glutinous rice. Eaten during special times of year, like New Years, and in other dishes throughout the year

Obachan - One word for grandmother

Oishii - Delicious, tasty, nice

Okaasan - Mother

O-Shiruko - a soup made out of red beans

Sobo - One's own grandmother

Taiyaki - Fish-shaped cake made from waffle or pancake batter and filled with sweetened paste or custard

Tempura - Seafood or vegetables that have been battered and

deep fried
Tengu - Legendary creatures, demons
Wagashi - Confection usually made with mochi, bean paste, and sometimes fruits
Wasanbon - Fine-grained sugar pressed into shaped cakes
Yokai - Supernatural monsters/ghosts

DREAM LAND

More about the Euthanasia Coaster

The Euthanasia Coaster is a real thing, in theory at least. Designed by Julijonas Urbonas, a designer, artist, writer, and engineer, and built and displayed (in scale-model version) at the HUMAN+ exhibition in Dublin, Ireland in 2011.

I happened upon an article about it and instantly, my mind jumped to considering how someone with no want to die might react to find themselves on, literally, the last ride of their life.

For more information:

http://www.julijonasurbonas.lt/p/euthanasia-coaster/
https://www.youtube.com/watch?v=ZEklVDlqwbQ
http://en.wikipedia.org/wiki/Euthanasia_Coaster

ORDER IN

On Souls and the Afterlife

In early May of 2012, my father suffered at heart attack at work, died, was brought back but locked in a coma on life support, and never recovered from the oxygen deprivation to his brain. We had a week in the hospital with his resting body before making the difficult decision to remove the life support and allow him to pass.

One day during that week, I leaned close to his ear and whispered "Hi dad, it's me, Michelle." He opened his eyes and pulled his head away from me, looking very confused as if he didn't know who I was. I noticed his eye color was different, a much lighter blue compared to his usual hazel (blue-green) eyes. A thought hit me, could the wrong soul inhabit a body? Did the resuscitators bring back someone else? I realize now his confusion was most likely due to brain damage, but the idea stuck. Where do our souls go when they die? Can they come back from there? Is it possible for a mix-up to occur?

LAST NIGHT WHILE YOU WERE SLEEPING
On Suicide

Years ago, on a Valentine's night drive, I crossed the infamous Fremont Bridge. The bridge was a popular place for jumpers, people wishing to end their lives, until a suicide prevention gate was erected on both sides, effectively stopping the problem. On that night however, no gate existed.

In the glow of a street lamp, I could see a man dressed in dark clothes, climbing over the railing. He came to sit there. I drove on, finished whatever business I had going over the bridge in the first place, and drove back.

A policeman was talking to him, but he was still sitting, facing out into the dark void that hovered above the water below.

I drove on and have wondered about him ever since.

Did he jump? Was the officer successful in talking him down from the edge? Why did he climb up there in the first place? Did someone break his heart on Valentine's Day? Had his loneliness become too much?

The stresses of life overwhelmed an uncle of mine. He was a kind person, he had served in the military, he dressed up as Santa Claus for many of our childhood Christmas celebrations. He gave a lot to others. I know little about his death. I know the how, but not the *why*. Who ever knows the entire story anyway?

The sighting of the Valentine's jumper and the suicide of my uncle have made me think about those considering suicide. How do we not see their pain? Or do we see it and write it off as normal? Did they ask us for help in a way we just couldn't translate?

Or are we too caught up in our own existence to pay attention to the person next to us?

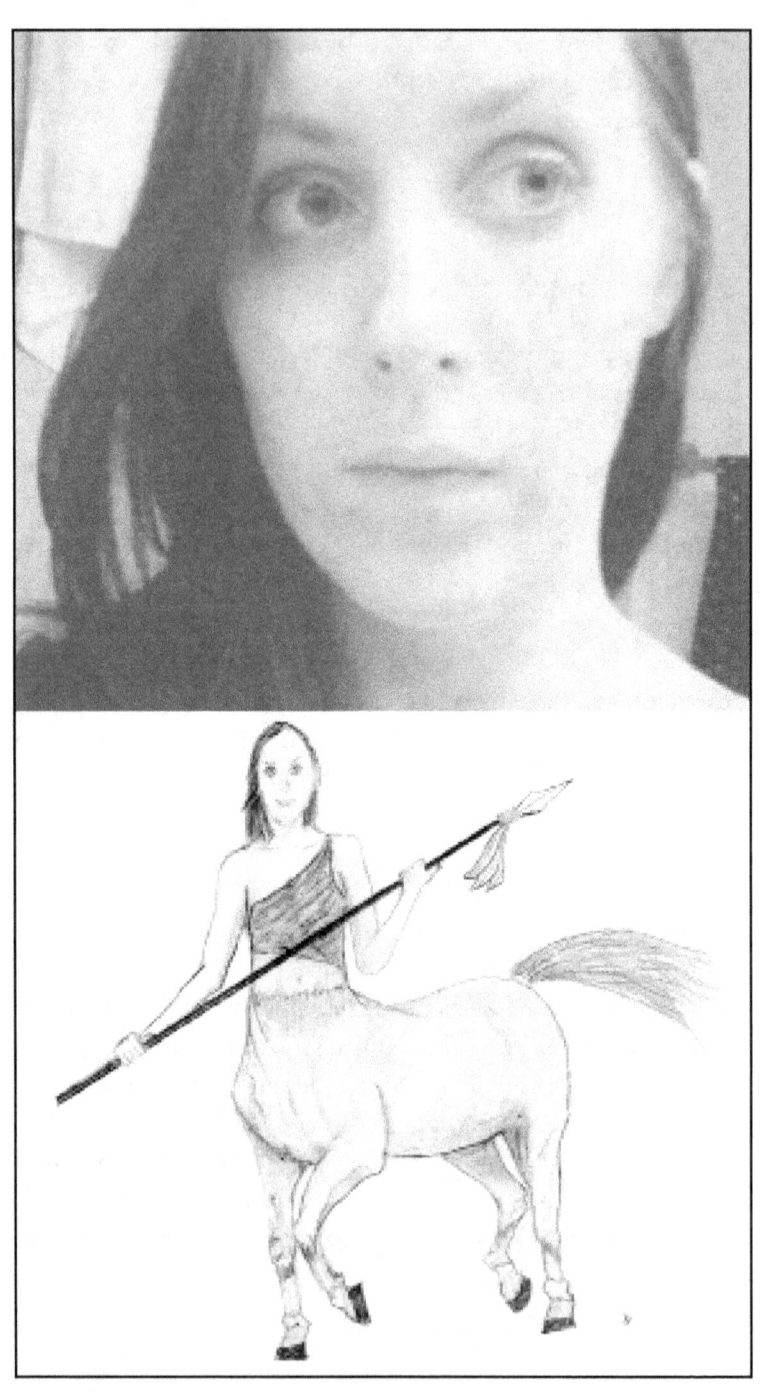

CENTAUR MICHELLE BY JONATHAN LAMBERT, AUTHOR

ABOUT THE AUTHOR
MICHELLE KILMER

Michelle is also the author of the zombie novels When the Dead and Mistakes I Made During the Zombie Apocalypse, co-author of The Spread: A Zombie Short Story Collection, and has also penned several short stories published in other anthologies. She is a co-editor of GIVE: An Anthology of Anatomical Entries.

When she is not writing, Michelle lifts weights, sings, plays guitar, camps, hikes, snowshoes, eats chocolate, reads, and designs websites.

She lives in Mill Creek, WA with her twin sister, two attack cats, and a broken heart.

MICHELLE ACCORDING TO OTHERS

...talks to strangers
...one of her nicknames is Moo
...once tried to self-eject from the Splash Mountain ride
...is the evil twin (this is a lie)
...makes some mean shrimp tacos (totally true)
...once hadn't farted for seven years (a lie I told as a child)
...has a wicked sense of humor
...is Scandinavian
...knows how to build rad boobie traps
...is a very special girl
...a recovered obsessive-compulsive
...doesn't have fans, she has friends
...was, at one time, frightened of yellow traffic lights

ABOUT THE ARTISTS

DARRELL TOLAND
ILLUSTRATOR - MIRIELLE

Darrell Toland has worked in television and won 5 Emmys for Motion Design work. He has a BA in Fine Arts, writes and illustrates children's books, and creates a weekly webcomic called Stix and Bones.

He lives in Seattle, WA with his wife, two daughters, and a bull terrier named Roxy who enjoys biting the garden hose. In 2014, Darrell built a 12-foot-tall robot and placed it outside to guard his house.

SARAH ALTENBURG
ILLUSTRATOR - OBACHAN

Sarah is an illustrator, graphic designer and artist at large. Nothing is safe from being turned into art at her hands, whether it is greenery from the garden becoming garlands for Beltane or receipts transforming into paper cranes.

When Sarah is not hot gluing paper flowers, cloth scraps, and cardboard into fancy Steampunk hats or beading up a storm she can be found backpacking or skiing in the Cascade Mountains with her husband and dog.

Sarah, her husband Derek, their Dog, and two cats currently live in Bothell. In order to support her art and tree hugging habits Sarah works at REI where she gives advise on what to wear while doing yoga on a mountain or kayaking on rainy afternoons.

ROB SACCHETTO
ILLUSTRATOR - HOUSE HUSBAND

In 2006, Rob started an online service in which he hand paint people as the living dead, called Zombie Portraits. He has zombified over 2500 people all over the world. He then started Zombie Daily, a blog with a new, original zombie drawing or painting every day! He has several book deals including "The Zombie Handbook: How to Identify the Living Dead and Survive the Coming Zombie Apocalypse", which last year was translated to Spanish, and titled "Apocolipsis Zombie" and his next book, "Zombiewood: The Celebrity Dead Exposed". Rob is also featured in the documentary "Zombiemania" and provided the morphing zombie portrait drawings for himself and the other noted zombie experts interviewed, including George Romero, Tom Savini, Max Brooks and Greg Nicotero. His zombie art has been licensed for use on everything from puzzles to skateboard decks, T shirts, journal covers, comic books and many other products, including a full 56 Zombie card deck for Bicycle playing cards and Comic book covers for IDW's new Zombie comic book series by Jonathan Mayberry, Rot And Ruin. View his work at www.zombieportraits.com.

JERI BRACKETT
ARTIST - NEGATIVE

Jeri Brackett has been creating art, including poster lettering, calligraphy, and computer graphics, off and on since she was young. She is currently studying Graphics at Everett Community College. In her free time she enjoys making hide purses and crocheting.

KRISCINDA LEE EVERITT
ILLUSTRATOR - AN ENTRY FROM SATAN'S JOURNAL

Kriscinda Lee Everitt is a writer, editor, and occasional artist. She's been published by Permuted Press, Postscripts to Darkness, Evil Girlfriend Media, and Monsters and the Monstrous. As an editor, she's worked for The Fourth River, Autumn House Press, and Nightscape Press. She is the founder/Editor-in-Cheif of Despumation, a literary journal that publishes fiction based on/inspired by extreme metal music. She lives in Pittsburgh, PA with her husband, Anthony, and their two cats, Gudrun and Aud the Deep-Minded. And the Spook Brothers.

RACHEL HANSEN
ARTIST - ORDER IN

Rachel Hansen works in the health and wellness field and is currently studying human anatomy and its movement. She has always been drawn to strange things like science fiction, fantasy and horror.

NICK GUCKER
ILLUSTRATOR - FAIR HOUSING

When he's not busy whispering to insects, trying his hand at taxidermy or watching weird Japanese monster movies Nick Gucker can be found hunched over his art table dreaming up disturbing nightmares and freakish delights.

His art has appeared in the pages of Strange Aeons Magazine and TheMagazine of Bizarro Fiction. His illustrations have decorated the pages of ALL-MONSTER ACTION! by Cody Goodfellow, the novelette 'The Eye of Infinity' by David Conyers for Perilous Press, The Aklonoimicon anthology from Aklo Press, a re-issue of H.P. Lovecraft's "Under the Pyramids" as well as book covers for Blysster Press authors Clyde Wolfe, R.L. Reeves, M.R. Mitchell and the 2011 and 2012 "De-Compositions" horror anthologies. His artistic contributions can be found in online publications including Lovecraftzine.com and Thisishorror.co.uk. Nick has also been the staff artist and board member of Crypticon Seattle horror convention since 2009. His unique, one-of-a-kind custom commission pieces have graced the walls and limbs of various and sundry patrons of the arts.

TRAVIS BUNDY
ILLUSTRATOR - BYE BYE BRIGHTEN

Travis Bundy was born into the fragrant cultural void known to the world as Tacoma, WA. He has been drawing and creating ever since he was old enough to hold a crayon. When he's not toiling under the boot of "the man" or drinking himself into an early grave, he continues to challenge himself in all artistic endeavors. He plans to do so until he is found expired and sprawled out over his art desk. I can only imagine that the stench will be atrocious.

Currently, Travis lives and creates in "Fry Bread Hell" (aka Auburn, WA). He shares a lovely little home with his amazing wife, as well as 2 retarded dogs and 4 spiteful cats. He is also the creator of the critically acclaimed comic book "Jeff" and is the Artistic Director and Submissions Director for Creator's Edge Press, an independent comic company based in Puyallup, WA.

TOM KERNS
ILLUSTRATOR - ERIS OF EARTH

Tom Kerns can build just about anything out of Legos. He has been writing and illustrating his own comics for as long as he could hold a pencil. Comics include Power Boy and The Adventures of Pointy and Handy. When Tom is not building or drawing, he enjoys attending church functions.

JAMES LACROIX
ILLUSTRATOR - LAST NIGHT WHILE YOU WERE SLEEPING

James Lacroix is a comic book artist from Milwaukee with a focus on punk rock and alternative themes. His aesthetic is often reminiscent of Jamie Hewlett. James writes and draws the independent comic series Critical Mass, which is published by Creator's Edge Press, and runs a webcomic at Baconmoosecomics. com.

MORE FROM WTD BOOKS

WHEN THE DEAD

There is no way out for the residents of Willow Brook Apartments. Outside a plague is spreading while behind the walls, neighbors are forced to become friends…or enemies.

When the Dead…will introduce you to a doomed family, a dying child, an egomaniac, a murderer, and many other undesirables (including the undead!!) in three floors of secured-access chaos.

THE SPREAD

You don't know when it will change your life, or how, but the zombie plague is spreading quickly and in ways that no one could have imagined.

Featuring short stories that showcase the many ways in which a disease can overwhelm a city, The Spread will get you thinking of how mundane acts can become deadly.

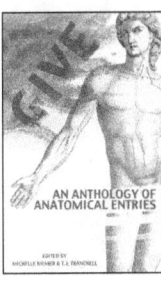

GIVE: AN ANTHOLOGY OF ANATOMICAL ENTRIES

Have you ever loved someone so much, you'd give your left eye for them? Does two of a kind mean one to spare? Are *you* an organ donor?

GIVE: An Anthology of Anatomical Entries explores, from head to toe, the varying reasons why and how someone might donate an organ. Horror, Science Fiction, and dark humor blend in this collection.

MISTAKES I MADE DURING THE ZOMBIE APOCALYPSE

In an undead world, death is only one mistake away.

How does one survive the zombie apocalypse? 17-year-old Ian Ward couldn't tell you because he is dying in one. From a closet in a second floor bedroom of an abandoned house, he recounts his tale of "survival" in a backwards journey through the choices that put him there.

whenthedead.com   facebook.com/whenthedead   @whenthedead